The Wonder 2

Deep Blue

A BASELINE PAPERBACK

© Copyright Nov 2016
James Devo

The right of **James Devo** to be identified as the author of
This work has been asserted by him in accordance with the
Copyright, Designs and Patents Act 1988

Peter Menich Cover design Book 2 Michael Rea additional
design work

A CIP catalogue record for this title is
available from the British Library

ISBN–978-1-911124-27-6

Dedicated to

JD Snr, the man with so many stories
but so few happy endings

CONTENTS

Part 3
A Fairytale of Chinsey

Part 4
Friend Only to the Undertaker

THE DUTCH
1.
...EAR MOUNTAINS
2.
3.
CHIN
The
Drama
5.
AND
6.
MAISY

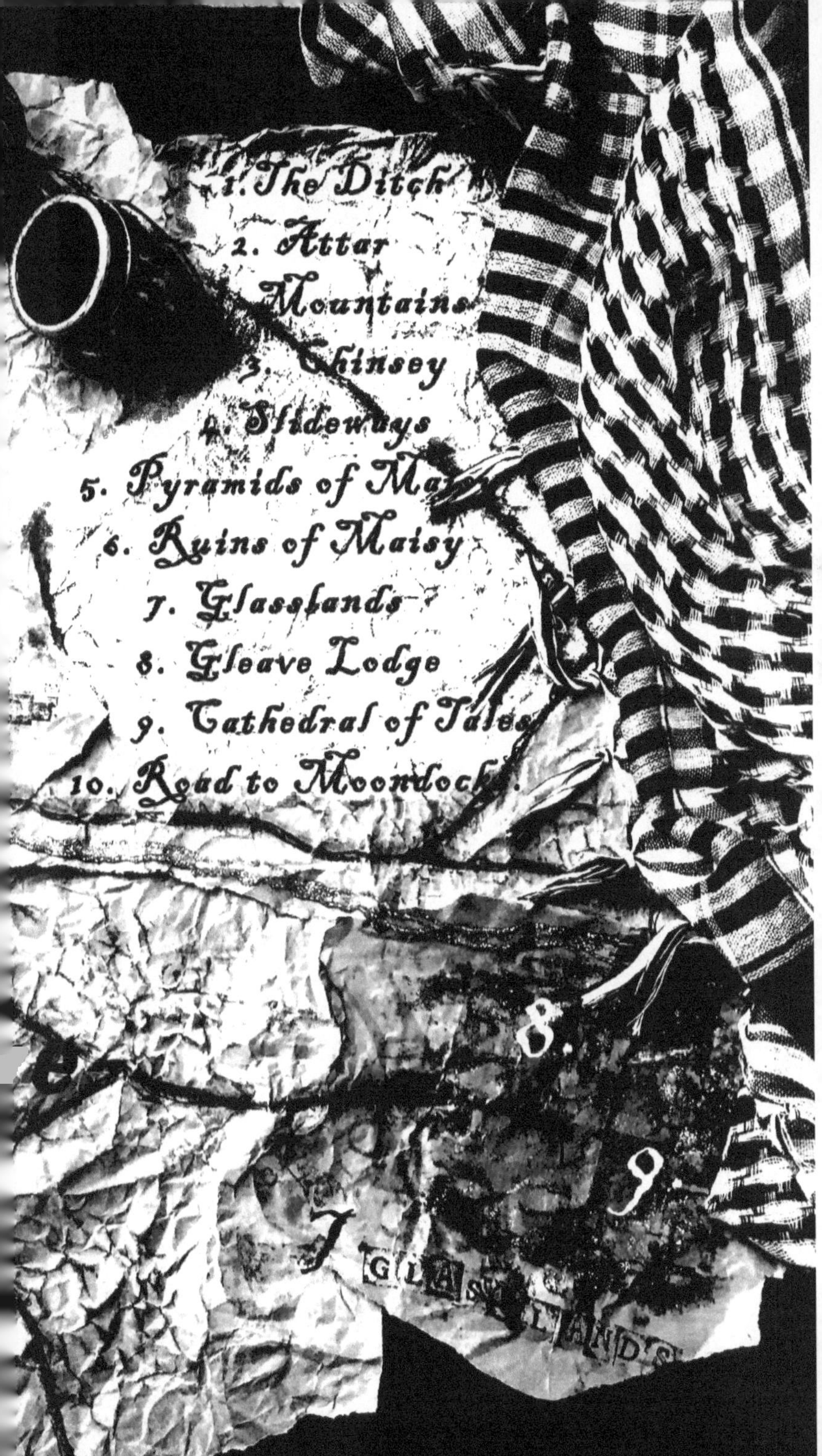

1. The Ditch
2. Attar Mountains
3. Chinsey
4. Slideways
5. Pyramids of Mars
6. Ruins of Maisy
7. Glasslands
8. Gleave Lodge
9. Cathedral of Tales
10. Road to Moondoch

Teddy's Letter
Somewhere in the Glasslands
The Gramarye Region
Grand Quillia

June 1856

Dear Aunt Josette,

I'm not sure you'll ever get this letter. I don't have the money for a stamp and I don't know where you live. Also, I haven't seen a post box for months now.

You see, Professor Rickenbacker, who used to rent a room from you, well, he's not a Professor any more. I mean, he is. It's still his name. Professor Rickenbacker. But he doesn't work at the university any more. Now he's a terrorist. I don't know if this is a promotion or not, or if the Professor even wants to be a terrorist, but the Grand Quillian Empire says he is, and so that means he is.

Hence not having seen a postbox for months. We are now on the run, being chased by some soldiers led by a Colonel Quine and a Doctor Axelrod. We are in The Gramarye, which is a small and rather rotten part of the Empire that I doubt you have heard of, but there's lots of Wonder here. You know what Wonder is, right?

Professor Rickenbacker and his friends, Sir Evan Mandell (dead posh), Pinkerton (a boxer) and Lady Elena Melody (she makes me feel funny) found something called a Gargoyle Key, which could get us into the Cathedral of Tales, which is in the Glasslands, which is where Pearly used to be.

Wait. I'm getting ahead of myself.

We had this Gargoyle Key thing and then these Reclaimers, mercenaries who work for the Empire, well not EXACTLY the Empire, the Trade, who are like this really big company who buy things for the Empire or something, yeah, so anyway, these Reclaimers chased us. They were led by this really ugly burnt bloke called Spicer and they were called Bunce (a girl that looks like a boy), Tork (a man who looks like a giant) and Conway (a dabbler who looks like a butcher). You know what a dabbler is, Auntie. It's someone who uses the power of the Wonder to make things – you know, grenades, guns, lifts, buildings, street lights, toasters, everything really important.

We were staying in this lodge in the Glasslands (it's not as nice as it sounds). It was an old hunting lodge in the middle of a forest made of glass that had these crazies called Humps living in it who attacked us and tried to bite me but then we escaped – and this lodge was where we escaped to.

It was owned by this really nice lady called Laurel Gleave, who came from a bad family but she's not like that, and she had some friends, Mister Brennan, his son Alf, a smelly man called Kendrick and some soldiers called Beasley and Hilt. Hilt has a sword stuck to his hand, which is weird. It happened at something called the Meander Valley Massacre when all Hilt's soldier friends, called the Torchlights, were killed by Reclaimers working for the Trade.

Yeah, so we thought everything was alright but then Lady Melody betrayed us and Spicer and his Reclaimers got in the lodge. Tork killed Alf and Hilt killed Tork and Spicer killed Beasley and next thing Kendrick ran off because we were surrounded by Colonel Quine and Doctor Axelrod's soldiers so we went to hide in the basement. Sir Evan Mandell was shot in the head and it was really sad and then we found a secret passage that was all scary.

Then we found a hidden city (there wasn't a postbox there either). It was called Pearly, like I said earlier, and we were attacked by this metal thingy but Brennan made it blow up and then Spicer and his Reclaimers found us again so we ran off and Conway, the dabbler, got squashed by the floor. Honest.

Then someone spoke to me in my head and told me I'm the chosen one, which was nice. I know you always thought I was little bit slow, Auntie Josette, but I think I'm really onto something with this chosen one thing. The someone who said I'm the chosen one was called Mister Elephantine and he was made up of all the people that ever lived in the city we were in, before they were all killed by the metal thingies. Mister Elephantine really hated Laurel because her family had helped the metal thingies or something, but I still really like her anyway.

Anyway, Mister Elephantine asked us to help him find some fairy so that he could help us do something or other about something called the Threat that made the metal thingies with the Gleave family and want to attack the Gramarye again. So we escaped to the underground city called Pearly.

Unfortunately Spicer and his Reclaimers found us again. Spicer wasn't all ugly and burnt anymore and has turned into an Elf because we unlocked the city – Professor Rickenbacker mentioned it but I didn't really understand. Yeah, the Reclaimers found us and started shooting at us and then Kendrick turned up with Sir Evan Mandell. Even though Sir Evan Mandell is dead! He's still dead and he's gone all nasty and wants to kill us too now, because Colonel Quine and Doctor Axelrod did something to him. Made him not dead but evil instead, basically. Mister Pinkerton is very sad because Sir Evan Mandell was his very best friend.

Hilt ran off and found some ponies and now we're running away to Chinsey, the main town in the Gramarye. I think we're going to catch an ice yacht on the slideways to take us all the way to Ashburton Station. Which is good because my feet are killing me from walking in the underground city called Pearly and my rear is chafing from riding the ponies.

Anyway. I hope Uncle Frank is well and that you don't have lice as much anymore.

Best Regards
Teddy (Creslow) Esquire

PART 3

A Fairytale of Chinsey

The Story of Mister Elephantine

Once upon a time there was a market. One day, a farmer nobody had ever seen before came to market to sell his cattle. The stranger said his name was Mister Elephantine.

All the traders in the market were very nervous that day because the King was coming to visit the next day, and so they decided to ask the stranger to test their wares, to see if they were good enough for royalty.

First, Mister Elephantine visited the baker. The baker gave Mister Elephantine a cake to taste. There was not enough sugar, the icing was too hard, and the bottom of the cake was burnt.

"What is it like, Mister Elephantine?" asked the baker.

"It is perfect," Mister Elephantine answered. "Fit for a King."

Next, Mister Elephantine visited the tailor. The tailor gave Mister Elephantine a suit to wear. The jacket sleeves were too short, the trousers legs were too long, and the material was threadbare.

"What is it like, Mister Elephantine?" asked the tailor.

"It is perfect," Mister Elephantine answered. "Fit for a King."

Finally, Mister Elephantine visited the carpenter. The carpenter gave Mister Elephantine a chair to sit upon. The legs were different lengths, the back was too low, and the cushion was too flat.

"What is it like, Mister Elephantine?" asked the carpenter.

"It is perfect," Mister Elephantine answered. "Fit for a King."

The traders in the market were very pleased at what Mister Elephantine had told the baker, the tailor and the carpenter. They helped Mister Elephantine sell all his cattle for a very high price, and the stranger was very rich by the time he bid them all farewell.

The next day the King came to market.

First, the King visited the baker. The baker gave the King a cake to taste. The king took one bite of the cake and immediately spat it out.

"What is it like, your Majesty?" asked the baker.

"It is awful," the King answered. "Nobody should eat this," and he ordered that the baker be baked to death in his own oven.

Next, the King visited the tailor. The tailor gave the King suit to wear. The King put one arm in the jacket and one leg in the trousers, and immediately took it off.

"What is it like, your Majesty?" asked the tailor.

"It is awful," the King answered. "Nobody should wear this," and he ordered that the tailor be hanged by the neck with rope made from his own material.

Finally, the King visited the carpenter. The carpenter gave the King a chair to sit upon. The King sat down but immediately stood up again.

"What is it like, your Majesty?" asked the tailor.

"It is awful," the King answered. "Nobody should sit here," and he ordered that the carpenter be buried alive in a box made from his own wood with his own tools.

When the King left the market, the traders were very sad, and they decided to ask Mister Elephantine what had gone wrong, but nobody could find him. They looked everywhere but nobody saw the stranger again.

This is why good little boys and girls should never listen to flattery from strangers.

CHAPTER 11

The Spirit of Bester
The Hodgkinson International Line
The Gramarye Region
Grand Quillia

June 1856

It has been said that the Grand Quillian Empire was built on the back of the slideways, an extraordinary network of iced tracks. The slideways were curved upwards on either side like a chute, the required frozen temperature maintained by Red Wonder, which also powered the spinning buffers on the ice yachts that kept the slideways constantly slippery.

Originally created in Grand Quillia itself to carry goods from the centres of industry and sea ports to the capital at speed while minimising the risk of banditry by virtue of both the cold ice and the high velocity of the yachts, the slideways were rolled out across the growing Empire. Wherever the Empire planted its flag, the slideways were sure to follow, initially carrying troops, then colonists and, finally, commerce.

The ice yachts themselves terrified the less advanced natives, and impressed on others Grand Quillia's dominance over their land and over nature itself, as well as demonstrating the power of the Wonder. Preceding the bulk of the yacht itself, an enormous V-shaped blade suspended from the prow by a great arc cleared the slideway of obstruction. Next were the spinning buffers, giant chamois leather balls at the ends of eight pronged propellers, perpetually spinning to keep the slideway as slick as an ice rink. Another set of buffers were in place either side of the yacht outside the hull and another at the rear, all powered by Red Wonder. As the cold air was pushed upwards by the buffers, it hit the warmer air and filled enormous sails which reduced the need to rely on the supply of Wonder the yachts carried, except for starting and stopping the enormous vessels on their journeys. Vents were positioned around the decks exerting force from the Red power generators below to keep the yachts on the straight and narrow, so a billowing stream of red smoke followed the yachts wherever they went.

The Spirit of Bester was one of the larger ice yachts in Grand Quillia's Eastern Imperial Fleet, stretching to nine hundred and twenty feet and weighing forty thousand tons. She carried one thousand first class passengers, six hundred second class passengers, and one thousand five hundred third class passengers, all in insulated cabins, and three thousand steerage, who were crammed into the frozen bowels of the yacht closest to the ice. Two thousand crew members kept the yacht at speeds up to eighty-four miles per hour. She was considered the pride of her line. Her older sister ships, The Spirit of Zelazny and The Brackett Flyer, although smaller and sleeker, were unable to boast the unadulterated splendour of their younger sibling.

The Bester started her journey in the Grand Quillian capital, its holds full of the joys of the motherland for homesick colonists, and more fodder to populate the Empire; farmers, traders, opportunists, mercenaries, bureaucrats, archaeologists, prospectors, hunters, missionaries, theatre troupes and labourers. Recently, groups of tourists had started travelling to the more exotic reaches of the Empire to see the Pyramids of Maisy, the spice markets of the Gramarye, and even the mysterious phenomenon of the Glasslands, garnered with the snowdrop spire of the Cathedral of Tales.

In the more remote areas, Captain Conrad, the Bester's commanding officer, would keep the speed up between the larger towns to avoid the unwanted interest of wild natives or criminal elements, although he would occasionally slow at the edge of the Glasslands to watch the Humps flee in terror. Conrad had no idea that his junior officers would occasionally stop briefly if there were any local traders, as they could pick up an attractive financial incentive from both the native tradesmen and the more gullible tourists, eager to spend their shillings on crystallised leaf jewellery, glass apple paperweights, and even jars of translucent grass, sometimes arranged into approximations of local landmarks.

The first officer on duty two days before the Bester's arrival in Chinsey was Trevor Gower, who was made aware one bright sunny afternoon that some of the passengers and even a few of the crew had reported seeing the snowdrop spire of the Cathedral of Tales move. Now if these people were stupid enough to think an ancient building could shuffle about, then he would be happy to liberate them of a hard-earned shilling or two, so, after checking with the captain's manservant that Conrad was sound asleep, he gave the order to reverse all vents and slow the ship, to allow passengers a chance to see the spire for themselves, and for any quick thinking locals to launch an iceboard to sell anything to hand. Obviously, he would make it be known to all but the captain that he was the one to thank for this unique opportunity.

Hilt saw the red smoke burst above the trees as they reached the edge of the Glasslands, where they tied the ponies. It looked about four miles away, around the other edge of the woods, and would probably reach them in twenty minutes if it was slowing, as he suspected.

The Glasslands stopped abruptly, the glass trees giving way to verdant living plants. It had been a relief to smell the warmth of living vegetation again, but it did not last. As they approached the enormous slideway, the plants had withered and died from the extreme cold emanating from the ice. In the more civilised parts of the Empire, there were barriers to protect the land either side of the slideways from the environmental damage, but nobody had ever considered doing the same somewhere like the Gramarye.

As they broke the tree line, they could see a small camp on the opposite side of the icy chute, a trickle of smoke smearing sadly into the sky from a paltry fire in the middle. At the edge of the slideway was a collection of large leather covered disks, about ten feet across and a hollowed out tree trunk with wooden stabilisers on either side, like a rudimentary canoe, its base also wrapped in shiny animal skins, with one end attached to a coiled piece of thick rope, the other end topped with a winch.

A few figures wandered around the camp, unaware of the group that had just emerged from the woods. Brennan put his hands around his mouth and called to the camp, but nobody turned in their direction. Pinkerton pulled his pistol and fired once into the air.

"That should do it," he said sagely.

One of the camp occupants looked across the slideway and raised their rifles.

"That did it, alright," Hilt groaned.

"Hang on a minute," said Laurel, "I think I know that one."

"Is that Jobby Stern?" Brennan asked.

Rounds struck the trees behind them.

"So can someone let your friend Jobby know that we are friends, please?" Rickenbacker suggested.

"Good friends, eh, Laurel?" Hilt mumbled.

Laurel rolled her eyes and started waving her arms frantically above her head.

"Jobby! It's me!"

One rifle was lowered.

"Jobby!"

"I hope none of the others is his wife," said Hilt.

"He isn't married," Laurel assured them.

"That's what he told you."

There was a glint of glass as Jobby raised his binoculars before indicating to his friends to lower their weapons.

"Your friends had better hurry up or we'll miss our ride," said Pinkerton, watching the red smoke above the trees.

The camp occupants picked up the canoe and carried it to the edge of the chute

"Here they come," said Brennan, moving to the side of the ice despite the cold.

"About time," grumbled Hilt.

Jobby climbed into the canoe, and his friends launched him down the side of the chute. The hiss of the canoe's belly on the ice got louder as it approached.

"Watch out!" Jobby shouted as the canoe began to slide up the side closest to them.

As the canoe started to slow, Jobby twirled the anchor above his head and let it fly towards the others. It landed with a loud pop of Wonder and sunk itself into the ground, before the powered winch at the other end of the rope dragged the canoe up the final few yards of the slideway.

"Jobby!" said Brennan eagerly, as the well-insulated man clambered out of the canoe and hugged the old man.

Jobby Stern was wrapped in layers of animal skins and fur, with a pair of enormous mittens he pulled off to reveal gloves underneath. He unwrapped the scarf from around his face and pulled back his hood to reveal a large, square head, tired eyes, a long moustache and a heavy set of jowls.

"Brennan, Laurel. We saw the smoke from the lodge and feared the worst," Jobby said, nodding to the others in turn. "What happened?"

"The worst," Laurel said. "How are you, Jobby?"

"Good. Fine. What are you doing in the woods? Where are the Humps? Did you see the snowdrop move?"

"Yes. We need your help, Jobby."

"Name it," Jobby said, grinning towards Pinkerton. "Laurel and I are special friends. She's fed me and the gang several times. It's amazing what she can cook up with so little."

"We can swap recipes later," Hilt interrupted. "We need to get on that ice yacht."

"Hello, Hilt," said Jobby without looked at the man. "As polite as ever, I see. How's the brigadier?"

"Dead. Alf is too."

"Alf. My God, Brennan..."

"We need to get on that yacht," Brennan said to Jobby, tears in his eyes. "We need to get to Chinsey before the people that killed my son."

Kendrick was relieved that Mandell was riding so fast and so far ahead. He could hardly see the misshapen form of the dead knight galloping ahead through the crystal trees, which was good, as Kendrick felt that he had vomited up everything bar the content of his bowels as he had watched Axelrod yank out bones and slide in others between muscle and sinew, saw away limbs to slot others into place, hammer out jawbones and wrench in replacements. What was left was less than human, despite the fact that he was cobbled together from many different people. In place of bolts and screws, the Wonder kept the different parts of the corpse together, and any open pieces of skin were hidden beneath different pieces of armour Mandell had scavenged from the Hump camp. As the man thing had scanned the ground with his mismatched eyes, he had mumbled words that had taken Kendrick some time to translate, now that the knight was missing all but three teeth, had a jaw too large for his skull and a tongue too small for his mouth.

Evan was repeating his own mantra, "Kill the sniper, fuck her bones, kill Laurel, fuck her bones, kill Hilt, fuck his bones," over and over again, and he had kept it up even as he climbed onto the back of one of the remaining ponies. It was as if he had forgotten Kendrick existed, which was one of the few things in his life that Kendrick was pleased about.

He hoped everybody else from the past few days would do the same.

As the troops left the empty lodge, Quine shook his head at Axelrod.

"I knew I should have killed that little man," he said to the Doctor.

"Don't worry. I'm sure Mandell will do that for us, if he hasn't already."

"Do you really think your patchwork killer will be able to find someone as sly as Rickenbacker when the man has evaded some of the best Trade agents?"

"Sir, I'm pretty sure I know where Rickenbacker is."

"You do?"

Axelrod pointed above the trees at the cloud of red smoke from the ice yacht rising above the trees in the distance.

"Bring me a crow," Quine commanded his second. "I need to send something by Murder."

"But if the smoke is over there, why are we heading in this direction?" Elena asked, pointing at the red smoke.

"The train is slowing down," Spicer replied.

"How do you know? From the smoke?" Bunce asked.

"It's expelling more smoke as it slows down. I don't know why it's slowing down but it is. And the red Wonder it needs to slow down and then get started again, it will need to replenish. And there's somewhere to refuel in this direction."

Elena and Bunce looked at each other, Elena shrugging as Bunce shook her head.

"I had no idea you were such a yacht spotter, Spicer," Elena said, smiling.

Spicer spurred his pony on without looking back at the two women. All he knew was that the direction he had chosen to take felt right, as if it were a path he had taken before, despite the fact that nobody but Humps had been this way for thousands of years. He had a feeling that he was going to catch the ice yacht from the direction he was heading, the way a child has a heady excitement when his parents take him out for a surprise and he suspects they are taking him somewhere he has always wanted to go. Everything else about the smoke from the yacht and the refuel point had fallen into his head as he spoke, like colours in a painting by numbers. He knew none of it made sense, but everything was fitting together perfectly.

Crossing the slideway on the canoe had been terrifying enough for Teddy, especially when he had been told that if any part of him were to touch the ice then it would be ripped off, like the tender meat from a boiled chicken. But to sit on these leather encased round sleds that didn't even have sides to keep you in, launch oneself onto the ice at a ship at least seven floors high, surely that was suicide, pure and simple. Jobby had assured them that the crew of the Bester would throw down netting for them to climb up, as they expected the traders to be there, and were keen for them to board for a cut of the profits; a cut the traders were happy to share, as they had already made a profit when Laurel had provided them with the Trade ponies in return for their carriage across the ice.

The ginger trader upon whose iceboard Teddy had been placed grunted through his scarves at him, and Teddy decided that this meant he should ready himself.

The ice yacht thundered across the ice into view, its sails furled, and Red Wonder pumping to slow the behemoth. The netting was cast through the smoke over the side and suddenly they were off, crackling across the ice with a loud swish. Teddy clung to the trader's enormous back besides an enormous duffle bag that tinkled as though it were full of glass. The boy had premonitions of the iceboard flipping over, catapulting him onto the ice, strips of him being torn from his bones as shards of glass shaved off chunks of skin, the passengers of the yacht pointing and laughing.

But then they were alongside the yacht, and slowing as the trader grabbed at the bottom of the netting until they were slowed enough to hold on and let the netting go taut. He tied the board onto the ropes and hauled himself upwards. Teddy's hand was engulfed by the grip of the trader's enormous mitt, and he was heaved onto the netting, which the boy grasped with all his might.

"Good luck," said the trader from beneath his scarves and hood, and he was off scaling the netting. The ropes swung and bounced against the side of the yacht as the man climbed, and tears crept from Teddy's eyes as he was slammed against the freezing metal of the hull.

As the trader ascended into the red smoke above, Teddy stole himself to take a look. To his left he saw Pinkerton helping Rickenbacker up the ropes towards the first open walkway that could provide entrance. They had agreed to let the traders head up to the top decks so that they could display their wares to the first class with money to spend, while Rickenbacker and the others would enter the lower decks under cover of the red smoke. Steerage was found in the freezing bowels of the yacht, and the passengers were unlikely to report stowaways to the crew, so it was the best place for them to start. To Teddy's right he could see Hilt struggling with his one hand to get up the ropes, ignoring

Laurel's offer of help so that she could concentrate on Brennan. Seeing the two old men, the woman and the man with one hand should have inspired him, he was sure, but Teddy still couldn't get his legs to move and his body seemed to be getting heavier by the second.

"Mister Elephantine?" he whispered. "Are you there?"

But there was no reply, in his ears or mind. He could hear nothing but the whistle of the wind, the clattering of the sled against the ice, the ropes buffeting the hull and his own ragged breathing.

"Mister Elephantine?" he tried again.

"Teddy!" he heard, and looked up to see Rickenbacker calling to him from over a barrier, "Come on, Teddy, you can do it."

"Get a move on, boy," called Pinkerton.

Teddy looked up through a gap in the smoke and saw the traders clambering onto the top deck. He felt a wave of nausea as the yacht's height seemed to tilt towards him. Teddy closed his eyes again and decided to die there, hanging on the side of this yacht that he couldn't remember the name of, heroism and chosen one be damned. He'd eventually fall, and his body and the stupid box holding Mister Elephantine would stick there until they were minced into the ice by the next yacht, and that would be the end of it.

The ropes started juddering again. Teddy's arms, legs and fingers started to quiver with the strain, and he decided that death would definitely be much easier. The decision seemed to free him, and he held his breath, preparing to let go as the netting shook more violently. Then he felt a strong arm around his waist, and opened his eyes to spy the whiskers and ruddy skin of Pinkerton beside him.

"Let me give you a hand," said the big man, and they started to ascend together, the bulk of Pinkerton behind the boy. They reached the walkway and Pinkerton put his shoulders beneath Teddy's feet to launch him to safety, feeling his wound open once more.

The Trade platoon had lost a third of its men in the Glasslands, and almost all of its ponies. Quine and Axelrod took mounts and rode behind the men as made their way down the gravel path of the Gleave family lodge.

"I could holiday here, you know," Quine said to the others, waving his hand over his shoulder. "No children, no women, a decent lounge."

"Perhaps you should return here and renovate it, Colonel," Axelrod suggested.

As they emerged back onto the road through the woods, Quine saw Franks on a steed ahead and called him over.

"What are you doing on a pony, Franks?"

"Riding, sir."

"Get off that animal at once. I want you to lead the men on the march from the front," Quine commanded, and he turned his pony to trot away.

Axelrod smirked at the little man's horrified face and followed the CColonel to the rear of the platoon as they formed up. Franks felt tears come to his eyes as he dismounted, not due to his embarrassment at being chastised in front of the men, but at the idea of marching miles back to Chinsey in a pair of knickers much too small for his girth and groin.

Laurel, despite the cold, had found herself breathless with excitement at the sled ride across the ice. After the oppressive murkiness of their journey beneath the Cathedral, it was a thrilling relief to feel the wind in her hair, to see people who were definitely real and not trying to kill her. And the opportunity to take a trip on the Spirit of Bester, one of the most well-known and luxurious yachts of the Grand Quillian merchant fleet made her heart race as she envisioned a hot bath, a well cooked meal and clean clothes.

But as they stepped from the walkway into the dark stinking steerage decks, her heart sank.

The stench of rotten food, curdled milk, sweat, shit and piss hung in the air, filling her nostrils, throat and lungs like a thick soup. Icicles hung from the ceiling, from the ragged sheets hanging between the hard wooden bunks and the bunks themselves. The wretched passengers - men, women and families, accompanied by the occasional cat, dog, and one lone parakeet - shivered in the cold, their breath hanging in the air. Parents clung to their children beneath thick fur coverings, while a few small fires burned in old food cans, warming foul stews and broths. A vague red glow throbbed in the air from the nearby Wonder generators, with extra illumination provided by smelly candles crafted from the fat of animals that could never have smelt this bad when they were alive.

Large eyes peered out from dark sockets in sallow faces, yellow skin hanging from their skulls. Their clothes were frayed and filthy, some hinting at Sunday best, the poor reaching for the finery they hoped to attain in the new world.

"This is heartbreaking," Laurel mumbled, as they picked their way through the detritus of humanity.

"Welcome to real life," Hilt said, and she wanted to hit him.

She had lived the life of an orphan, she thought, looking at the children wrapped in their parents' arms. These

people were trying to look after each other while they headed somewhere they hoped would offer them the chance to
better themselves. She had sold herself when she was barely a teenager, sold her body - and not just dancing, either.
And then she had tried to make things better, make people
better. She had sown other people's bodies back together
with sheep intestines on the battlefield, young soldiers yet to
shave who had signed up because life offered them nothing
else but crime. She looked around and saw her real family,
not her blood relatives, the mysterious Gleaves who had left
her to rot until they were in the ground themselves. These
were her kin who clung to each other for support, picked
each other up and dragged each other back down again.

"Is there anything we can do for them, Professor?"

Rickenbacker reached into his bag to retrieve a scrap of
material smeared with a gluey concoction of Wonder.

"This might help," he said, handing it to Laurel. "Just
knot it tightly and it should provide some warmth. It can be
undone and used again."

Laurel looked at the scrap and then looked deep into the
gloom, spying a gaggle of children attached to one another
under a stained cotton sheet. She approached them slowly,
the material in her hand, and they cowered away from her.

"It's alright," she assured them, "I have something that
can help you warm you up."

She took the two ends of the material and tied a loose
knot, unsure how hot it would get in her fingertips. She
pulled it tight and it immediately flooded the area with a
fresh warmth, like morning sun, without burning her hand.
One of the braver children crept forward, reached out tentatively and snatched it from Laurel's grasp.

"There you go," she said, smiling.

"So much for keeping a low profile," Hilt said, looking at the wide eyes turning towards them.

"That's nothing," said Pinkerton, before climbing onto the nearest bunk. "Listen up. If any of you take that scrap of warmth from those children, I will personally freeze you to death myself. Is that understood?"

Everybody turned away from the group and Pinkerton decided to take this as a good sign.

"Are we quite finished do-gooding?" Hilt asked. "I would like to find some food that won't kill me and a bed that won't give me crabs."

And with that, Hilt led the others through the huddled masses towards the only door they could see, hoping it would lead upwards.

The crow network was another backbone of the Empire, and it generally followed wherever the slideways went, so that the crows could follow them to other Imperial centres. Using Green Wonder to control their minds, crows would be given a message letter by letter that would be translated into caws, the language of the crows. Crows had been chosen as the birds were essentially pack animals, aggressive with crows from other areas and flocks, known as Murders, so the message could be kept within the Grand Quillian Murder. As the crow did not migrate too far, the Green Wonder enabled the already intelligent birds to pass the message on, and their incredible hearing meant that the crows could pass messages between each other across extraordinary distances.

Within the Empire, the crow network was known as the Murder, and the phrase 'as the crow flies' did not always mean the straightest distance between two places, as they followed the slideways, but it did generally mean the quickest, as there was no faster way to send a message within the Empire than via the Murder.

The message sent by Axelrod to the Chinsey Trade Headquarters took twenty minutes to arrive at the Headquarters' Murder Exchange, and then took another twenty minutes moving up three floors into the A.I.R. office.

The Alien and Insurgent Research department was often seen as a law unto itself, especially in the colonies that were run by the Trade, as they reported directly to the Grand Quillian government as opposed to the Trade. Therefore, most Trade officers and their ECOs were not very forthcoming in sharing information with them until they had to. Their bureaucratic powers were absolute, their physical and Wonder powers had never been advertised, but everybody in the know knew that they were the concealed strong arm of the Empire. AIR was only aware of Rickenbacker due to their meeting with him at the Necropolis dig four years previously, when they had closed him down. His history as a troublemaker had only been of local interest, and they were therefore happy for him to be managed by the Trade in the area. But the news from Doctor Axelrod about Rickenbacker's infiltration into the Cathedral of Tales and his pilfering of a Gargoyle Key, coupled with his knowledge of the mass grave at the Necropolis, troubled AIR. So they contacted two agents via the Murder, who happened to be in the area of the Glasslands, and told them to command the Spirit of Bester to stop for refuelling, where they would board the ice yacht and detain this local problem named Rickenbacker, who seemed to have ideas above his station.

The door from the bunks led to steps up to the steerage refectory, where the long tables and benches were busy with families gossiping, arguing, gambling, playing chess, backgammon and drinking much like any village square, illuminated by large portholes on either side. The distance from the ice, the proximity of the kitchens and crush of people served to warm the area to bearable temperatures.

Rickenbacker and the others approached a large serving hatch into the kitchens as surreptitiously as possible, Hilt concealing his blade behind the bulk of Pinkerton. The hatch was secured with a barred shutter bolted closed with a padlock, so without a word, Hilt bent down and pulled the shim from his spurs. Within seconds he had popped the lock and Pinkerton slipped his fingers beneath the shutter to raise it.

"I haven't seen you down here before," said a man behind them.

"And you won't see us down here again," Hilt replied, without looking back. "Lift the shutter, Pinkerton."

"Leave it where it is," the man said again, before spitting the last word, "Pinkerton."

They turned to see three undesirable individuals, one armed with a club, the others with knives. Pinkerton turned back and lifted the shutter.

"Gentlemen, why would you care what my friends and I are up to?" Laurel asked, smiling.

"Because there's a premium on grassing up stowaways, darling. Maybe we'll let them have your friends and keep you for ourselves."

"Why not give them a warm hankie to show we're friendly?" Hilt said to Laurel.

"You're an arsehole, Hilt."

"I'm the arsehole you should be worrying about," said the man with the club.

"Tell me, Sir," said Pinkerton, "do you know what the opposite of a stowaway is?"

"Er..."

"It's someone who should be on the yacht who isn't. And that's exactly what you and your friends are going to be when I throw you through that window."

"It's called a porthole," Hilt corrected Pinkerton.

"Shut up, Hilt, or you'll go with them."

"I think we're all a little overtired," Rickenbacker suggested.

"Be quiet, old man," said the man with the club.

"So when we get out of here, can we find a cabin? A good one?" asked Laurel, ignoring the men.

"I am still here," the man with the club pointed out as his friends shuffled cautiously.

"Why?" Hilt asked as he raised his blade to the man's throat.

Laurel slipped beneath the shutter, followed by Brennan and Teddy.

"Bye now," said Laurel. "Nice to meet you."

Pinkerton helped the Professor through the serving hatch and turned to stand side by side with Hilt.

"I lost a dog today," Pinkerton told the three men, who turned from staring at Hilt's blade to look at each other.

"The dog is at the lodge," Hilt told him, rolling his eyes.

"It might not be."

"I promise you that dog is at the lodge."

And when Hilt and Pinkerton turned from each other to confront the three men, they found they had already moved on.

Jobby and the rest of his traders disembarked and the Bester fired up her generators, unfurled her sails and slid slowly forward.

As they made their way further into the ship, steadily ascending through the decks towards warmth, a better class of passenger started to emerge. In third class Rickenbacker and his group met small time traders, skilled labourers, the occasional youngster in a brand new, ill-fitting Trade uniform, and some young families accompanying their junior bureaucrat fathers. The accommodation was broken into thin-walled cabins, fully insulated against the cold, lit by Wonder and made homely with mattresses, pillows and even sinks. The smell of smoked fish, onions and boiled cabbage permeated the decks, except for the rich throat burning scents around the smoking rooms.

"Can't we stop for food?" Teddy asked. "Some toast or something?"

"Surely the Chosen One wants more than third-class grub," Hilt chided him. "You can aim higher than toast."

"I like toast," Teddy mumbled back.

The doors between second and third class were not locked, and Rickenbacker suggested they find a cabin in the second-class decks, but something had stirred in Hilt. He was determined to get into first class, and Rickenbacker was certain it was not the need for the high life that spurred Hilt onwards, but more the pleasure he would take in depriving somebody in first class of their luxury. There was a zeal in his eyes, a bloodthirstiness that Rickenbacker did not find reassuring, so when Hilt said he would scout ahead for a first class cabin before coming to get them, Rickenbacker felt both a sense of relief for himself and a dread for whomever had whatever cabin they were about to inherit.

It was not that Captain Conrad was not a morning person, it was more that he hated being woken up. And he definitely didn't like being woken with a message received via the Murder ordering him to stop at the next refuelling depot to pick up two AIR agents who would search his ship for a group of criminals who had apparently stowed away. AIR agents were generally arrogant and intrusive, liable to make the captain feel like he was relinquishing some command of the Spirit of Bester. But the consequences of ignoring an order from AIR did not bear thinking about, so he gave the order. He decided to stay in his cabin for the rest of the voyage and let that jumped up first officer Trevor Gower deal with the agents. It might teach him some manners.

The refuel depot nearest the Glasslands stood at the base of a steep incline, impassable to Humps, and offering no view of the snowdrop spire. It was known as Wyman's Base, and was manned by two Hodgkinson Line employees named Ed and Spike. Neither man was particularly blessed with intelligence, patience or charm, happy in their role of transferring Red Wonder from the company's containers into the generators of passing yachts.

Due to its close proximity to Chinsey, Wyman's Base was not particularly busy, so Ed and Spike spent a lot of their time taking pot shots at Humps on the hilltop, playing cards, brewing their own alcohol and bickering over women that they would never have the nerve to talk to.

Ed was the first of them to notice the two strangers approaching side by side on a pony and trap. Spike was dozing in a hammock having drunk three pints of homebrew for breakfast.

"Strangers!" Ed informed him.

"Shut up!" Spike shouted back, although Ed wasn't far away.

"And the Bester is late," Ed continued, checking his timepiece.

"Shut up or so help me you will be spitting out my toenails because I'll have kicked you in the arse."

Ed heard this insult two or three times a day, it being Spike's favourite ever since somebody had threatened him with it some months ago in some Chinsey dive.

"Strangers are getting closer," Ed commented.

Ed always had been the more observant, mainly because Spike could only really concentrate on one thing at a time. Ed sometimes managed two or even three.

"Right!" Spike shouted before aggressively tumbling from his hammock.

He pulled himself up and squinted down the slideway, discerning the smoke of the Bester.

"I see the Bester," he told Ed, then followed his colleague's gaze and pointed. "Strangers."

Ed nodded.

"Two men shouldn't share a pony trap. Or an umbrella either. It ain't dignified," Spike continued. "You deal with them." With that, the man returned to his hangover, grunting as he attempted to climb back into his hammock.

Ed scratched his head and considered sitting down to wait for the strangers, but decided that would take too much effort.

Spicer, Elena and Bunce surveyed the scene from their ponies on the hilltop above Wyman's Base, careful to avoid the rotting Hump corpses littering the ground. The descent to the refuel depot would be arduous but not impossible, as long as whoever was responsible for picking off the Humps didn't take any interest in them. From what they could see, the two men below were too busy to notice them. One appeared to be asleep, while the other seemed to be completely entranced by the approaching pony and trap.

"Who are they?" Bunce asked, looking at the approaching travellers.

Spicer shrugged.

"I doubt they're friendly," Bunce continued. "If I still had my rifle, I could pick them all off within seconds."

Spicer bit his lip. Bunce did not say much, but even when she did it was not entirely helpful. That said, he was pleased it was Bunce by his side as opposed to Tork or Conway. He doubted Tork could have handled his transformation, and Conway was less than useless, a hyperphysicist who could only dabble with other people's creations. Since his change, Spicer had felt less inclined to take revenge on Rickenbacker's band for the death of his comrades, and a deeper sadness and rage was now mixing in his chest regarding the loss of Pearly, somewhere he had never visited populated by people he had never met. He looked into the distance at smoke from the approaching yacht.

"As long as we get down there before that yacht leaves, everything should work out."

"And you're sure Rickenbacker is there?" Elena asked.

"I'm sure the Gargoyle Key is."

"Those yachts are big," Bunce informed them. "How will we find it?"

"I don't know, Bunce," he replied.

Spicer had already forgotten the woman's first name.

AIR Operative 1066 noticed the figures descending from the Glasslands first, handed the reins of the trap to his colleague, Operative 80K, and retrieved his field glasses from their case in the bag at his feet. He looked through the lenses and made out two unidentified females and one male. Something in the manner of the way the male moved bothered him, so he flicked the latch to allow the gel of Green Wonder to flow across the glass and his vision was extended as though he were ten feet from the objects of his interest. And then he recognised what made the man different, something extremely disquieting that required immediate elimination, then a full report, followed by more investigation and, finally, a cover up. He would leave the reporting to 80K, as his partner appreciated that side of things. 1066 was a lot more hands-on, a people person. He raised his hand to indicate for 80K to stop the trap and reached for the high-powered rifle. He had not had the opportunity to put down Elf for some time.

"They've stopped," Ed said.

"Shut up," Spike replied.

"One of them has a big gun."

"I bet mine's bigger," said Spike, climbing from his hammock again and reaching for his blat gun. "He'd better not be planning on shooting any of our Humps."

Spicer continued down the sharp incline of the hill by jumping and tumbling from tree to rock to plateau, grabbing anything to slow his descent. He hardly heard Bunce call to him from above.

"They've got guns," she repeated.

He slid to a halt behind a large rock, got his breath back and looked back up the incline to see the others take cover. He edged carefully around the rock on his belly and spied the pony and trap, now stationary. One man was sitting in the trap holding field glasses to his eyes as the other raised a rifle. There was a loud ricochet inches from Spicer's head, and then he heard the sound of the rifle below. He crawled backwards into cover and drew his Twirler as the sound of more gunfire echoed from Wyman's Base.

Operative 80K did not doubt that 1066 had seen Elfkind. He was just a little surprised, which was why he wanted to see for himself. He placed one finger in the ear nearest 1066 to lessen the noise of the rifle while he held the field glasses with his other hand. When his partner fired the first shot, he felt the pony grow skittish, but now it knew the sound of the rifle wasn't hurting it, it would relax, 1066 would get a clear shot, and then they could get on with the job in hand.

Then he heard through his unobstructed ear the unmistakeable sound of a blat gun. Shots peppered the trap and the bottom of his trousers, and he wondered why somebody would be so stupid as to think a blat gun fired from the hillside would actually reach them. Next, the pony reared up in terror, and there was a deafening snap as the trap collapsed to one side on top of one of its wheels. 1066 was catapulted into 80K, squeezing the rifle trigger as he fell. The pony spooked and immediately made a break for it, its hooves tangling in the mess of tack from the trap. It stumbled forward, one of the limbers cracked, and the pony fell, screaming as it went. 1066 pushed himself off 80K and reached for the pistol inside his jacket. The blat boomed out again. As the pony thrashed around on the floor, 80K saw one of the men from Wyman's Base strolling towards them, calmly racking his blat gun and firing again. 1066 had his Twirler in his hand but as he spun the chamber, shot struck the side of his head and his shoulder, throwing him against the back of the trap and on top of 80K again. 80K grabbed his partner's Twirler and aimed past the thrashing limbs of the pony at the man with the blat. He fired three times and hit the man twice in the chest, and then the pony rolled backwards onto 80K, crushing his leg, pelvis, stomach, chest and, finally, his head in quick succession.

Ed saw Spike drop to his knees and drop the blat. He ran towards his friend as he saw the pony free itself of the tack, turn tail and gallop away from him. Then he saw the badly wounded man, blood pouring from a head wound, raise a high powered rifle from the floor and fire from the hip. Ed felt a chill in his chest as he flew backwards through the air. He lifted his head to see Spike fall face down into the floor and the man with half a face drop the rifle from his dead fingers. As Ed watched the pony gallop into the distance, he wished very hard that he was riding it home, and then he died.

By the time Spicer and the others reached Wyman's base, the pony was long gone, leaving just tracks. The red smoke of the Bester was starting to reach them as it braked, its bulk still out of sight behind the incline they had just descended.

"What happened?" Bunce asked as she surveyed the scene.

"Luck?" Spicer replied, following the sniper to the corpses in the tangled mess of the wrecked trap.

Bunce pulled the high-powered rifle from the dead operative's hand and checked it over.

"A Simon Insley Gee Zero with telescopic sights. Thank you very much," she said, taking it apart to return it to its case.

"And Alien and Insurgent Research passes and identification papers. Very useful," said Spicer, closing the second body's jacket and handing one set of documents to Elena.

"Why do you think AIR operatives shot at you?" Elena asked, her eyes scanning the papers.

"My good looks?" Spicer replied, fingering the points of his ears.

"You need a hat," Bunce suggested as she rooted through the Operative's bag. "Ooh, this is interesting."

She handed Spicer a bound folder as red smoke started to overwhelm them.

"Rickenbacker's file…" he said, flipping through it. "Looks like Axelrod knows the Professor is on the Spirit of Bester."

"What's the Spirit of Bester?" Bunce asked as she transferred her attentions to bodies of Spike and Ed.

"That is," Elena replied, pointing at the hull of the enormous ice yacht as it hove into view.

Laurel and Rickenbacker leant against the barrier of the second-class promenade as they looked through the clouds of red smoke at Wyman's Base sliding into view below them. They stood apart from the other passengers, attempting to cover the sight of Pinkerton slumped against the barrier on the floor, exhaustion exacerbated by the pain of his wound beating him down. Brennan and Teddy watched people exercising in the gymnasium, completely bemused.

"It looks like we are refuelling," Rickenbacker said, seeing the crew busying themselves to take on more Red Wonder from the tanks below.

"Is your life always like this, Professor?" Laurel asked the old man.

"Recently it has grown rather frantic," he conceded. "I find it difficult to find the time just to breathe."

"What do you think this big new threat is?"

"I pray it isn't whatever unleashed those mechanical beasts on Pearly."

"We beat one. Couldn't an army beat them?"

"Those beasts were unleashed thousands of years ago. God knows what their creators would be capable of now."

"And Mister Elephantine thinks the Fairy are the ones to help us, of all people..."

Rickenbacker frowned in warning at Laurel, touching a finger to his lips as a figure approached, the sun at his back. He was dressed in the unmistakeable black and red of the Trade, wearing an officer's long frock coat and a shako, its peak pulled low over the eyes as the plume of black feathers stood proudly above the cylindrical cap. As the man approached, Rickenbacker noticed that one sleeve was empty and pinned under the shoulder, and that the man dragged one leg behind him, dead straight.

"What's wrong with whiskers there?" asked the man, looking down at Pinkerton.

"Hilt?" said Laurel, looking the man up and down.

"You are addressing Captain Harvey Shackleton, you are my nurse," Hilt replied. "Now please bring the rest of the servants along to the first class parlour suite B62 where dinner is served."

"Dinner?" Pinkerton groaned from the floor.

As they helped the boxer to his feet, they did not notice the jetty being lowered towards Wyman's base, or the corpses lying around the defunct pony trap at the base of the hillside.

First Officer Trevor Gower was surprised at the appearances of the AIR operatives. He knew they generally travelled incognito but these three looked and smelt like they had been sleeping rough for some time. That said, the man in the ill-fitting hat and the woman wearing the two-gun rig made a very good-looking pair. Even their leathered up henchwoman was not too bad to look at either, if a little boyish.

They had boarded at Wyman's Base, a trail of destruction in their wake, and had immediately asked if the Bester had made any unscheduled stops in the last twelve hours. Gower couldn't deny it, so he told them about the trader stop on the other side of the woods. They had glanced knowingly at each other and shown him two wanted posters, one of an older gentleman, the other of a bewhiskered heavy. If they had known Gower for the man he was, they would've known that the bounty of hundreds of shillings would be incentive enough. Instead, he felt extremely intimidated. Their weapons seemed to be the only parts of these weary people in good repair, and the boyish henchwoman seemed to be sulking. He looked at the posters, desperately racking his brains for any memory of anyone that looked vaguely like these purported stowaways. He even attempted to use his imagination, picturing the old man with the other's whiskers, and the whiskered one clean shaven, but he drew a blank. So Trevor decided to do what came naturally to him when dealing with authority figures. He offered to bribe the AIR operatives with one of the best suites on the ship, and he was extremely relieved when they accepted.

He would put them up next door to Trade Captain so they would see that they know how to treat the military on the Bester. He called for a porter and asked him to escort the operatives to first-class parlour suite B61.

CHAPTER 12

The Spirit of Bester
The Hodgkinson International Line
The Gramarye Region
Grand Quillia

June 1856

Nothing says civilised like a long hot bath. It's not about the cleansing of the body. That can be done with a cloth and a river, perhaps a little soap. Having a long hot bath is about opportunity. It is about being in control of your life, having the money to afford decent plumbing and the time to stay still for as long as you want. To ruminate or vegetate. Bliss.

Laurel closed her eyes and lowered herself further in the bath, feeling the bubbles tickle her face before she submerged her whole head. As her ears filled with water, she found herself counting the times she had heard the pop of raw Wonder in the last thirty-six hours. Raising her head again, she heard the murmur of strangers and the door of the adjoining cabin open. She felt a pang of jealousy. Their neighbours must live like this all the time. They had no idea how lucky they were, how special this was. Even the word 'decadent' sounded better than normal people's language.

She looked around the bathroom, taking in the graceful carved marble shapes of the double sinks, the colouring of the tiny tiles, the plush cotton towels hanging from the warmed oak racks. Her mind flickered back to the moving mosaics beneath the Cathedral of Tales and she considered what opulence the wealthy of Pearly must have had to hand. But then she thought of their gruesome deaths at the grinders and sticky fire of the praying mantis beasts.

Despite the steam in the room and the warmth of the water, she felt a chill.

She considered calling for someone to come in, soap her back, warm her loins and soothe her soul. Pinkerton perhaps, or the boy. Just a little fun to relax the muscles and stretch the bones. Give in to a little selfishness. Then she saw the figure of Mandell, of what he had been in the cellar of the lodge and what he had become, how close they had been, how they had become one for that brief moment of bliss and now he wanted to kill them all, separate them from each other, from life itself.

She had accepted the legacy of the lodge because it connected her to a family. It meant she belonged somewhere. The fact that Brennan and Alf (poor Alf) came with it only made it more attractive. Brennan had looked after her like a doting uncle, while Alf had been a little brother. She had found what she needed, something to take her away from the lunacy her life had become, the love life of the battlefield nurse. There was no commitment, no future, as much romance or physicality as she fancied, and as the nurse she still had some control, something she really only pretended to have when she was a dancer, when she had relied on her body, kidding herself that the men's lust meant she could pick and choose.

And now she was here, in a borrowed bath surrounded by fugitives having been told by dead Elf that her family were killers. Even the lodge was destroyed. And it was up to her, as Laurel Bristow, Luscious Legs Laurel and Sister Bristow, to help these people save the world. She was not clear what she was saving the world from, but save it she would. After all, she had been an orphan, still was really, and the world was all she had.

That and this nice warm borrowed bathtub full of bubbles.

Pinkerton could feel the herbs and Wonder from the medicine Hilt had procured working through his system. The bullet hole was clean, thanks to Laurel, the medicine had both stemmed the flow of blood and alleviated the throbbing pain, so the only discomfort he now felt was from the soft king-size bed and silk linen.

The old boxer preferred a hard bed, if not the floor. Sheets were unimportant, and the best pillow was his trusty blat gun. He liked the chill of the night air tempered by the embers of a dying fire, and ideally the loving warmth of another body; ideally a dog, but a large cat or overweight woman would do.

He also felt uncomfortable because a gentleman should never hog the bed when there was a lady in need. And the Professor was an older gent, as was Brennan, who had also suffered a terrible loss.

But they had insisted, and as he had been weakened by his wound he had been unable to argue.

He wished Mandell had been there to talk it through. He wouldn't have let the others treat his partner like an invalid, whether it was true or not. Evan would have insisted the lady take the bed and then he probably would have taken her in it.

But Mandell was the one who had put a hole in him, tried to kill him, wanted to kill them all.

Pinkerton had spoken to the Professor about it and he understood that the thing that had attacked them was no longer his partner in crime, but it was still hard to take, harder even than accepting that he was dead.

Pinkerton had met Sir Evan Mandell, son of Prince Edmundsen of the Bullen Protectorate and brother of Lord Ethering of the Great Quillia Parliament, due to a recurring problem in the man's life; women.

Pinkerton had received a lot of attention after he had won the Langtry Common fight, eventually accepting one Francis Settler as his manager, trainer and promoter. Pinkerton had decided on Settler after investigating both the man and his reputation, discovering that he was an avowed family man and that all his surviving prize fighters were very rich and rather famous. Settler did indeed look after Pinkerton very well, arranging excellent bouts, some of which tested Pinkerton's skills, most of which attracted attention and all of which Pinkerton won.

The night that Mandell entered the boxer's life taught Pinkerton a few new things about Settler, and reinforced others.

Pinkerton was fighting an individual named Frederick Banks, known as Footlocker Freddie due to his fighting style, which was to plant his feet firmly in the centre of the ring and stay there. The bout was in the large back room of a public house called the Archer and Apple, located on the High Moors of Grand Quillia, and for the first time, Settler asked Pinkerton to fix the fight. He didn't ask him to lose it, that would be at most unethical, and at the very least ungentlemanly. No, Settler was having some cash flow issues. He had cash, Pinkerton was not to worry about that, he just had no flow, so Settler needed a favour. He knew that his man was going to win, he was a natural after all, a joy to watch, not some lead head like Footlocker Freddie, who won his bouts by virtue of being able to absorb blows. Put simply, it would really help Settler if Pinkerton would not win the fight until a specific time. Settler would put the money he did have on the precise minute that Pinkerton would send Freddie to the ground. Then Settler could collect big time.

Settler wouldn't normally ask but it was his daughter Iris' birthday and he wanted to really treat her after the fight, show her off, prove to her what a big success he was.

His manager had done Pinkerton a lot of favours, and had improved his boxing no end. He had also added to the victor of Langtry Common's fame, so although it was not strictly gentlemanly, Pinkerton agreed to knock out Footlocker Freddie at a specified time. Settler was thrilled, promising to introduce the boxer to Iris, the apple of his eye, after the fight and would check the odds before laying his bet after the fight had begun. He would give Pinkerton a signal one minute before he should deliver the ultimate blow, so nobody could accuse them of setting it up beforehand, and he could get the longest odds as nobody expected Footlocker to last too long. The signal would be one finger raised in the air.

And so when the night of the footlocker fight came around, Pinkerton discovered Settler was not above a little fiddling, but that he was definitely a family man, as he doted over his daughter.

The fight began, and once Pinkerton had probed Footlocker's defences he reckoned he could knock out the less-than-animated fighter whenever he wished, so he took his time, pulling his punches as he skipped around Freddie, avoiding almost everything thrown at him, while he kept a close but surreptitious eye on Settler, seated in the front row.

After the first five minutes there was still no signal from his manager, so Pinkerton started to worry. He understood that he was the favourite to win by a wide margin and therefore the longer Footlocker stayed standing, the better Settler's winnings. However, this was affecting Pinkerton's reputation, and Footlocker already looked ready to fall without the help of Pinkerton. But Settler wasn't moving. There was no sign of any sign at all. In fact, Settler didn't even seem to be interested in the fight at all. He glared across the ring into the seats beyond. Pinkerton let Footlocker land one on him and stumbled onto the ropes, scanning the crowd. He noticed a young lady who bore a definite resemblance to Settler, who Pinkerton surmised was his manager's beloved daughter. Pinkerton did a lap of the ring around Footlocker, let the man connect with his chin once more, and took another look at the Settler girl.

She was blushing, fluttering her lashes and generally cavorting in a way no father would appreciate, with a dashing ne'er-do-well who seemed to be doing very well for himself, judging by his manner and effect on all the women around him, not just Iris Settler.

Pinkerton's manager glared at the man, his face slowly turning purple as he saw red, and Pinkerton realised that the last thing on Settler's mind was the fight, no matter how much money was riding on it. Pinkerton resolved to remedy the situation immediately. He danced around his hopeless opponent, dropped his defence and offered the man his chin. It took a while, but Footlocker finally noticed and took advantage of the situation, smacking Pinkerton across the chops to send him sprawling in Settler's direction. The manager's finger went up. Pinkerton pushed himself from the ropes and counted down to delivering the final punch of the evening.

As his fist connected with Footlocker's face and his opponent took to the air, Pinkerton looked past Freddie and immediately knew he had made a mistake. The finger hadn't been a signal to him. It was a warning to his daughter's suitor, and Settler's look of surprise and frustration said it all. Footlocker hit the floor out for the count and Settler was in the ring.

"You stupid, mutton-chopped loser! I didn't give you any signal. You just cost me and my friends a lot of money," he hissed at his fighter. "You owe me, Pinkerton."

"Right you are, boss," Pinkerton replied. "Just name it."

As Pinkerton's fist was raised into the air by the referee, Settler put his lips to the winner's ear.

"Kill that lascivious little creep whose hands are all over my daughter."

And that was when Pinkerton discovered two new things about his manager; that he was crooked, and that he was no gentleman.

The Footlocker Freddie fight was Ten Fingers Pinkerton's last professional bout. Instead of murdering Iris Settler's courter, he introduced himself to Sir Evan Mandell, and after the two of them saw off the various henchmen of Francis Settler together, Mandell took Iris' virginity and Pinkerton gained a new partner. Their relationship was cemented when they were made aware of the significant price on their heads, and they left Grand Quillia together soon afterwards.

Since then, Mandell and Pinkerton had saved each other's lives countless times, usually in situations that arose due to Pinkerton's acute gentlemanly honour and Mandell's acute womanly pursuits.

But as Pinkerton lay in this sumptuous bed aboard the Spirit of Bester, he couldn't sleep because he knew that he had failed his friend. Evan had been shot dead, and now Pinkerton would have to kill him.

The Professor had finished loading his pipe, and was just bringing the match up to light it when the door to the parlour's private promenade deck opened and Hilt stepped out. Neither man acknowledged the other, Hilt moving to the barrier to stare out over the Gramarye as it edged past them, while Rickenbacker puffed on his pipe.

The buffers rumbled as they spun and there was the constant crackle of the ice, but it felt quiet.

Hilt pulled a pack of cigarillos from the frock coat he was wearing, flipped it open with his thumb, and removed one with his lips.

"Would you like a light?" the Professor asked without looking up from the glowing bowl of his pipe.

Hilt moved closer to the Professor, who lit the cigarillo, Hilt shielding the flame with his hand. His eyes looked into the Professor's face as the match flared.

"Is there something you want to say, Mr Hilt?" said the older man.

He was waiting for another barbed criticism or casual putdown and was surprised when Hilt exhaled smoke, paused, and said, "I want to know about the Brigadier's last moments."

Rickenbacker considered his words, looking into the past.

"He had that small pistol…" he began.

"The Schrödinger. No range, terrible aim, slow to reload…"

"Spicer disarmed Teddy. The Brigadier fired once before the Lieutenant put a bullet between his eyes. It was not undignified."

"A soldier's death."

"Spicer had no choice."

"Old Beasley was a danger to the end."

The two men smoked on in silence.

"He was very precious to you, wasn't he?"

Hilt moved back to the barrier, his face in shadow.

"We were the last of the Torchlights," he said. "Now it's just me."

"Weren't there other survivors of Meander? Civilians from Maisy?"

"Not according to my sources."

"Your sources?"

"The Trade officers I spoke to."

"Spoke to? Have you killed a lot of people, Hilt?"

"What's a lot? I doubt the amount I've killed add up to the population of Maisy, or one street worth of Pearly's dead."

"Did the Brigadier help you?"

"Help me?"

"Help you dispose of the Trade officers? Help you take your revenge?"

"He helped me. He helped me to stop."

It was during the famous storm of 1851, December, at the Grayson Hospital, sixty miles from the centre of the capital. The walls were so thick and the shrieking of the inmates so frenzied that the sound of the rain could not be heard inside the secure asylum, although the corridors occasionally echoed with the bass rumble of thunder.

Sheet lightning illuminated the cell, the blood splatters up the wall turning silver during each flash. Hilt looked down at the disembowelled corpse, its mouth lolling open and the eyes wide, and wiped his blade on the body's sleeve. He bent over, scooped some water from the bucket on wheels, and wiped the blood from his face and hair. Then he slid the blade back into the groove he had cut into the handle of the mop, placed the mop head in the bucket and wheeled it out into the hallway.

He had come in over the roof and climbed down into a quad where the doors were left unlocked. He had already memorised the route to the patient's cell, an ex-Reclaimer who had been looting Maisy at the time the paralysing floor had struck the Meander Canyon.

It was just a simple matter of keeping his cover and re-tracing his steps. He shuffled along, keeping his head down and the bucket on wheels in front of him. He watched the feet of passers-by, not knowing or caring whether they were patients or wardens, not stopping. And then he saw the ragged bottoms of a pair of trouser legs above bare feet, and he looked up to see the unmistakeable scarlet dress uniform of the Torchlight Cavalry. As he tried to hide his growing incredulity, his eyes fell upon the pips of a Brigadier, and he knew it was Beasley.

Hilt stopped and pulled the mop from the bucket. He wet the floor in front of his former commanding officer and took in his surroundings. Three wardens struggled to push one patient into a nearby cell, while another patient leant against the wall, giggling with one hand down his trousers as he watched the scene.

Beasley stepped into the puddle and stopped, looking down at his wet feet.

"Brigadier," Hilt whispered, moving closer.

The man raised his head but kept his eyes to the floor.

"Beasley, it's me," Hilt said, trying to move his face into the man's line of sight. "It's Widdershins."

Beasley lifted one foot from the floor and flapped it down again in the water. Then he did it again.

"You remember Widdershins, Maisy. The Moon Docks." He glanced at the three warders as they locked the door of the cell. "The Meander Canyon."

Beasley continued to tap his bare foot in the puddle, watching his toes get wetter. Hilt put a hand on the man's wrist.

"You. Don't touch the freaks."

Hilt ignored the warden and squeezed Beasley's hand.

"I can get you out of here," he said.

"Oi, loony lover," the warden continued, stepping towards the two men.

Hilt raised his sword, the blade still in the mop handle, and pointed it at the warden's face.

"Leave us alone," he warned.

"Or what? You'll wet my hair?" the warden chuckled, slapping the cosh in one hand as his two colleagues stepped up either side of him. "Come here, you."

The lead warden stepped forward and Hilt kicked the bucket towards him so it slid across the floor into the man's shins. The man called out in pain as Hilt flicked the mop handle from his weapon, the mop head hitting another warden in the face. The remaining warden froze, looking at the blade flash in the lightning. Then he turned and ran down the corridor, pressing a whistle to his lips so that the piercing sound rang out down the corridors.

"Beasley," Hilt said, louder now, "we have to go."

He put his hand under the Brigadier's armpit and looked down the corridor towards the door to the quad he had entered through, but knew the old man wouldn't make it to the roof. As he looked in the opposite direction where the whistler was fleeing, the first warden launched himself at Hilt, wrapping his arms around the warrior's elbows and running him into the wall. Hilt's feet left the floor and all the air was forced from his lungs as he was smashed against the tiles. The other warden, his nose a bloody mess from the mop head, raced forward, grabbing Hilt around the knees. All three men slid to the floor into the puddle at Beasley's bare feet. Hilt tried to raise his sword but he was pinned. He tried to butt the warden, bite him, do something, but the man knew what he was doing after years in an insane asylum. The other man lay across his legs, stopping him from kicking out or getting any sort of momentum. And then the man with his arms around his elbows and chest started to squeeze tighter, crushing all the air out of Hilt, whose head started to swim. The screams of the patients seemed to diminish, so all he could hear was the whistle as it moved into the distance, his own blood pumping in his ears and the splish-splash of the Brigadier's feet in the puddle of water.

Then he felt the arms around his body tighten as if in shock and go loose. He flapped his arms free and shook his head to clear it. He heard a clang of metal and felt hands help him up. He leant against the wall as his sight returned and heard Beasley's voice.

"Here comes the cavalry."

Hilt looked around. The bucket was over one warden's head, blood mixing with water on the floor. The other warden had the end of the mop head sticking out of the back of his neck. The random patient still had a smile on his face and his hand down his trousers.

"We need to get out of here, boy," the Brigadier said.

"Yes Sir," Hilt replied, saluting. "Could you make it over the roof?"

"Of course I could," Beasley said proudly, "if I had a pair of boots."

Hilt reached down and took the enormous ring of keys from the first warden's belt.

"So you know what we need?" he asked.

"An army to charge the gates," Beasley replied.

And that night, two hundred and thirty four patients escaped from Grayson Hospital, including a homeless man in a dirty uniform who had been found sobbing uncontrollably in the streets of the capital, and who hadn't stopped for his first two years in the hospital. Nobody had ever learnt his name, and nobody believed he was a Brigadier.

Brennan was in the smaller room of the parlour room suites, generally set aside for travellers' servants, seated on the small chair next to a meagre bed, a bottle of whiskey open in front of him and an empty glass in his hand. The booze felt good, offering him a relief from the pain by blurring his thoughts, letting them run together like so much coloured paint mixing together and turning grey. He'd feel the shadow of Alf and then think of his wife, which would lead him to his youth with her, warming his soul as the alcohol warmed his guts.

Brennan had been born at the lodge and thought he would die there, just as Alf had, and just as his father had. He could hardly remember his father ever even leaving the Glasslands, which was lucky for anyone outside the Glasslands.

The Brennans had served the Gleaves for generations. The Gleaves visited the lodge frequently, leaving their house in Chinsey with another family of servants to join the Brennans. Even when they were not around, the door was always open to adventurers on a quest to find the treasures of the Cathedral of Tales, the secret of the snowdrop. Old Man Gleave would grill the visitors about what they thought they would find and how they would enter, wheedling out the information, never giving anything away that could save a life. Brennan clearly remembered the few times he had managed to steal into the sitting room, the skeletal figure of Oliver Gleave seated by the fire, his talon-like fingers wrapped around his ebony stick as his pale blue eyes drank in the doomed, a cruel, mocking smile on his lips as he bathed in the pointless hope of the strangers. Occasionally the old man would venture outside to the edge of the Glasslands and watched as friends he had invited would hunt and kill Humps, returning with an ear or finger as a trophy for their host, which Brennan's father would place in a display cabinet in the dining room. The lodge was an evil, foreboding place while his father was alive, and whenever Gleave visited, it got darker.

Brennan's father did not see any problem with Hump killing, or culling, as he called it. He had a cruel streak which his son did not inherit, and a drinking problem, which he did. He would beat his son at the slightest infringement of any of the multiple rules he had imposed upon Brennan, and if his mother got in the way, she would feel his fists too.

As a boy, one rule banned Brennan from the sitting room if Old Man Gleave was there, and each time he had he had been caught by Missus Gleave, a beautiful woman some forty years younger than her husband, who had never told on him. As Brennan grew up, he suspected she had been bought by her husband as breeding stock, as kindness, which she emanated from her every pore, was not something Gleave seemed to recognise as an asset. Missus Gleave had even introduced Brennan to his wife, having taken the teenager into Chinsey to carry her packages. Missus Gleave seemed to hate the household in Chinsey, and kept herself apart from the old man's life there. Even at the lodge, if she was not expressly required in the sitting room, she would keep herself to herself, knitting in the main hall, nodding to visitors as they moved around the lodge. When she was with child, she spent almost her entire pregnancy at the lodge, but was spirited away one night when the child was due. Brennan was never sure if she was taken or went of her own accord, but he never saw her again.

Old Man Gleave still came occasionally, outliving Brennan's father by a few years, and then his visits also dried up. By then, Brennan and his wife looked after the lodge for Brennan's mother, still taking in the occasional adventurer. When his wife was pregnant with Alf, having not heard from the Gleaves or any of their representatives for so long, they started to change the lodge. They tried to bring light to the blood-stained building, life to the dead woods. When Brennan's wife died, he struggled to keep the love in the walls, not able to leave now that his mother was an invalid in an upstairs room and he had a babe in arms.

But he had managed to make the lodge a home. His son had grown and his mother had passed away. He wished the adventurers luck and warned them about the dangers, sharing other rumours he had heard when they passed through.

And then one day, when Alf was about to become a teenager, Laurel had arrived. She was the spit of her mother, a stunning beauty with warmth in her eyes, a lost soul relieved to find a home. She loved the lodge, loved the excitement of the visitors, and was desperate to belong. Brennan knew that she was the missing ingredient the lodge needed, the female touch, and she was what Alf needed too, a female role model. It all fell into place.

As Brennan started to age and the Humps' fear for the lodge was forgotten, he worried that he would be unable to keep them at bay, and then Hilt and the Brigadier had arrived, one with the necessary skills to ward off the evil of the woods, the other with some glamour and class for the old place. Kendrick had also moved in at some point, a blemish that never seemed to completely clear up, and everything had been well with the world.

And then the darkness had returned, as though his father and Old Man Gleave had returned to scoop out the love he had nurtured in the building they had used to gloat at those heading for certain death. Now even his home was a smouldering wreck.

Brennan took one last drink and decided it was time to go.

As Brennan passed him, Teddy shifted to ensure the man wouldn't see what was in his hands. He watched as Brennan held the door open for Hilt and Rickenbacker as they returned from the promenade. Brennan headed outside alone, and the two men headed to their separate beds while Teddy returned to concentrate on Mister Elephantine's box.

"Mister Elephantine?" he whispered, gently shaking the box.

His fingers skimmed across the surface of the box, looking for a lid, a latch, a join, anything.

"Mister Elephantine? It's me. The chosen one."

He put his ear to the surface and listened intently.

"I need to know more, Mister Elephantine," he said.

The unmistakeable tone of Mister Elephantine cut through his brain without touching his ears.

"Shut up, Teddy. You don't need to talk when you talk to me. I've told you before."

"Sorry," said Teddy, before apologising again with his mind.

"Where are we, Teddy?"

"Can't you tell?"

"I told you I do not have the same capabilities now we have left the Library of Senses. Are we in touch with the Fairy?"

"No."

"Then where are we?"

"On an ice yacht."

"A what?"

"On a yacht on the slideways to Chinsey."

"I do not understand a word you are saying. Why didn't we fly to meet the Fairy?"

"Fly?"

"Please tell me we have the money to fly?"

"We can't fly."

"Why? Are you too scared to fly?"

"Probably."

"Oh great."

"I mean, nobody can fly."

"Nobody? Do you mean that the Gramarye has lost the knowledge of flight?"

"I suppose so."

"This worries me."

"Yes."

"How can we defend ourselves against the Threat without air force?"

"We have guns. Pinkerton has a blat gun. Well, he did have. And Hilt has a sword stuck to his hand."

"Teddy?"

"Yes, Mister Elephantine?"

"I am going to leave you now. I'll be back when we reach the Fairy. I can already feel Elf close by."

"But I wanted to talk about being the Chosen One. I mean, am I doing a good job?"

"Oh, Teddy. You. Are. Spectacular."

And then Teddy felt Mister Elephantine leave his mind, so he decided to have a little sleep. He was pleased he was good at being the Chosen One. Perhaps he should get some business cards printed up like that Mister Kendrick.

"Teddy Creslow. Chosen One."

Brennan reached the promenade barrier and gripped it hard with both hands. It was getting dark, and the Glasslands were sliding further into the distance, the snowdrop spire hardly discernible against the night sky. The horizon glowed with the lights of Chinsey, and Brennan looked up to see less stars in the night sky, blotted out by the light pollution, something that never happened at the lodge.

He used to step out with his wife every night and she would recite stories of the stars, their names and the tales behind them. If he had known she wouldn't be there for Alf, he would have written down every word. He should have written them down anyway. He should have written down everything, everything that ever passed her lips.

But that didn't matter anymore.

He heaved himself over the barrier and felt the wind in his hair and the rumble of the yacht on the slideway. He kept his eyes on the stars, searching for one that could be named after Alf one day. Perhaps there were three close together, one for each of them, now that they were all dead. Because Brennan knew he was dead now. He may have been breathing, but he was dead without his wife, without his son, without their home. He had pretended to himself that Teddy needed him, but the boy was the chosen one. He had the protection of some all-powerful being in a box, a being that probably already had countless stars named after him in many skies. And Laurel would be fine. She had been before and she would be again. She would find the right man and fall in love and they would have a child and live happily ever after.

He could feel the tears on his face in the chill of the wind and wondered if that would be his last sensation, his own pain stinging his cheek. Would the fall kill him? Would he slam into the hull on the way down? Would he die when he hit the ice, or would he survive, crippled and stuck there, slowly freezing to death begging for the next yacht to pass, crushing him to death? Whatever happened, he had failed everybody who had ever loved him and didn't deserve to live.

He took one last lingering look at his wife's stars and closed his eyes, so that they would be the last thing he ever saw.

And with that, Brennan took his hands off the barrier and closed his eyes.

He heard a door close behind him and waited for someone to wrap their arms around him, give him one last hug and let them know he loved him, so he could take their affection to the grave.

"Do you need any help?" came a voice.

Brennan cracked open one eye and glanced to his right, automatically grasping the barrier with one hand. Somebody he didn't recognise, someone he had never seen before

from the suite next to their own, was regarding him curious-
ly, a man wearing one of the Bester's complimentary bath
robes with the hood up so that his face was in shadow.

"I'm fine," Brennan replied. "Please leave me alone."

"You don't seem fine to me."

"Well I am."

The stranger moved to the barrier on his suite's side and
leant against it, looking out.

"What are you doing?"

Brennan thought it was pretty obvious what he was doing, and was starting to resent the stranger. His final moments on Earth were being ruined by someone in a dressing
gown.

"Please go away," he snapped at the man.

"It's sad, isn't it?" the man remarked, looking up at the
night sky. "The stars are going out."

Brennan frowned. Could the man read his mind?

"I've had a hard time the last few days too," the man told
him, "learnt a few things about the world, myself, worked
out what's important."

"I've lost everything," Brennan replied, "and learnt
nothing."

"I'm sure that's untrue. Loss is a great teacher," said the
man, removing the hood of the bath robe to reveal a pair of
pointed ears, much like those Brennan had seen throughout
the Cathedral of Tales, on the people in the mirage in the
main hall, one some of the Gargoyle creatures and on Mister
Elephantine himself.

"You're Elf."

The man looked surprised to be recognised.

"How did you..?"

"I know what happened to your people," Brennan said, and as he spoke he felt a pang of guilt at the realisation that his grief was so petty, his self-loathing selfish.

"I just found out myself. I didn't even know I had a people."

"What happened?"

"I didn't even look like this yesterday," the man replied, "I think my parents tried to hide it, to cover up how I looked, but yesterday it seemed to re-assert itself."

"Yesterday?"

"Why don't you come back over the barrier so that we can continue this conversation? I don't like the idea of you disappearing mid-sentence. I've seen a lot of death and it's not something I've ever got used to."

The man put out a hand for Brennan to take.

Brennan considered his own life against this stranger's, his own tragedies against this man's history, his parents protecting him, something Brennan had not been able to do for his own son. But then he thought about the praying mantis and his fatal hammer blow, about Mister Elephantine's warnings about the threat, about all the deaths that had occurred here when this had been Pearly, and he grasped the stranger's hand.

"I'm Brennan," he said, holding on tightly.

"My name is Valentine."

The name meant nothing to Brennan, despite all these apparent coincidences. And if this man had been with the Trade at the lodge, or one of the Reclaimers, surely he would have let him fall, if not pushed him into the abyss.

"Shall I help you over, Brennan?"

"Thank you, Sir," Brennan replied, and Valentine climbed into parlour suite B62's promenade deck to help Brennan back over the barrier.

The two men regarded each other. Valentine raised his hood again, as though embarrassed by his ears.

"So," said Valentine, "What do you know about the Elf?"

He looked back out over the Gramarye.

"I know they were betrayed at Pearly, and that whatever did for them is coming back to finish what it started."

"Finish?"

"The end of the world. Apparently, the Fairy of all people…"

"How do you…"

And then the door into B61 opened, and Brennan was shocked to see Lady Elena Melody standing on the promenade deck in a bathrobe that matched his new friend's, the Elf he knew as Valentine.

"Lady Melody?" Brennan said.

"Spicer, what's…"

Elena's hands dropped towards where her guns normally sat. Brennan looked at his saviour with incredulity.

"You're Spicer?"

"Bunce!" Elena shouted as Brennan launched himself at the Reclaimer.

Geraldine Bunce was oiling her new weapon on the parlour suite's dressing table, a truly beautiful piece of craftsmanship, the perfect partnership of cutting edge Wonder and precision firepower. She had heard about the gel dispenser on sights but had never seen an example. She'd been out of the regular army for a long time and had been forced to make do and mend with her weapons as a Reclaimer.

She had met Spicer on her first job out of the army. Although Bunce had been invalided out on bitter terms, she still needed the comradeship only the military could offer her, so she been having a drink in a pub frequented by the armed services on the Western Isles, an area where the occasional insurgent meant a high proliferation of army bases, the isles being so close to the Grand Quillia heartland. As most of her postings had been overseas in the disputed territories between the people of the Ditch and the Empire, nobody knew her so close to home, so they had no idea of the reality of her being kicked out. When the recruiter looking for possible Reclaimers approached her, she was relieved and excited. The recruiter has been an attractive woman, and they had slept together in the carriage used to transport new recruits to the camps. Despite their intimacy, Bunce had neglected to tell the woman why she had been forced to leave the army. Nobody wanted to hear about a sniper taking down fourteen of her own side. She had not been court-martialled, as her commanding officer had forgotten he had ordered her to take down anything that approached over the horizon, and she was so well hidden nobody could find her to tell her to cease fire until it was too late. Sometimes being so fast was not a benefit.

Her first job as a Reclaimer was at the clearance of Red-church, with a sniper's rifle she had pawned her neighbour's furniture for. Redchurch was a remote farming community on the farthest of the Western Isles which AIR had discovered had been supplying sustenance to insurgent groups who did not consider the Western Isles a part of Grand Quillia, and so some irregular forces were despatched to 'grill and season' Redchurch. The Reclaimers would enter the community, kill the livestock, torch the crops, and salt the earth to stop anything being grown there again, hence 'grill and season'.

The Reclaimers were all issued with bright yellow sashes so they could identify each other, and they had been told what was needed to be done, but not how to do it as a unit, and so Redchurch was soon being pillaged by a dissolute band of ruffians, which happened particularly due to the seeming defencelessness of the farming community.

About two thirds of Redchurch had been grilled when the Reclaimers approached Quakers Farm, a large house at the top of a hill. At the base of the hill was a small orchard, and the rest of the land was recently ploughed, offering hardly any cover.

As the rest of Redchurch had capitulated so easily, the majority of the Reclaimers had grown lazy and arrogant, exacerbated by the ale they had stolen. Weighed down with loot, a group of twenty Reclaimers simply strolled up the lane towards Quakers Farm, weapons holstered.

Being new, or 'fresh meat' as most of the others called her, Bunce had easily kept herself apart from the old hands. Her army training was still drummed into her, and so thoughts of looting or harming civilians were not something she took to with ease. She was also sober, and the potential for danger the farmhouse offered from its high ground and lack of cover on the approach was clear. She decided to settle into an apple tree in the orchard to watch things play out.

From her vantage point, she could see the dark smoke engulfing Redchurch, the villagers beating back the fires that raged around their homes. Then she noticed two men to the west of the farmhouse on their bellies, identifiable as

Reclaimers by their yellow sashes, who seemed to have the same idea as Bunce and were biding their time, using the ploughed up earth as their cover.

One was enormous, covered in furs caked in soot from the various fires he had ignited. The other was spryer, and seemed to be twisting the top of his head. Just as Bunce realised he was adjusting a wig, she felt her ears pop, there was a flash of bright red and an explosion erupted in the middle of the lane. Reclaimers and their body parts were blown into the air and plopped down into the surrounding mud. Armed men appeared at the farmhouse windows and opened fire on the few Reclaimers who were still alive in the lane as they scrambled for cover, cutting them down with ease.

Bunce's training immediately kicked in and she looked down her rifle and picked out three insurgents who were moving down the lane towards the Reclaimers. She fired, putting them down within five seconds. Then she found her next two targets on the roof of the farmhouse and took them out before bullets starting whizzing around her. She let herself drop from the tree as branches and leaves rained to the floor, and she took cover behind a low wall. She took a breath, peered over the wall and took more fire. She noticed two riflemen on the second floor keeping her pinned down and before she ducked back into cover, she saw the front door open. It would take the insurgents minutes to reach her if she stayed still, and she couldn't take them out without drawing fire from the riflemen in the house. It was time to retreat.

It was at this point that she noticed some of the Redchurch villagers approaching the orchard, armed with clubs and scythes, and Bunce decided that joining this bunch of Reclaimers may have been an unfortunate misstep, despite the recruiter being an above average lover.

She turned and fired her rifle through the trees at the villagers, hoping to scare them off by winging two of them, but the others just scattered for cover. She glanced back over the wall and snatched a view of the insurgents getting closer, one of whom was carrying a Red Wonder grenade. More bullets ricocheted around her from the farmhouse, and she came to the sad conclusion that her last ever lover was only above average.

Then the bullets slamming into the wall ceased, and she heard the echo of a blat gun firing over and over again, before her ears popped and there was another explosion. She looked over the wall and saw the man in furs racking his blat gun while he looked down at the smoking remains of the insurgents. She could hear Twirler fire from the farmhouse, the windows now empty of riflemen. She turned back to the villagers in the orchard to find them running headlong in the opposite direction.

"Hey you!" she heard from over the wall. "Boy!" Bunce turned to see the furry man approaching. "You're pretty handy with that rifle, son!"

The big man frowned as he looked Bunce up and down.

"Oi, Lieutenant!" he called over his shoulder, pronouncing it 'leftenant'. "This sniper's only a bleedin' bird, innit?"

Bunce had been mistaken for a boy many times, and it didn't particularly bother her. She looked in the ornately framed mirror of the parlour suite's dressing room and toyed with her short hair. She did look boyish, she admitted that, and she wondered what Elena preferred, what Elena thought of her looks, and she prayed that Elena did occasionally think of her.

Then she heard Elena call for her from the promenade deck, but unfortunately it did not sound like an invitation to a romantic interlude, so she drew her pistol before heading for the door, leaving her new rifle in pieces on the dressing table.

The roar from the promenade deck surprised everybody in Parlour Suite B62, especially as it appeared to emanate from Brennan.

Pinkerton was still laid up, Laurel still soaking and Teddy had no inclination to move in the direction of screaming, and so Hilt was first out of the door, Rickenbacker close behind.

Both men were taken aback by the chaos that greeted them. Brennan's hands were around Spicer's throat, the younger man's feet off the floor and his back bent over the barrier, seconds from toppling to his death. Lady Elena Melody straddled the divider between the two private promenades, her hands grasping towards the melée.

Bunce and Hilt raised their guns simultaneously as they entered, training them on each.

"You!" Hilt scowled when he laid eyes on Elena, unable to stop himself from taking in her naked long legs as he raised his blade to the soft skin of her throat.

"Drop the sword," Bunce commanded, taking cover behind a bench.

Spicer's eyes flickered across all of them as his face turned from red to purple, his hands too busy clinging desperately to the barrier to defend himself against the throttling he was receiving from Brennan.

"Stop," Rickenbacker called, stepping between the two raised, humming Twirlers to lay his hands gently on Brennan's shoulders. "This will not change anything," the Professor reasoned. "He did not kill your son and this will not bring him back."

Spicer stared into the man's eyes as he saw the rage dissolve into grief. Brennan's hands relaxed and he stepped back, allowing Rickenbacker to separate them.

"You are a good man, Mr Brennan," Rickenbacker said, his hands still on the man's shoulders. "Always remember that."

"I'm sorry," Spicer managed to rasp out between gulps for air. "I'm sorry for your son. I didn't kill him but I am sorry."

Brennan seemed to fold in on himself, shrink in his sadness.

"Your man killed him," Brennan mumbled. "One of your Reclaimers."

"Tork is dead. He was a soldier who…" Spicer started to reply.

"He murdered a child."

"I understand," Spicer replied. "Believe me, I understand and I'm sorry."

Hilt smirked, a cynical snarl on his face, as Rickenbacker turned from Brennan to look at Spicer. The Professor's face dropped as he recognised the Lieutenant for what he was.

"You're Elf," he uttered, raising a hand towards Spicer's face as though he didn't believe what he could see.

"Apparently," Spicer answered, nodding as he straightened the robe, feeling more naked than ever.

"But you are Lieutenant Spicer, are you not?" the Professor asked, discombobulated.

"Yes, I am. I was. I don't know what…"

"I thought you were scarred. That you were… I had no idea you were Elf."

"Neither did I."

Rickenbacker continued to stare in amazement at Spicer.

"Who cares? Let's kill him anyway. He'd kill us all if he had the chance," Hilt said, his eyes still on Elena. "And then we can finish this traitorous bitch."

"I'll drop you where you stand," Bunce warned the man aiming the pistol at her head.

"You have no chance, boy," Hilt replied, and Bunce found herself doubting her ability to pull her trigger first.

"This is all much more important than our feelings. This is bigger than all of this," Rickenbacker said. "Lower your weapons. Everybody."

Nobody moved.

"We don't need to kill each other," Spicer said. "We need to find out what is happening, what happened at the Library of Senses…"

"You know its Elf name," said Rickenbacker.

"So he's good at crossword puzzles," said Hilt. "We should drop him. For Brennan."

"You have already dispensed with Alf's killer, Hilt. The boy's death is avenged but he is still dead. More death improves nothing."

"Bunce," said Spicer, regaining his composure.

"No. No way," said the sniper. "Look at him. He's a murderer. He wants to kill us. He'd enjoy it."

Hilt shrugged, almost concurring.

"Hilt. Please," Rickenbacker implored. "Whatever has happened before, Lieutenant Spicer can help us. If he's Elf, then he may know things, be able to understand things that..."

"He's a Reclaimer," said Hilt, shaking his head. "He helps nobody unless there's money involved, unless there's something in it for him."

Brennan raised himself up to his full height, a serenity passing over his face as though he had reached an epiphany. He raised his hand and placed in gently on Hilt's Twirler as he looked deep into the man's eyes.

"Hilt," he said quietly, "the Professor is right. Let them talk."

"Brennan," Hilt started to reply, "You of all people..."

"He saved my life. Spicer..."

"He did what? What are you talking about?"

"Don't kill them. Don't hurt them on my account, or for Alf. In my son's name, lower your weapons."

Spicer stepped towards the divider and gripped it as he addressed Bunce.

"I order you to do the same, Corporal."

Hilt let the barrel of the gun drop while the chamber continued to spin.

"You played me, woman," he said to Elena, his eyes following his blade as he slowly lowered from her throat to her breast, her hips, thighs, until it was pointed at the floor.

Bunce stood up and holstered her weapon.

"You had something I needed," Elena said to Hilt. "You had the Gargoyle Key."

"No. I didn't."

Elena climbed back over the barrier and moved to Spicer's side.

"Are you alright?" she asked.

"I'm fine," he replied, before turning to the Professor. "Do you still have the key?"

"Of sorts. Shall we adjourn to your cabin to discuss?"

CHAPTER 13

The Road to Chinsey
The Gramarye Region
Grand Quillia

June 1856

Kendrick had lost sight of Mandell for some five minutes or so, and he was working up the nerve to make a break for it, turn off the road and escape, when he rounded a blind bend and found the former knight on his feet surrounded by corpses, one of which was Sir Evan's pony.

"Ambush," said Mandell, as he fired one shot after another into the bodies' skulls.

"You or them?" Kendrick asked.

"Bandits," Mandell said as he holstered his gun.

The former knight looked worse than ever. Some of the Hump bodies Axelrod had used to stitch up Mandell had not been fresh, and so his skin was brown and green in places, sagging away from the rest of his body. Kendrick noticed one of his partner's eyes was falling back into his head.

"Your eye," he couldn't help but say, pointing. "It's falling in."

And then Kendrick watched as Sir Evan poked his fingers into the socket and straightened his eyeball.

"Better?" Mandell asked, shaking his head to test the rest of his head for any issues. "Must have been the ride."

"Perhaps we shouldn't ride quite so fast then," Kendrick suggested. "I mean, we might not even be able to find them anyway."

"Don't you know where they are?" Mandell asked, and Kendrick realised he had made a mistake as the knight's hand moved to his cutlass. "Did you lie to Doctor Axelrod?"

"No, no. I know where we can find them," he stuttered, raising his hands in his defence. "I just don't know when we can find them, when they will actually be there."

"Move aside."

Kendrick pushed himself towards the rear of his pony and Mandell mounted up. The stench made Kendrick belch stomach acid into his mouth, and the smell stuck there. Kendrick knew then that it would stay with him forever.

He spat at the bandits' corpses in frustration, but the spittle hit his own boot, and he wanted to scream and throw himself to the floor and pull at his hair and kick at the ground. Instead, Mandell clicked his tongue and the pony trotted on.

"Put your arms around me," Mandell told Kendrick, and, holding his breath, tears springing to his eyes, the little man wrapped his arms around the dead body with which he was sharing a ride.

Mandell spurred the pony into a gallop, Kendrick's head snapped back, and with horror he felt his fingers sink into the rotting meat of the once honourable knight.

Elena and Spicer had both dressed before joining Bunce, and they entered the lounge of Parlour Suite B62. As they crossed over the promenade barrier and entered through the external door, there was a knock at B62's door into the corridor, and Brennan opened it. A porter stood there with a food trolley, which Brennan signed for, then brought inside before closing the door and raising the cloches. He had found his grief and anger had made him hungry, and was thrilled at the smoked fish and freshly baked bread laid out before him. Laurel was perched on the edge of Pinkerton's sick bed, drying her hair with a towel embroidered with the Hodgkinson Line brand, her eyes on Spicer. Hilt was reclining against a wall, his blade already having carved a hole in the floor next to his foot, while Rickenbacker and Teddy sat at the small coffee table. Bunce leant against the wall on the opposite side to Hilt, her eyes on the man's blade, while Elena and Spicer were offered a seat on the chaise longue.

Pinkerton did not know which of the Reclaimers had killed Sir Evan. The boyish girl with the large rifle seemed most likely, but it wasn't gentlemanly to scowl at a lady: something that Hilt had obviously never learnt, judging by the eyes he was making at Lady Melody.

Despite everything, it was nice to see Elena again. After all, Pinkerton reasoned, she could have poisoned them or murdered them in their beds at the lodge, but she hadn't. She had asked how he was when she had entered, and they had touched on how things had changed, especially for Mandell. Pinkerton told her that he would kill whoever had transformed his friend into the undead stalker he had become, and Elena gave him a name, which he rolled around in his head so that he wouldn't forget it. Someday soon, somehow, he vowed he would kill Doctor Axelrod of the Gramarye Trade.

Elena ruffled Teddy's hair, pleased to see he was still alive, and nodded respectfully to Rickenbacker before she sat down next to Spicer, studiously avoiding Hilt's gaze.

Spicer stared at the box Teddy had placed on the table, his hands still wrapped around it.

"It doesn't look like much, but…" Rickenbacker started.

"It's changed since we last saw it," Elena said.

"The Gargoyle Key not only granted permissions to enter various parts of the Cathedral, or the Library of Senses, as you rightly call it," Rickenbacker explained. "It was also a power source, which is now being used to power what you see before you. I don't really know. It is the deep Blue Wonder, more powerful and complicated than anything I have seen before."

"May I touch it?" Spicer asked.

His hands reached for it but Teddy pulled it away.

"Teddy is quite protective of it," Rickenbacker said. "The box took a liking to him."

"I'm the Chosen One," Teddy told Elena.

"That's good, Teddy," she replied. "Will you let the Lieutenant see it?"

Teddy reluctantly unlocked his fingers and Spicer stroked the side of the box gently.

"My God, I can feel its warmth, like a crowded carriage. So many people," he whispered.

Teddy didn't like this at all. He was the Chosen One and he didn't want this Elf man interfering in his relationship with Mister Elephantine. He hoped Elephantine wouldn't change his mind and go with the Elf man instead. He liked being the Chosen One, although it hadn't really amounted to much so far.

"Who is this man?" he asked Elephantine, careful to just use his mind.

"Why are your lips moving?" Elena asked him.

"Is Elephantine talking to you, Teddy?" Rickenbacker asked.

"Yes. He doesn't like the Elf man," Teddy mumbled.

"You're not very popular, Spicer," Hilt said without looking up.

"Who is Elephantine?" Elena asked.

"According to Elephantine himself, he is a representative of the surviving Elf of Pearly. That box holds the essence of all the survivors," Rickenbacker answered.

"*All* the survivors?" Spicer asked, lifting the box to eye level to stare at the patterns on the size.

"Perhaps I should introduce myself," said Elephantine, his voice echoing in all their minds.

"Oh great," Hilt tutted.

"Oh my," said Elena, the colour draining from her face.

The top of the box started to glow an eerie blue, and Spicer placed it carefully back on the table.

"What's happening?" Teddy asked, tempted to snatch the box away.

Mister Elephantine's face appeared in two dimensions, an actor's mask flickering with St Elmo's fire, a haughty look on his face. Spicer saw ears like his own flanking the visage in front of him as it considered him.

"You're Elf," whispered Spicer in awe.

"Of course I am Elf. I am one and many. I am the last defenders," Elephantine replied without a hint of welcome.

"I am the final survivors, prisoners of Pearly, heroes of the Gramarye. You may call me Mister Elephantine."

"He always talks like this," Hilt said, rolling his eyes. "Where one word would do..."

"And I recognise you, Elf," Elephantine said, glaring at Spicer. "I know your family."

"You do?"

"Of course I do. Your blood were the milksop brigade. The dastards. The poltroons."

"Dastards?"

"They ran, my boy. Your brethren ran. When Pearly was under attack, they fled, skedaddled, left the rest of us to our fate in our greatest hour of need."

Spicer winced at Elephantine's words.

"How do you know?" he asked.

"Because I was there then and you are here now, wherever we are. You're sitting in front of me and my little prison box, your consciousness wrapped in flesh and blood, your lungs pumping and your heart beating. You can touch and feel. You can breathe." As if to make a point, Elephantine seemed to pause for breath. "You're alive, you little shit."

"He's a charmer, isn't he?" said Elena, sitting back.

"I am not here to charm, my girl. I am here to save the world."

"Is that all?" she asked.

"I sensed there was Elf present," Elephantine said. "That is why I am here. His ancestors deserted their race but now he can make amends. We shall meet with the Fairy people..."

"The Fairy! You're going to save the world with Fairy?" Bunce interjected.

"We shall meet the Fairy and they will help us rally our forces, uniting the Elf so that we can repulse the threat," Elephantine continued.

"Tell me about my family," Spicer said, his hands clasping the table in front of him. "Please."

"You wouldn't know, would you? Your history hidden from you, living in fear, your culture decimated as a result of your own cowardice..."

"I am not sure this is the best way to rally one's forces, Mister Elephantine," Rickenbacker offered calmly. "If you have a problem with this man's past, perhaps you should conceal yourself until we reach Chinsey and find the Fairy."

"A good point, well made, Professor," Elephantine nodded, "Perhaps I should share my knowledge and begin the journey to reunite our people. Build bridges burnt, welcome the black sheep and the dark horse. Open my arms and lead my people. Look into my eyes, Elf."

"Spicer? Are you sure this isn't some trick?" Elena said, placing her hand on his arm.

"He is an invasive bugger," Hilt warned. "Likes getting in people's heads."

"If I can learn something about what happened," Spicer said, "about what will happen, then I have to."

"Of course," Rickenbacker nodded. "We should learn as much as possible."

"Why hasn't he ever asked me to look into his eyes?" Teddy grumbled. "I am the Chosen One."

"Very well, Mister Elephantine, show me."

"Let me see your history. Let me see where you have been, what your people have done since they left us behind. Look into my eyes and share your bloodline's failure."

Spicer took a breath and looked deep into the empty sockets of Elephantine's mask.

"Many aeons ago, the people of the land you know as the Gramarye discovered the Wonder. Over time, they learned to harness the power of dragon bones, initially using the energy inherent in Red Wonder, then, as they grew in confidence, they started to utilise the life-changing capabilities of Green Wonder.

"And then, for the first time in recorded history, there was the Threat.

Led by the people of Pearly, the Gramarye started to experiment with the miraculous abilities of the deep Blue Wonder, to use against the Threat.

The Threat was seen off, the Gramarye survived and Pearly was left with the legacy of the deep Blue.

As the people of Pearly started to use the deep Blue Wonder in abundance, there was a proliferation of Elf births from human parents, and these Elf seemed to be affected by the specific Wonder their parents utilised the most. Warriors who had used deep Blue weaponry begat Elf children, who were better shots and had quicker reactions. Farmers' Elf offspring knew instinctively the optimum areas for different crops. Even the Elf descendants of parents in more menial professions - greengrocers, librarians - were able to remember their customer's preferences or the exact page for a reference faster than those not affected by the deep Blue, their non-Elf counterparts. And the progeny of a combination of deep Blue-using skills would have more to offer, a fresh mix. A butcher and a nurse would produce a highly gifted surgeon, and suchlike.

"Eventually, Pearly was populated by these talented Elf who had been gifted by the deep Blue, working for the betterment of mankind. Each generation was an improvement, another step towards superiority in every way. The Elf would inherit the earth, with the help of the Wonder.

"Of course, some of our unevolved human brethren were threatened by the dominance of the Elf, by the obvious supremacy of Elf in the ascendancy, and they fled, or made things awkward for us, arguing that it wasn't natural. Even some Elf did not appreciate the skills apparently foisted upon them by their parents' choices and the power of the Wonder, refusing to accept their caste, the standing that had been bestowed upon them, and they too left the Gramarye.

"Pearly became the world's centre for hyperphysical learning, and the more we studied the Wonder, the greater the possibilities for expansion, the broader our horizons became. We could take the gift from the dragon bones past and spread it around the world, improve humanity, bring Elf blood to every corner of the globe. Pearly was just the beginning.

"But there was a rift. The Pearly Assembly, made up of humans, Elf and others, fought amongst themselves. Some wanted to expand beyond the Gramarye, while others were cautious about the Wonder and its effects, considering its side effects and unknown long term consequences. They thought we should learn more about this fallout, as they called it, before letting it spread, and that the potential it had given us should be used to assist the rest of the world, not lead it. They argued that the jewel of the Gramarye, the Elf capital Pearly, should be just another pack animal, not the luminary it had undoubtedly already become. They said that the superior did not have a right to rule.

"One terrible day, Pearly found itself the target of terrorist attacks when seditionists destroyed the Spider Generator and the city was plunged into darkness. Only those Elf who knew to distrust the world knew what to expect and were ready for it. There was an uprising against the Assembly, and a War Council was formed of pure Elf blood, including many of the souls within this box.

"The War Council proposed purging the city of all but Elfkind as a means of defence, but many of the civilians of Pearly stood united against us. They left our wonderful city en masse; people we needed, the Intelligentsia, the bureaucrats, many of the hyperphysicists who had built the city, they scattered into the world, taking our secrets with them. Whole brigades of the armed forces, squadrons of the air force scattered to the winds, too scared to stand alongside us and prove our superiority.

"They left us in disarray, defenceless, and then our enemies sent in the beasts, the killing machines you saw in the Library of Senses, burning and grinding the city before them. The Elf were decimated, culled, cut from existence, until only the War Council remained, holed up in the snowdrop spire, at the mercy of the treacherous humans who weeks before had stood alongside them feeling the benefit of the Wonder, the same humans who had been saved from the Threat by the only people brave enough to use the deep Blue in their defence. We rallied our forces and amalgamated our power to create the final barricade, the gargoyles. The humans made our last rallying point our final resting place, blockaded with the beasts and fatal traps while they completely destroyed Pearly and annihilated our culture.

"We locked our essence away using the deep Blue and seeded the world with the Gargoyle Keys, praying the other Elf would return, that they would come to our aid, free our souls and rebuild Pearly, but nobody came. We were left to rot in the snowdrop spire while our brethren pretended we didn't exist, so ashamed that they hid their own bloodlines to conceal us.

"Your forebears hid their Elf heritage, scared of their responsibilities, unwilling to admit their obvious supremacy. Your parents must have been terrified when baby Valentine, the youngest Spicer, was born with his beautiful Elf ears for all to see. So they burnt them away, preferring an ugly human, a blemished, damaged child, to a proud Elf.

"And then the Gargoyle Key was returned to us, and deep Blue Wonder seeped back into the Gramarye, bringing with it the hidden memories of the death of Pearly for all to see. And because you were here, you, warrior Elf, with your genetic improvements, your Elf blood pulsing through you to make you the perfect soldier, you were cured. Your enhanced nervous system fixed your scars, wiped clean the cloak of disfigurement your own parents inflicted upon you. The deep Blue returned to you your real face.

"You are no longer some soldier of fortune ashamed of his mercenary past, Valentine Spicer. You are reborn as your true self, a descendent of the bloody Yossarians, one of the great warrior castes of Pearly. You need to make amends for your bloodline, Yossarian. You need to help us. You need to rise up from your knees and lead us all against the Threat, show the world why they turned to us originally, return the

Elf to their true standing as the best humanity can be. We need you, Yossarian."

The lids closed on Elephantine's hollow eyes and the mask folded in on itself, shimmering back into the box. The blue glow faded to leave the parlour suite strangely still, and the space between each person seemed to grow in the darkness left in its wake.

"Erm, but I'm still the chosen one, right?" Teddy asked. Everybody ignored him.

"You all heard that?" Spicer checked.

"Whether we wanted to or not," Hilt grumbled.

"Wish I had some of that Elf blood in me," Pinkerton grunted from his bed, his hand moving to his bandages.

"He didn't say why he wants the Fairy involved," Elena said.

"I was brought up near a Fairy colony. They used to tell me stories that nobody else seemed to understand. Perhaps there's a special relationship between the Elf and Fairy..."

"The Fairy have a strange connection with Wonder. I was once invited to the post mortem of a Fairy and they have no heart," Rickenbacker told them. "They just have a chamber that contains Blue Wonder, and when they die it disappears. It's quite extraordinary."

"You cut open a Fairy?" Laurel asked incredulously.

"Well, not me, precisely..."

"Why not?" Hilt asked. "What other use are they?"

The room went quiet except for the crackle of the ice and spinning buffers outside.

"Should we tell the Trade?" Elena asked. "I mean, if this Threat is as dangerous as your Mister Elephantine says..."

"You've betrayed us to the Trade once, Lady Melody, why not go for a second?" asked Hilt.

"You're an idiot," Bunce told him.

"Try me, boy," said Hilt, without looking away from Elena.

"The Trade couldn't catch us with a full platoon," Pinkerton gloated. "What use will they be at the end of the world?"

"Perhaps we should speak to the Grand Quillian Viceroy," the Professor suggested.

"That makes sense," said Elena. "My husband, Lord Drew Hynes Melody, knew the Viceroy. I've met Sir Windsor Dunkley a few times and he was a bastard every time, but that was nothing personal. I could try to get us in."

"So when we arrive in Chinsey, we'll take Mister Elephantine to the Fairy colony and you can seek a meeting with the Viceroy," Rickenbacker suggested.

"I'm not sure how excited the Viceroy would be to see an Elf in his reception room," Spicer suggested. "It may be more useful for me to join you when you meet the Fairy."

"And if the Gleave name is as…" Laurel paused, searching for the right words, "…dramatically involved with Gramarye history as Elephantine said, perhaps I should go to the Viceroy's too? I've never been to an Viceroy's before."

"What is this?" Hilt asked. "Are we all some happy family now?"

"If what Mister Elephantine says is true, that this great Threat is coming, we need to work together," Rickenbacker reiterated. "You're welcome to go your own way, Mister Hilt, but I think we need you."

"Come on, Hilt," Laurel said, moving towards Hilt. "You're good at this stuff."

"He killed Beasley," Hilt said, staring at Spicer.

"It was him or me," Spicer replied.

"It should have been you," Hilt told him.

"It almost was. He was fast. If it hadn't been a Schrödinger he was using…"

"I warned him about that…"

"He was a soldier, Mister Hilt," Rickenbacker said. "Perhaps his time had come."

"Who are you to say…"

"Hilt," Brennan interjected, "what do you think the Brigadier would want?"

Hilt flinched at Brennan's words, his face like thunder.

"I am willing to go through with this for the greater good. It is what my son would want. Beasley would too."

Muscles flexed in Hilt's jaw and Laurel put her hand on his arm before moving her arms around him to hold him. She could feel him relax.

"Fine. Then I suppose I should go to the Viceroy's too."

"You have a blade for a hand, Hilt…" Elena started.

"If your contacts or guiles can't get us in, I'll find an alternative way in."

"I'm not sure…" Elena continued.

"I can make him listen. As Laurel says, I'm good at this stuff."

Bunce could see the worry etched into Elena's face, while Spicer seemed completely unaware, lost in his own thoughts.

"I'll come to the Viceroy's too," she suggested. "I can watch your back."

"I can watch my own back," said Hilt.

"I wasn't talking to you."

Spicer tore his eyes from Mister Elephantine's box and looked up.

"So the Professor, the Chosen One and I will head for the Fairy colony. Anyone else?"

"I think I'll go with Laurel," said Brennan, "if she'll have me."

"Of course, Brennan. I don't know what I'd do without you."

As Rickenbacker looked up at the old man, he saw Brennan's eyes flicker towards Hilt and understood that Brennan would attempt to keep the peace. He had managed twice before, and as both the warrior and he had lost the most at the lodge, it made sense.

"And I'll stay with the Professor. No offence, Elena. I know you betrayed us and all that," Pinkerton explained, "but as a gentleman, I can forgive you for that. It's just I don't have the wardrobe to visit the Viceroy's house."

Elena smiled back at him.

"So one final point," said Spicer, "we boarded using AIR identification documents."

"We're stowaways," Laurel told the handsome Elf proudly.

"And AIR agents will undoubtedly be waiting at Ashburton Station, so how do we get off this yacht?"

Mandell slowed the pony and Kendrick was able to relax his grip.

"What did you say?" the knight asked.

"What? I didn't say anything," Kendrick replied, confused.

"I heard you."

"You heard me what?"

"I heard you say something."

"But I didn't."

"You did. I heard you."

"So what did I say?"

"What?"

"What do you think I said to you?"

Mandell pulled on the reins and the exhausted pony came to a halt.

"You told me to attack."

"What?"

Mandell pushed back with his arm and Kendrick fell to the ground. He scrambled backwards on his elbows, waiting for Mandell to pull a weapon, to end this nightmare.

"You told me to attack. You said it was time. You told me to attack the Trade platoon."

Mandell looked confused, the first time his face had registered an emotion since his death, even when he was sexually assaulting corpses.

"Honestly, Mandell, I didn't say a word. Perhaps someone else is trying to communicate with you, but it wasn't me."

"Someone else?"

"Axelrod perhaps? I don't know."

"Why would Doctor Axelrod tell me to attack the Trade Platoon?"

At the exact same moment that the corpse of Sir Evan Mandell heard voices, Major R. Franks, still wearing Laurel's undergarments, discovered the benefits of leading the Trade Platoon from the front.

The platoon had left the Glasslands some miles back, and were marching four abreast down a dusty back road of the Gramarye back towards Chinsey, Colonel Quine and Doctor

Axelrod bringing up the rear. The Colonel had noted that the good Doctor had grown quieter than usual on the ride back, almost nervous, since they had left the Glasslands behind. The Doctor scanned either side of the road, which was flanked by low hedgerows bordering flat pastureland populated by the occasional scraggy sheep. He noted a ragged yellow jacket hung incongruously from a branch that jutted from the bushes as the road rose slightly over a slight ridge.

From the back of his pony, he could see for miles, as far as the treacherous Attar mountains that marked the extremity of the Grand Quillian Empire, where it skirted the realm of the People of the Ditch.

Following the dangers presented by the woods and its Hump population, Quine was puzzled by the beads of sweat breaking on Axelrod's forehead. He didn't like sickly people.

"Are you alright, Doctor?" the Colonel asked, frowning.

"I will be presently, sir," the tall man replied, his eyes narrowing as he looked back at the Colonel.

"Gastric, is it?" Quine continued smugly. He had a strong constitution, and, despite the rich spiciness of Gramarye cooking and the less-than-desirable level of hygiene, he had had diarrhoea but twice and only vomited once, and then only into his own lap. He rather enjoyed watching new arrivals struggling with their bowels. The fortitude of his own guts proved to them what an old hand he was, what a true man of the world he was. The Empire could do with more of him.

"No, no," Axelrod, appearing to fiddle with his belt, loosening it probably, the Colonel assumed, to allow for bloating.

"You seem a little out of sorts," Quine gloated.

"You seem a little dead, Colonel," Axelrod replied.

"I beg your..."

And then Doctor Axelrod pulled the pistol from his belt and shot Colonel Quine in the head. The shot threw the fat man over his pony's hindquarters, and he landed with a satisfying thud.

At the sound of the shot, the rear of the column turned to investigate just as the loose dust and stones of the road beneath them erupted. Hands burst from the earth, clasping and stabbing at the men of the Trade Platoon, dragging them to the ground before the soldiers could unsling their rifles or draw their pistols. Axelrod watched as a legion of undead rose from their shallow graves directly beneath the road, where they had laid in wait for the exhausted platoon to return from the Glasslands, just as he had planned. He had also hoped the Gargoyle Key would also be in his possession, but one couldn't have everything.

When Axelrod had used his necromantics on Sir Evan, he had not been surprised that the Colonel had not been suspicious. Most of the Trade knew that the People of the Ditch used legions of undead. The Trade hoped to counter the legions with the Immolators, their pyrotechnics in the event of death being a potent last line of defence against the dried out corpses against them. Quine had not questioned the Doctor's abilities because different hyperphysicists had different specialties. Besides, Axelrod had been imbedded in the Trade for some years, passing himself off as not only a colleague but a friend of the foul bisexual officer, and the man had been completely unaware that there was a spy who dreamt about killing him. The Ditch High Command had ordered him to bide his time and Axelrod had followed orders, until he recognised an opportunity. He could secure the Gargoyle Key, destroy the platoon at Chinsey and weaponise the Key before reinforcements could reach them.

He was surprised that he didn't feel more, he thought as he regarded the Colonel's body lying in the dust. He watched the Trade Platoon being cut to pieces ahead of him as the legion rose up among them, anyone attempting to run being shot down with their fallen comrade's weapons. The platoon would be dead within minutes, and then Axelrod would have to get to work reanimating them to join their killers on the march on Chinsey. He considered whether he should bring back Quine, but could see no value in the Colonel, dead, alive or anything in-between. Axelrod ordered the remaining Immolators to stand down before dismounting, and he took his necromantic tools from his saddlebags, considering his task ahead.

The undead platoon and legion would arrive at Chinsey where other agents would aid their entry into the town. The Doctor would take control of the Chinsey Ballroom, and thus the Immolators, so that they too could stand shoulder to shoulder with his undead legion. He would find the Gargoyle Key and unlock its secrets.

It would be a fine day for the Ditch, a mortal strike against Grand Quillia, securing the capital of the Gramarye, the centre of Wonder for all the Empire, before taking control of the whole region.

Meanwhile, at the front of the troop, Franks had heard the screams behind him and had immediately started running without looking back, the knickers chafing his chubby thighs. As shots rang out amongst the screams, he threw himself over a hedgerow and lay there, his lungs burning as he tried to catch his breath, urine leaking into Laurel's knickers. He peered beneath the low shrubbery back at the road and saw the platoon, his men, being slaughtered with ease by the ungodly demons rising from the underworld. He saw his comrades hacking at each other in their terror, firing blindly into their own ranks at an enemy already dead. Franks saw Axelrod calmly dismount, no hint of panic on his face, just a cool complacency. Franks had never liked the Doctor, but he had never suspected he could be a traitor. The Major had to get back to Chinsey and warn them, protect his wife from these undead beasts and beat back the invader. He started to crawl along beside the road, keeping his head beneath the top of the hedgerow to stay out of sight, desperately stifling his sobs of terror.

The first thing everybody saw of Chinsey was the blotched watercolour sky, caused by the factories on the outskirts belching out reds and greens that bled into yellows, browns and greys. It was sold to infrequent tourists as alluring, but most visitors found it oppressive, as though the red brick factories themselves were blowing away in the wind.

As the Spirit of Bester grew nearer to the town, Laurel leaned over the promenade barrier so that her feet hardly touched the floor and squinted ahead through the wind. The square blocks of the factories, topped at each corner by enormous chimney stacks, sat next to subsidiary tracks of the slideways, like tumours on arteries. Workers in brown-stained smocks loaded barges using cranes powered by the Wonder, waving their arms to give direction as though they were genuflecting towards their wares.

Then came the tenement blocks, overflowing with the living detritus of Chinsey, the factory workers whose existence revolved around their workplace and their nearby homes, desperate for their families to remain clinging to civilisation. The tenements seemed to lean into each other like whispering co-conspirators, their cheap foundations crumbling into the earth. From afar, they looked like the victims of a dirty protest, their walls and windows smeared with brown stains the colour of sewage from the factory smoke. As the Bester moved closer, Laurel could make out women beating brown and yellow clouds from clothes as the children played in the dust, the skin of their hands and feet matching the filth.

"So this is progress," Hilt said from behind her.

"It doesn't have to be like this," the Professor said, joining them at the promenade barrier, his eyes dark.

"So once you save the world from the Threat," Hilt continued, "are you going to save humanity from itself?"

"Are you angry with every single person, Hilt?" Laurel asked.

"Some more than others," Hilt replied, his eyes flashing towards Elena.

The tenements had given way to streets of terraced housing, the effluence from the industrial district largely restricted to a light dusting across the roofs and gutters. Outside toilets sat in shared yards, the plumbing of Chinsey served by the same ancient tunnels that concealed the subterranean Ballrooms that were used to control the Immolators.

"I miss my lodge," Laurel said, almost to herself, and felt Brennan's hand on her back.

"We all do, Laurel," he said softly, glancing at the marks his boots had left on the barrier the night before.

The roads got broader, and the terraces became mews and squares around verdant grass. Hansom cabs awaited passengers, and perambulators were pushed by uniformed nannies. Hilt watched suburban life play out before him and felt alien, a deviation like a smack round the face of a child. He thought of the simple farm near Maisy, his mother, his friend Kip Evans, of a life not lived.

He felt eyes fall on him and looked further down the promenade to see Spicer looking back at him. The two warriors regarded each other, sharing an incongruity and darkness that Hilt put down to the Elf's prying mind. He closed down the part of his memories of what he had lost and looked back at Chinsey, a town that now needed the very skills that set him apart.

Elena put a hand on Spicer's.

"Valentine?"

"I'm fine. It's hard..."

"What is?"

"I can feel things I've never felt before. I don't even know if feelings is the right word for it. I feel something more than sympathy."

"With Hilt?"

"At that moment, yes. We are both warriors, me by blood, him by necessity."

"You believe Elephantine?"

"I am a Yossarian. My heart tells me that is true. But there is something not to trust about him. Not everything he says is in all our interests."

"I don't like to trust anything dead," said Elena. "It reminds me of my ex-husband."

Spicer smiled.

"That's the Trade building where we lost the Key," Bunce interrupted, stepping between them to point at the colonnaded building, one window still boarded up from Rickenbacker's attack. Spicer slipped his hand from beneath Elena's and indicated the ruins at the front of the building.

"And there's more of what came before. The ruins of the Elf."

"Let's hope the rest of Chinsey doesn't end up the same," Elena commented.

"We should get ready to disembark," Rickenbacker called, as the final destination of the Spirit of Bester hovered into view.

Ashburton Station in Chinsey was named after Lord Ashburton, hero of the battle of Stickley and author of "Cooking with Spice: Victual to aid digestion and fortify the constitution". The edifice had started as a regular way station with two berths, a warehouse and a hot dock, where the ice yachts could be moored, the ice melted, the water drained away and any structural issues could be addressed. Over time, as Chinsey had become a more important hub of the Empire, Ashburton Station had grown into a small town itself, with its own laws, warehousing, hotels and public houses. Most of the original red brick frontage was now covered at the lower floors by market stalls and money changing booths, while from the higher windows fluttered the clothing of different cultures from the Empire, reflecting the thousands who passed through the gateway of the Gramarye.

It had traditionally been straightforward to disembark at Ashburton, but boarding an ice yacht of the Hodgkinson Line that would transport its passengers directly into the heart of Grand Quillia itself was the epitome of bureaucracy. Different passes, visas, documentation, recommendations and certificates were needed for every official on the route from the station entrance to the gang plank, and each one seemed to represent a different organisation. Station security, the Trade, the Gramarye council, Hodgkinson travel operators, the Repatriation Society, Peregrination Incorporated and the Grand Quillian Orienteering and Rambling Association all demanded paperwork, stamps and signatures from the corresponding office to allow entrance to an outbound yacht. Entrance to the Gramarye, meanwhile, involved nothing more complicated than flashing some form of identification to the border guard before fighting back the various porters, pickpockets, cabbies and cut-throats until one was safely aboard whatever conveyance one had arranged to remove one from Ashburton itself.

However, on this particular afternoon, the passengers of the Spirit of Bester were met by a Trade Squad and some cooler individuals that a few of the more dicey travellers may have recognised as agents from the Alien and Insurgent Research Department, with plans to stop every individual on the Bester and search the entire yacht. Luckily, within minutes of the gangplank going down, First Officer Trevor Gower disembarked to inform the AIR operatives that not only had they lost their colleagues and their assistant, but the flagship of the Hodgkinson Line had also mislaid two of its lifeboats about ten minutes from Ashburton Station.

Teddy had hoped and prayed that the exit from the Bester would require minimal effort on his part and involve a lot less drama than the boarding. His prayers paid off on the first count, but were not fulfilled on the second.

The lifeboats on ice yachts were required to ferry passengers and crew from a stricken vessel while also ensuring that no soft warm flesh came into contact with the slideway. Therefore the designers had utilised the same sail methodology used to propel the yachts horizontally to lift the lifeboats into the air, allowing the occupants to glide to safety beyond the slideway. Catapulting large boats from a ship was not ideal for built up areas, but the perceived wisdom was that if there were a problem in a built up area, there would be enough help around so the lifeboats would not be needed.

Pinkerton was already in the high-sided lifeboat and helped pull the Professor in behind him as Teddy pushed from the deck. Then the boy passed Rickenbacker Elephantine's box and clambered in to await the last passenger.

"Everything will be fine," Spicer informed the other Reclaimers.

"This feels strange," Elena said. "I'm normally the one going it alone."

"Don't let Hilt..."

"Not going to happen," Bunce assured Spicer.

"Once we've met the Fairy, we'll reconvene at the rendezvous point. Good luck with the Viceroy."

He leant forward and pecked her gently on the cheek, aware of Hilt's eyes burning into him.

"Good luck, Valentine," she said, feeling her eyes moisten.

"See you on the other side," Bunce nodded, turning towards the other lifeboat.

"Are we ready?" Hilt asked impatiently, watching Spicer climb into Rickenbacker's craft.

"Hold on tight," Brennan warned Teddy from the other lifeboat and then Hilt pulled the lever.

They all felt their ears pop, a muffled "puh" like some-body had blown into a bottle followed, and then there was an explosion of Red Wonder. The lifeboat swung out at right angles to the deck, so that it hung above the slideway, before it was catapulted up a chute and into the air. Brennan watched the tops of the occupants' heads snap back as the boat was flung into the air, and then nod forward as the sail unfurled like a parachute. Bunce peered down her rifle sight and could see Spicer wrestling with the rigging hanging from the sail, struggling to manoeuvre the craft towards the tenements in the distance. The townsfolk looked up in surprise at the wooden boat drifting between the buildings towards downtown. Bunce put the sight back into her kit, threw it onto the other lifeboat and climbed aboard.

"May I be of assistance?" Hilt asked Elena.

He picked up the large bag they had purloined from the suite, threw it into the boat and offered Elena his hand.

"She can manage," Bunce told him, taking Elena's hand and pulling her in.

Hilt shrugged, checked the rope attached to the lever was secure, took one last look around the deck and climbed aboard, careful to mask the tremor in his hand. The inside of the high-sided lifeboat felt like a cocoon, but Hilt still didn't feel safe. He resented the fact that his life was in the hands of the Wonder again, but he'd be damned if he was going to show Elena fear. He let out a breath and took up the rope leading to the lever.

"You there," came the voice of a crew member on deck. "What do you think you're doing?"

"Ready?" Brennan asked, and when the others nodded, Hilt pulled the rope.

The lifeboat swung out immediately, knocking Hilt off his feet and jostling them all to the left before it sprung into space. Hilt tumbled across the bottom of the boat and slid into Elena's lap as they were all rammed against the rear of the boat. The sail unfurled and there was a puff of warmth as Red Wonder blew out from beneath the rigging and caused the sail to billow, full of warm air. The boat slowed and Hilt rolled off Elena.

"Excuse me," he said, and found the barrel of Bunce's Twirler in his face.

"Never do anything like that again," she warned him.

"Call off your guard dog," Hilt told Elena. "It was an accident."

"Bunce," said Elena, her hand on the Reclaimer's arm, "we have more pressing issues."

Brennan grabbed the two lengths of rigging, wrapped them twice around each hand and looked out over the high edges of the boat. They were some forty feet up, the Bester already resembling a toy boat on trails of spilt milk, as they glided over the suburbs, heading in the opposite direction to Rickenbacker's lifeboat, towards uptown Chinsey.

"Lady Melody," Brennan called, "I need directions."

Elena joined him in the centre of the lifeboat and scanned the horizon, getting her bearings.

"My God, we're high," she remarked, and Brennan flashed back to the night before when he had hung above the slideway from the wrong side of the barrier of the Bester.

"This is nothing," he told her. "Now which way? We don't want to stay up here all day."

"There's the music hall so that patch of green must be Wadsworth Park, which the Viceroy's house backs onto. I think."

"You think?"

Bunce watched as Elena as her nose grew red, her face flushed and she grew goosebumps in the wind. She looked over at Hilt, expecting to see him admiring Elena too, but he was seated deep in the lifeboat clinging to the stolen baggage, his eyes locked on the floor.

"Don't like heights?" she asked him.

"Tell our pilot not to land in the Viceroy's front garden," Hilt growled. "We need some time alone with him before he calls in the troops, boy."

"Brennan knows what he's doing," Laurel told him, gazing over the edge of the lifeboat with a smile on her face. "Ignore Hilt, Bunce. He hates everybody."

Bunce looked from the nauseous warrior to the buoyant curves of the woman who seemed to think everything was a game. She wondered how she had ended up here, still alive.

"Hold on to your hats," Brennan warned his passengers. "We're going in."

Brennan pulled up the sail, and Bunce relished Hilt's face as it grew paler. The lifeboat dipped towards the ground and she felt her own stomach lurch. Above the edge of the boat, sky turned to chimneys, then roofs rushed past, followed by windows and tree tops. There was a gasp of heat, Brennan dropped the sail to let it fill one last time and the lifeboat slowed. It hit the ground, staccato beats thundering around them as the wooden vessel was dragged across the cobbled street. Brennan heaved up the sail, and minutes seemed to pass as they rumbled down the street until they hit a wrought iron fence and came to a halt. Everybody rolled to the rear of the boat in a heap of limbs and luggage.

In the quiet that followed, Bunce heard gasps of awe, cries of terror and whinnying horses.

"Let's go," Brennan said, extricating himself from the others and grabbing the two suit bags. The three women followed him out and they raced away from the upturned and scarred lifeboat as a crowd started to form.

"Where's Hilt?" Laurel asked, looking back over her shoulder to see the warrior warily climb over the edge of the lifeboat. He looked thirty years older, and dropped heavily to the cobbles then steadied himself against the boat. The crowd retreated as they saw the heavy blade in his hand, and then he saw the others and raced after them, the military frock coat flapping around his ankles.

Meanwhile, some of the more audacious downtown residents approached the lifeboat that lay upside-down in their midst with a selection of tools to start stripping the vessel of all its fixtures and fittings. They clambered over the hull and started to lay into the battered wood, pulling back planks and yanking out screws.

"There's someone 'ere!" called one of the communicative members of the group, and the group stepped back to right the lifeboat. It rocked back onto its hull and the salvagers looked inside.

"Get back, you graverobbers!" roared a large man with impressive whiskers.

There were exclamations and curses as the man pulled himself out of the boat and turned back to pull out his comrades.

"Who are you?" asked one of the salvagers.

"Does it matter?" asked the man with the whiskers, a bloodstain caked onto his shoulder. "Are you alright, Professor? Teddy?"

The older gentleman and his boy checked themselves over as they were helped out, looking for cuts and breaks from the crash landing. A good-looking warrior climbed out behind them.

"Sorry about that," said Spicer to the others.

"Be off with you, your scavenging rats!" Pinkerton growled.

"Wait," said Rickenbacker. "If you want this boat, it's yours," he said to the tallest salvager.

"Oh, yeah? And what do you want for it?" challenged the salvager suspiciously.

"Don't tell anyone you saw us," the Professor suggested.

"This is downtown, sunshine. I don't tell people I even met my own mother."

"And can you point me in the direction of the nearest Fairy lodgings."

"Handspans, is it? You'll be wanting the rookery," the man said, and pointed over his shoulder. "Straight down there, second on the left. You can't miss it. Biggest in Chinsey."

"Thank you, Sir," said Rickenbacker, and the four men stepped over the deep groove in the mud of the road caused by their landing and followed the man's directions. Just before they turned the corner, Teddy looked back, and was surprised to see that all that remained of the lifeboat was some splinters and shavings, the rest on its way to being repurposed in a variety of locales around downtown Chinsey.

Nobody really knew the point of the Fairy. There were more in the Gramarye than anywhere else in the Grand

Quillian Empire, more even than in the Capital, which was blamed on the abundance of Wonder. It seemed to attract them, like bees to a honeypot. They were known as handspans, due to their diminutive size, or dodos, as although the Fairy had wings, they seemed unable to fly, much like the dodo. With much exertion, they could flutter as high as ten feet, but it could not be described as real flight. It was more like a stag beetle, hesitant as though they were taking to the air for the first time every time they left the floor, their translucent wings beating to the sound of a slow raspberry.

They survived on scraps from the world around them, stitching clothes from rags and making furniture from rubbish. But they didn't seem to eat or drink, surviving only through their proximity to Wonder. They lived in piles of dust created by the nearby factories of Chinsey, the brown filth compacted into great termite mounds. Thousands of Fairy lived in each mound, or rookery, one family on top of the other. Twigs and sticks protruded from the rookery, giving the Fairy the opportunity to launch themselves into the air before flittering to the ground like fallen sycamore leaves. They were also used as something to grasp if they lost their momentum mid-flight. Clothes hung from them, drying in the wind, and they also proved a good defence against cats and dogs. They gave the rookery an appearance of a melted snowman crafted from brown snow.

Many years ago, mankind had stopped listening to the Fairy, viewing them as frivolous and obscure. Every word they uttered seemed an attempt to confuse, every tale was confounding, and the longer people ignored them, the more obtuse they grew, until nowadays it seemed they made no sense at all, to each other or to the outside world.

They were viewed as a nuisance, vermin, hardly any better than rats, but two things had saved them from being wiped out; their resemblance to mankind, and the fact that they could not be killed unless they were removed from a source of Wonder, when they would shrivel to nothing, simply disappearing, leaving no sign of their existence. In fact, witnessing the death of Fairy was seen as extremely bad luck, and so the dodo-wings were tolerated. If a Fairy rookery was established in a middle class area or somewhere embarrassing for the Empire, they would simply be removed to somewhere a lot more salubrious where there was a source of Wonder. The Fairy didn't mind. In fact, they didn't seem to notice, so busy were they tumbling drunkenly through the air while bickering nonsensically.

The only people who did take an interest in handspans were children. Little girls were drawn to them by their doll-like stature, only reinforced by their complete lack of genitalia, while some naughty little boys liked nothing more than tearing the wings from a lone Fairy, only to watch it grow back again while the little creature ran through a whole dictionary of swearing.

Valentine Spicer had been different. As he approached the rookery with the others, he felt an excitement growing in his chest. Spurned by other children due to his fearsome facial scarring, young Valentine had spent many hours amongst the stories listening to the Fairy. They didn't exactly welcome him, but they didn't tease him the way the neighbourhood youth had. And he had been fascinated by them. Their use of language suggested they were desperate to communicate precisely, while their demeanour implied that they had no interest in sharing their knowledge with anyone. They would tell tales that had no ending, or the story would continue past the initial topic only to stop on some random halfway point on an entirely different topic. To Valentine, cut out of most of the social mechanics of childhood, it seemed to make sense, in as much as nothing did. If he thought he understood, that he had a grasp on life, it would slip through his fingers, slide out of his own awareness as if he should never have been there in the first place.

Teddy, on the other hand, was not quite as keen. As they approached the rookery, he thought the Fairy swarming around their heap of mixed Red and Green Wonder looked like nothing more than flies around shit. Their faces wore gormless expressions, their bottom lips drooping open, while their stitched-together clothing looked like nothing more than hessian sacks of varying colours with neck and armholes.

He could feel a distinct warmth emanating from Mister Elephantine's box. A blue glow ebbed from the joints and he swore he could feel the object pulling towards the Fairy slum. And as they grew closer, the Fairy seemed to grow agitated, excited, calling their friends out from the rookery to join them in greeting their new visitors. They lifted from the floor to greet them, so the air was full of the sound of raspberries as their wings flapped together. Teddy thought the Fairy were cooing, like pigeons, but his eyes acclimatised to their high tone.

"The Blue," they were repeating, "the blue, the blue..."

Rickenbacker put a reassuring hand on Teddy's shoulder.

"Hold out the box so that they can see it," he suggested.

"The Storyteller box," they started to say amongst themselves as their eyes fell on Elephantine's box, "the living coffin, the traitors' gate."

They had reached the group now, and some started to grasp at Teddy and the box. Other clasped their chests and fell to the ground as though dead.

"What should I do?" Teddy asked, his voice trembling as little hands grabbed at his clothing and little feet landed on him. He worked hard to stop himself from batting them away.

"Tell them you're the chosen one," Pinkerton suggested, and the Fairy started to giggle.

"The susceptible simpleton, the credulous cretin," they said, laughing together. "The victim, the fool."

They shook their heads in disappointment and made faces even more idiotic than their normal expressions. More Fairy were coming from the rookery, and Teddy's heart started to race.

"Professor?" he asked, looking like an over-decorated Christmas tree, dripping with Fairykind.

They threw themselves at Elephantine's box, stroking it, hugging it, finding any way to soak up the blue glow. The weight of the little people started to tell on Teddy and his arm started to drop.

"Stop this!" Spicer called, stepping forward, "We are not here for your mirth."

All the Fairies' heads snapped in Spicer direction and they looked him up and down, their eyes narrowing. Some dropped to the floor to march up and down, others saluted. Some jousted with one another.

"A Yossarian, Elf warrior, killer blood," they whispered to each other, "travelling with the storyteller box, protect the traitor, stand up for those that should lay down."

"Where is Elephantine? Why doesn't he show himself?" Pinkerton asked the Professor.

"The box. They want the representative, the proxy, the collective," the Fairy said. "Take it, show them."

They started to pull at Teddy to drag him towards the rookery.

"Should I give them the box?" Teddy asked.

"Take it to the mound," Rickenbacker suggested.

"You'll be alright," Pinkerton assured him. "I'll flatten their home if they try anything."

"Big man. Whiskered brethren. Trimmed chin, fluffy lips."

"They're quite annoying, aren't they?" said Pinkerton, twisting his moustaches.

"Fairy," Spicer ventured, "I am indeed Elf and wish to find my brethren."

"The Elf mouth moves, he speaks, talks, requests, demands, blah blah blue."

"Can you help me?"

"Fairy and Elf work together, live together, love together, all friends, chums, mates, cousins, nephews and nieces, born together, grown together, betrayed together. All fall down."

"Can we perhaps just talk to one individual?" Rickenbacker suggested,. "To get to the bottom of this betrayal of which you speak?"

There was a huge flash of ice blue and Mister Elephantine was among them in all his finery. Teddy immediately dropped the box as if it weighed as much as Elephantine's body would, were it not a phantom.

"Don't panic, my friends," Elephantine smiled, "for Elephantine is here."

"Great," mumbled Pinkerton.

The Fairy all burst into paroxysms of giggles, pointing at Elephantine and clinging to each other to stay upright while their shrill voices filled the air.

"Shut up, you little bastards," came a cry from one of the tenement upper floor windows.

"I see you Fairy are as welcome here as you are everywhere."

"Break the box. Ruin the receptacle. Quash the craftsman of crafty calamity!"

"A lot of alliteration from meddlesome midgets lacking in luck and leverage," Elephantine said. "Now shut up, little playthings. I require you to contact my brethren."

"The deceiver commands! The villain demands!"

"What the hell is going on?" asked Spicer.

"I have never seen Fairy so agitated," Rickenbacker replied.

"They don't seem to like our travelling companion very much now, do they?" said Pinkerton, folding his arms.

"I've never known them to have an opinion about anything," said Spicer.

"Stop this immediately," Elephantine called as the Fairy surrounded him and commenced leaping through the projection of his body. With each jump, their ascendancy slowed by the wings, the Fairy grasped at the phantom, grabbing handfuls of Blue Wonder as though it were candyfloss and clasping it to their chests where it seemed to dissipate.

"Is he getting smaller?" Pinkerton asked.

"Yossarian!" Elephantine called. "Help me," he cried, as more Fairy pierced his body, laughing and yahooing.

"What's happening?" Teddy called. "They're hurting him."

"The Blue... the Blue..." they started to chant again.

"Teddy!" Elephantine called, reaching for his chosen one. "Get them off the box."

Without thinking, Teddy brushed the few Fairy from the box, and Elephantine, already reduced to three quarters his usual size, folded back into it, leaving a puff of blue that more Fairy attempted to make their own. The lad grabbed the box and slid it beneath his jacket, his arms folded across it. The Fairy, their ranks still swelling with new arrivals from the Rookery rounded on Teddy.

"Professor?" Teddy stuttered, his back against the wall of the tenement.

The three men surrounded the boy and started knocking back the advancing Fairy with their feet and batting them away with the backs of their hands.

"Spicer," said Rickenbacker, "You need to talk to them."

"Me?"

"They called you a cousin, brethren. They recognise you as one of their own."

Spicer shook his head in disbelief before raising himself to his full height and squaring up to the expanding swarm.

"Fairy," he demanded, "Stop this immediately. Or am I not a feared Yossarian?"

The beating of the wings grew louder and the view beyond was blocked. All was the bustle of the Fairy reaching for the box beneath Teddy's jacket.

And then Spicer surprised himself. He identified himself again, but this time his words were not his own. He spoke in a language he had never heard before, let alone used with a sing-song tone and soft R's and hard consonants.

The Fairy immediately stopped their advance, those flying dropped to the floor like bluebottles struck by a cloud of insecticide.

"He speaks," they hissed to one another.

The Fairy drew themselves together, climbing and clambering over and under each other.

"Follow the leader," they started to chant, "follow the leader."

One Fairy was jettisoned from the top of the throng before falling back into the mass of little arms and legs. Another was ejected straight upwards, and her wings started fluttering before she too dropped back into the huddle. The chant continued, growing louder as the writhing grew more frenzied. Another Fairy was elevated above the others, but this one seemed in better control. She flew straight up in the air, her wings a blur, and she stopped to hover steadily above the others. The orgiastic scrum slowed in their threshing and then stopped altogether. They soberly disentangled themselves from one another as the chant died down to a slow rumble. With no apparent organisation, the Fairy manoeuvred themselves into the shape of a five-pronged star beneath the female above them, who had started to glow with blue. Her scraps of clothing seemed to coalesce into something resembling grandeur; the grubbiness around her face left her, and her lank hair curled into a full-bodied style reminiscent of gentry.

"It is good to meet a Yossarian again," said the girl, her chin high. "Especially one that brings the deep Blue."

The three humans and one Elf looked at each other with astonishment.

"Who are you?" Spicer asked.

"My name is Carlson, but you shall not know me for long. Without more deep Blue I'm afraid I have but minutes before I descend back to my former state, back to a subsistence level of Wonder."

"Why did Elephantine ask us to come to you only for you to take his energy?" Rickenbacker asked.

"It is surprising to see an Elf travelling with a human after all that has passed."

"Professor Rickenbacker found Elephantine and allowed me to discover my true identity," Spicer told her. "I would also like an answer to his question."

"I take it you do not know your history then," said Carlson, shaking her head sadly.

"I saw shadows of Pearly when the Library of Senses came alive, and Elephantine told us tales..."

"Who is this Elephantine?"

"The man in the box. The man of Blue Wonder. He told us the Threat was coming and that we should ask the Fairy to help us rally the remaining Elf."

"The man in the box?" Carlson laughed. "That is no man. That is the storyteller box. A casket of dead lies."

"Lies?" asked Teddy, taking the box from beneath his jacket to look at it.

"It obviously had no idea that the Fairy fell victim to a terrible a famine of the Wonder. Or that we have such long memories. If this miniscule taste of deep Blue will allow it,

I will share with you the true story of Pearly, the death of the Elf betrayed to the murderous scum of the earth, the Gleaves."

Blundstone Hall, situated to the south east of the Trade headquarters, had been built by the architect Sir John Dulwich along the lines of Addington Hall, built for the Addington family on the outskirts of the Grand Quillian capital. The Trade had approached such a prestigious architect as they liked to prove that they had tamed and civilized their colonies, and nothing said Grand Quillia like a landscaped garden and a column or two.

Just as Blundstone Hall looked out of place in the industrial frontier town of Chinsey, so did the figure of Sir Ambrose Willis. He had met Elena's late husband Lord Runciman Drew Hynes Melody when they had both become a little too embarrassing for Grand Quillian society and been slipped surreptitiously into exile. Lord Hynes Melody's legacy of slave mines was echoed by Sir Ambrose's history in penal colonies. Whenever the Empire found an inhospitable and worthless rock in the middle of a tempestuous sea, Sir Ambrose had been the first to suggest it be populated by dissenters, criminals and debtors, before building a virtually uninhabitable penitentiary made with rock from his quarries and built by his firms. After one such remote gaol collapsed, killing most of the prisoners, and, more importantly in the eyes of the public, their guards and the guards' families, Sir Ambrose was posted as far from the Capital as possible, where he could be both ineffectual and forgotten. Lord Hynes Melody and Sir Ambrose would sit late into the night righting the wrongs of the world while ogling under-age women brought in for the purpose and beating the help.

Sir Ambrose had never married, although he had enjoyed many dalliances with married women, a few of whom had been reciprocal. Sir Ambrose had never been foolish enough to try anything with Lady Elena Melody, although he had regretted his lack of foolishness many times. So when he was told that she was at his door seeking an audience, he found it very hard to refuse.

"Sir Ambrose, thank you so much for taking the time to see me," Lady Elena said as she was granted an entrance into his study.

He was frailer than she remembered him, but his eyes were as alive as ever, like an owl's alighting on a mouse. His talon-like hands were crossed in front of him on the large leather topped desk, the joints bulbous, the yellowing nails long and sharp. Behind him hung an enormous portrait of himself in all his finery, rows of medals like soldiers on parade dangling from his chest, and a large white dome of a pith helmet boasting an explosion of dove feathers from one side. Beside the portrait, the Grand Quillian flag hung loosely, the red, gold and black merging together in the folds. Behind an enormous vase holding fresh blooming roses, the heavy velvet curtains were closed right, so no natural light could enter the oppressive and stuffy study. The stench of cabbage, stale breath, moth balls and a hint of urine caught in Elena's throat, and she felt she should hold her breath so it couldn't get any further inside her.

For the first time since she had left him chained to his bed, Elena wished Hilt was by her side. Instead she had left him with the others posing as her staff, and had last seen them being led into one of Blunstone Hall's various sitting rooms.

She felt like she was choking in the evening dress they had purloined from the suite on the Spirit of Bester. It was too tight, constricting her stomach and pushing up her breasts as though she were presenting them for exhibition to the lecher across the desk. He licked his lips before speaking.

"My dear Lady Melody, I will always find time for you, especially now your husband is no longer with us."

His voice sounded like fingernails on parchment.

"Thank you, kind Sir," she replied, feeling a chill creep up her back despite the heat in the room. "I sincerely hope that once you hear what I have to say..."

"You come to beg of me a favour, do you not?" he asked, moving his laced hands into a steeple beneath his chin.

"It is more of a warning, as opposed to a favour. Do you have access to the Murder here?"

"Of course I do. Does that bother you?"

"We need to send word to the Capital."

"You wish me to send a warning to the Capital? I understood you had been engaged in unsavoury adventures with ne'er-do-wells since your husband's passing," he nodded. "Is it for them you speak?"

"I represent nobody. All I care about is the safety of the Empire, Sir Ambrose."

"That is gratifying to hear, Milady. Most gratifying. Snuff?"

Sir Ambrose opened a drawer and retrieved an ivory snuff box. Leaving the drawer open, he unlocked the box and took a pinch of the powder inside. Elena heard snot move in the old man's hairy nostrils as the smell of cinnamon seeped in to join the stink in the study.

"No thank you, Sir Ambrose. I need to discuss this grave danger. The Gramarye, if not the whole Empire, is in terrible peril."

Sir Ambrose put the ivory box back in the drawer.

"And where did you learn of this terrible peril, my dear?"

"The Cathedral of Tales in the Glasslands..."

"Are you sure you won't join me in snuff?"

"Thank you, no. As I was saying..."

"I would be more inclined to listen were you to share this small vice with me."

Elena attempted to conceal her frustration with a smile.

"Very well, sir Ambrose. I would be happy to imbibe with such honourable company."

Sir Ambrose removed the ivory box and held it out to Elena, who took it.

"You know I've always been very fond of you, Elena."

Elena nodded thanks for the compliment as she opened the box, expecting another waft of cinnamon, took a pinch, held it to her nose and snorted. She felt a burning sensation in the walls of her nostril and a sour taste at the back of her throat. She moved to return the box to Sir Ambrose but her hand felt heavy, so it remained on her lap. She opened her mouth to talk but a wheezy groan was all that emerged. Her eyes flicked in terror to the powder in the open box on her lap and then to Sir Ambrose's face. He smiled at her, showing his crooked, tea-coloured teeth, as he removed an identical ivory box from the drawer and took another pinch of snuff.

"You are quite helpless, Elena," Sir Ambrose informed her. "Unfortunately I have already received a warning."

He pulled himself out of his chair, his eyes never leaving Elena's.

"A warning from the good Doctor Axelrod, who informed me of your treachery with your companions via the murder this morning."

He picked up the box from Elena's lap, snapped it shut and placed it on the desk.

"But I never thought you would present yourself to me directly. I have already let the Doctor know using the very system you were so keen to utilise yourself."

He rested his thin, ageing buttocks on the edge of his desk.

"Your willingness to deliver yourself to me bodes well for you as I could never really be bothered with the pursuit of women. I see no thrill in the chase," he reached forward to untie the front of her dress. "I have always found romance most tiresome."

She could feel his breath on her neck as he moved closer, could smell the brandy. He kissed her on the cheek and then moved his lips to her ear.

"But snuff cannot be a man's only vice."

He sunk his teeth into Elena's ear lobe. She tried to scream as she felt the blood drip onto the base of her neck, she tried to move, to get away, to do anything but she stayed slumped in the chair, her eyes locked on the portrait of the honourable Viceroy for the Gramarye.

"This place is amazing," said Laurel, looking around the sitting room at the paintings depicting landscapes of Grand Quillia, antiquities from around the Empire and trophies of most animals from across the globe. "Why couldn't the

Gleaves leave me anything like this instead of my lodge in Hump country?"

"I don't like it," said Brennan.

"It may be a little rich for your tastes, Brennan, but you have to admit..."

"I know what you mean," Hilt mumbled, his blade concealed beneath the greatcoat, his sleeve pinned to his chest. "If we're supposed to be her servants, then why have they put us in a sitting room?"

Bunce frowned. She wasn't *au fait* with social politics.

"Why aren't we below stairs with the other help?" Brennan asked, and they all looked to each other.

"Elena," Bunce heard herself say.

First one entrance, a double doorway leading into the hall, burst open, followed by another single door on the opposite wall, and eight Trade regulars entered, their rifles trained on the visitors.

"Drop your weapons, insurgent scum," demanded the Trade Captain at their head.

"I knew this was a bad idea," Hilt grumbled.

The smoke from the factory chimneys had descended on the tenements quickly, faster than a winter's night, forming a fog at ground level that the locals bitterly called 'mutton stew', due to its brown hue and thick density.

Carlson the Fairy smiled as it engulfed them and casually waved her hands at the wrists so the fog around her retreated, forming a dome around them all.

"This brutally ignorant use of the Wonder was not always the case. There was once another way, not the amateurish dabbling you see around you now," she said, shaking her head sadly. "Mankind once used the Wonder for the betterment of everyone. The whole world could have felt the benefits. Medicine improved, education was better served, faster communication and travel meant nobody was ever too far from their loved ones."

"Utopia," the Professor noted.

"But it did come at a cost. There was a ripple. A ripple that became a wave that crashed across humanity, changing it forever. Elfkind became prevalent in the Gramarye within two generations. These children seemed to have soaked up the Wonder. It permeated their very being. However, on the outskirts, especially in the Attar Mountains, many children were born stockier, shorter, and the Wonder seemed to have passed them by. The gifts brought by the Wonder had no effect. It was as if they were out of step with the rest of the Gramarye. These children, who became known as the Out-steppers, turned from the Wonder and concentrated on mechnology, clockwork. Machines. They used godless methods to improve themselves."

"The praying mantis beneath the Library of Senses," Pinkerton whispered.

"And what about you?" asked Spicer. "What about the Fairy?"

"As the Elf found or created more deep blue, so more Fairy flocked to the Gramarye. We were there to help the Elf, as the more deep blue there was, the greater we became. In fact we were the first to detect the Out-steppers' return."

"Return?" Spicer asked.

"They invaded the Gramarye and were eventually forced back beneath the mountains by the Elf led by the Yossarians, but at great cost. The Elf were weakened, the Wonder reduced to critical levels. Unable to support the quality of life to which the Gramarye, and especially Pearly, had become accustomed, the populace revolted."

"Just like Mister Elephantine said," Teddy offered, clinging to the box.

"But the storyteller box did not reveal whom he represents. He did not explain why that box of blue Wonder you hold is known as the traitor's gate."

"They lead the populace," Spicer said, his eyes darkening.

"With humankind, the Elf in the box turned against their own kind. Humanity had promised the traitors they could rule Pearly, and then they destroyed the city anyway, using captured weapons from the Out-steppers."

"But Mister Elephantine..." Teddy whimpered.

"Humanity had grown to hate the Elf. They found their ways patronising. And so they decided to annihilate them."

Pinkerton's mouth dropped open in horror as Rickenbacker glanced at Spicer, whose eyes had narrowed.

"The Library of Senses was left standing..."

"...as a trap to attract the last of the Elf," Spicer interrupted.

"The humans were led by a family called the Gleaves," Carlson continued before Rickenbacker interrupted her.

"That's why Laurel was able to use the Gargoyle Key."

"And why Elephantine hated her so much," Pinkerton added.

"And now the Gramarye is in trouble again," said Spicer, unable to look at his companions, his eyes locked on Carlson.

"Spicer being an Elf, Laurel being a Gleave. This all seems so lucky," Rickenbacker said, shaking his head.

"Deep Blue brings coincidental positivity to the world," Carlson told them.

"Coincidental..?" Pinkerton repeated.

"Luck," the Professor clarified.

"Serendipity," Carlson added.

"No."

They all turned to see Teddy. Tears were running down his face.

"I am the Chosen One. Mister Elephantine told me."

"He is a liar. A traitor. A murderer and a liar," snarled Spicer, "like everybody in that box."

"No. You're the liar. You're a Reclaimer," Teddy shouted at them. "And everybody knows you should never believe in Fairy tales."

"Teddy," said the Professor, offering a reassuring hand, "I know it must be hard to..."

"Damn you!" Teddy screamed. "I'll show you. Mister Elephantine and I will show you all," and he turned and ran, the smog engulfing him as soon as he stepped from Carlson's dome.

"I'll go," Pinkerton said, and, taking his blat gun from his shoulder, he too was swallowed by the fog as he pursued the boy with the storyteller box.

Spicer and Rickenbacker looked at each other with determination and turned back to face Carlson, who seemed to be hovering lower than she had been.

"So what about the Threat?" Spicer asked.

"The Elf are coming," she said, and giggled.

"Isn't that a good thing?" Spicer asked.

"At least you've got your Elf," Carlson said.

She had lost more height, and her hair was starting to lose its curl.

"The Blue Wonder..." Rickenbacker said. "The power it gave them is going."

"Carlson?" Spicer asked.

The raspberry noise started to accompany the beating of her wings, and looking down, the two men noticed that the star made up by the Fairy was fast losing its shape.

"Tell us about the Threat," Rickenbacker pleaded, knowing it was already too late.

"The dead will make dead when you should fret about the Threat," she said, her appearance almost back to how she started.

"The dead?" Rickenbacker repeated.

"The People of the Ditch use the undead," Spicer said, reaching out a hand to catch Carlson as she fell.

"And Axelrod had the skills to re-animate Sir Evan..."

"You look better with ears," Carlson told Spicer.

"Could Axelrod be working with the Ditch?"

"And what about the Elf? Am I the only returning Elf?"

"Your fingers smell of custard," said Carlson.

Aldo Kendrick had never been so happy to see the smoke stacks of Chinsey in his entire life. As the two of them entered the town and trotted past the factories, he prayed that a patrol would catch sight of his travelling companion and destroy him. But they passed into downtown, the low smog swept in to cloak the two of them, concealing them from prying eyes. Sir Evan Mandell brought the pony to a stop.

"So," Kendrick ventured, "what now?"

"Our mission has changed," Mandell said, not bothering to turn round. "The Doctor has new information."

"He has?" Kendrick said. "So you no longer need my skills?"

"You are right," Mandell answered. "I must scout Chinsey to ensure it is ready for invasion."

"Invasion? What about Rickenbacker?"

"Soon the whole city will be under our control. Then we can find the Professor and his box in our own time," Mandell replied. "Unless he is already in chains."

"Great. Good. So I'll be on my way then."

"Yes you will."

Mandell reached behind him and effortlessly through Kendrick to the floor. The knight pulled his spinner and pointed it at the small man sprawling on the floor.

"Wait," Kendrick suggested as Mandell spun the pistol.

From the nearby smog, the form of a boy barrelled into view, caught his foot on Kendrick and tumbled onto the floor, the small box in his hands rolling onto the cobbles in front of him.

"Is that the Gargoyle Key?" said Kendrick.

"You!" gasped Mandell's former partner as the gentleman pugilist named Pinkerton emerged from the brown hue, his blat gun already in his hand.

The Fairy lost interest in Spicer and Rickenbacker within thirty seconds of Carlson fluttering out of the Elf's hand, apparently forgetting about the Storyteller Box, Mister Elephantine and the source of the Deep Blue. The female Fairy had disappeared into the fluttering swarm, never to be seen again.

"Do you think we could use one of the Fairy to find your boy and the Storyteller Box?" Spicer asked.

"I'm sure their bloodhound skills are as minimal as their abilities to communicate. I suggest we return to the rendezvous point. If Pinkerton finds Teddy, and I'm sure he will, then he will meet us there."

Rickenbacker looked at the smog swirling around them and shrugged.

"Teddy could be three feet away and we wouldn't even know it," he said.

"A legion of Immolators could be three feet away and we wouldn't know it," countered Spicer.

Before they started off into the fog, Spicer noticed Rickenbacker's mouth twitch nervously as the older man nodded acknowledgement. As the rookery was engulfed by the mist, Spicer regarded his new travelling companion, Professor Hilary Rickenbacker, feeling a peculiar warmth emanating from him. He had been aware of the Rickenbacker legend for some years, the shadowy terrorist mastermind and daredevil adventurer who was only one hair's breadth from capture by the Trade. He had expected an evil magician type, all top hat, twirling moustaches and sword stick, and was amazed to discover an ageing academic and former ECO who seemed driven by honour, by some personal sense of justice.

Spicer had never been driven by anything apart from his own survival and relied on his pragmatism to get him through. Now he was obsessed with finding where the remaining Elf had gone, and discovering how to use these new senses that had infused his being since his Elf side had been awakened in the remains of Pearly. He could feel a righteous anger at the near genocide, but none of it was directed at the Gleave girl. He felt more antagonism towards the phantom Elephantine, twisting those around him to his own bidding in his desperate quest for power. When he thought of Laurel Gleave, he was touched by hope, of the possibility of change, of improvement. Somehow he knew she was not his enemy, despite her bloodline. As he considered legacies, he felt the strength of the Yossarians before him. He knew that they represented the battle for truth, that they could have never joined Elephantine and the other traitors, that they would rather leave Pearly than hand it to power-seeking despots and scum.

And then he felt the warmth coming from the Professor at his side again. Spicer knew there were things that Rickenbacker knew, and that he himself knew individually, that would bring all this together. He had never been so sure of a hunch before in his life. He felt it in his guts, his heart and head. He felt like he was on the verge of a missing piece that would explain why both of them had ended up here together, pushed together by the Deep Blue, why their lives had taken the routes they had.

"Why, Professor Rickenbacker?" he said as they passed more tenements.

"Why?" the Professor repeated.

"Why are you doing this?"

"Doing what?" the man replied, not looking at the Elf, concealing something.

"Why aren't you sitting in a study poring over books? Why isn't Teddy shining your shoes and your housekeeper pouring you tea? Why aren't you inspiring students with history? Why aren't you..."

"Living the easy life? Existing in a world where I accept the truth I am fed without questioning it?"

"Dissension is one thing. What made you take this route?"

"Are you asking me why I'm doing the right thing?"

"No, I'm asking you what made you fight for it?"

Spicer was aware of an empathy he had never known before. His own being was infused with a need for atonement, an all-consuming need to make amends, and he realised he was experiencing Rickenbacker's own feelings.

"What are you not telling me?" Spicer asked, reaching out and turning the Professor so that the man was forced to face him.

"I don't know..."

"What did you see? There's something you saw, something when you were an ECO, when you thought you were doing good..."

"Oh my God. How do you know?"

"Tell me."

Rickenbacker reached for a nearby wall to steady himself. Spicer took him by the shoulders and looked deep into the man's moist eyes. He felt his heart beat, swelling as though it would burst from his chest, sweat broke out on his brow and he felt nauseous and faint. He realised he was feeling the exact same sensations as the Professor, mirroring him in every way.

"The Immolators..." both men said simultaneously.

"I discovered the truth. Children snatched from parents, brought up in the ballrooms so they can be commanded, grown into their armour. Children..." Rickenbacker stuttered.

"Elf children. The Immolators are Elf," Spicer said, "That's why my parents burnt me. When I was born an Elf..."

"...they knew you'd be taken so they hid you..."

"...behind my scars."

Spicer let go of the Professor and his hands rose to his face, smooth now, untarnished. The two men looked at each other in shock.

"You were in my mind," said Rickenbacker, still slumped against the wall.

"And you in mine."

"I thought they used the ballrooms to discover those born susceptible to that form of Wonder, those who would take orders from the ballrooms. When I discovered they were taking children, babies really, stealing them from their parents and turning them into those terrible things. I didn't know the children were Elf."

"Who created the ballrooms?" Spicer asked.

"We never knew..."

"Elephantine and his mob. They must have created them when they brought down Pearly."

"And now the Trade use them to enforce their own control."

The two men shook their heads in awe.

"Men like Axelrod have the skills and knowledge to use the ballrooms. He must have worked out the Gargoyle Key was connected with them in some way."

"We have to get the Elephantine back and we have to destroy the ballrooms," Spicer said.

Spicer helped Rickenbacker upright and the two men regarded each other with mutual respect. They shook hands, realising for the first time that it was growing brighter.

"The fog is lifting," said Rickenbacker.

"Let's find the others," Spicer said. "We know what we need to do."

PART 4

Friend Only to the Undertaker

Chinsey,
Capital of The Gramarye region
Grand Quillia

June 1832

There wasn't a cloud in the sky above Chinsey, the latest boom town on the outskirts of the Empire. The sun was warm and the air was thick with the rich aroma of herbs and spices. Young Hilary Rickenbacker shielded his eyes as he looked up at the wooden scaffolding being erected across the dirt street from the newly built Trade headquarters. He watched the builders' mallets pummelling the remains of the centuries-old native structures, the construction teams tearing apart the bricks and rubble to provide the foundations for the new Imperial buildings. He puffed on his pipe pensively as the long thin shadow of a man slid into sight.

"Heart bleeding again, Hilary?"

Rickenbacker turned to regard his fellow Enchantment and Chicanery Operations cadet, Kevin Axelrod.

"Don't you think we should study the history of a region before we destroy it?"

"We're not destroying it. We're recycling it."

Axelrod sniffed. He didn't have time for Rickenbacker's high-mindedness.

"Why do you want to be an ECO, Hilary?"

"I want to learn about the Wonder."

"You can do that without becoming an ECO."

"I don't want to be an architect or a hyperphysicist. I want to find the source, see how other people, other cultures have used it through time. I want to see how it works, I want to know why it exists, I want to push the boundaries, make the world better for everybody. But I want to do all that without just stripping it out from any source we find. We should be economical with it. We need to be more careful."

"As I said, why do you want to be an ECO?"

Rickenbacker smiled gently and shrugged, feeling the cadet uniform's high collar chafe at his neck. He waved his pipe around, indicating their surroundings.

"Look where we are, Kevin," he said, eyes wide. "Not everybody gets to see this, these places, the edge of the known world."

"This isn't the edge of the world," Axelrod replied.

"Alright," Rickenbacker conceded, "the edge of the Empire."

Axelrod's mouth twitched and he raised a hand to cover it. He should be more careful. He should not point out to members of the Trade, proud Grand Quillians, that there is more to the world than their precious Empire. He should definitely not mention the People of the Ditch. And he should without a doubt never impart that he himself had been adopted on the other side of the Attar Mountains, in the Ditch.

The natives beyond the mountains did not call their homeland the Ditch. It was more a basin surrounded by treacherous peaks that had acted as a perfect defensive wall against the ever-expanding Grand Quillian Empire. The Attar Mountains had not only kept people out, but had also ensured that the people of the Ditch stayed at home. They had also discovered the Wonder, but they had discovered more Green Wonder, and so, as their hyperphysical studies progressed, they followed a more esoteric route than the Empire's use of Red Wonder for energy. The reanimation of the dead had become quite commonplace as the population of the Ditch started to dwindle.

The people of the Ditch would have been extinct many years earlier, but millennia previously there had been an influx of new blood, as refugees from Pearly struggled across the mountain paths, running from the Threat and from their own rulers.

The Ditch had taken in the Pearly Elf and humans, and the skills they brought from the extraordinary city of Pearly had been useful for hundreds of years. Indeed, many Elf were born in the Ditch, and they bided their time, knowing that they would one day take back Pearly. Christened the New Arrivals, they were a minority that dwindled, and were occasionally treated as such, but they had learned to fight over the years, and anyone who looked down on an Elf found themselves taking on the whole community.

The Threat that had driven the New Arrivals to their new home had not gone for good, even when Pearly had been obliterated. There were reports of mechnological beasts in the mountains, and slowly the people of the Ditch became insular as they withdrew further into the natural basin, scared of waking the Threat that had destroyed their neighbours' homes once before.

But a millennium of self-sufficiency was coming to an end. The crops were failing, the reserves of Green Wonder were drying up. The people of the Ditch would have to rise up from their remote strongholds to reengage with the world. Following the systematic destruction of the Elf in the Gramarye, and the subsequent distrust of the undead, the people of the Ditch knew they would not be welcomed, and so the only way forward was through subterfuge, to use the limited resources they had to expand into the Gramarye, repel the Grand Quillian invaders and tap the rich resources of Pearly.

The destruction of Pearly and the creation of the Glasslands were still engrained in the minds of the aristocrats of the Ditch, the ruling families that had led their people for thousands of years. The Emperor himself was only one generation away from remembering the arrival of the Elf, his father having been 1700 years old, kept alive by the power of Green Wonder, living the verdant life of the dead, as it was known in the local vernacular. Emperor Verlaine was 900 years old, and, prompted by the other families, he had agreed to send in agents to probe the Gramarye's defences, to dig deep into Grand Quillian society, find the weak spots to ensure that the limited means of the Ditch could be utilised to drive Grand Quillia out.

For two hundred years, the agents of the Ditch had investigated and planned while the embattled Elf born in the Ditch continued to fight for equality in their new land. And then one of these embedded agents, Kevin Axelrod, found a key to victory for his countrymen that would also motivate the New Arrivals into helping the people of the Ditch.

Axelrod had been smuggled into the Gramarye and had made his way to the Capital in Grand Quillia. Showcasing the hyperphysical skills that the Elf had taught him, he won a place at the ECO academy in the capital, and after four more years of study, the two best students were despatched to the Gramarye, so tantalisingly close to his homeland.

"Why do you think they've brought us here?" Axelrod asked Rickenbacker, looking up at the imposing Trade edifice, the bright yellow uniforms of the guards flashing between each thick column.

"The Gramarye has very rich deposits of Wonder. It was once the centre of the Deep Blue."

"I know all that," Axelrod snapped back. "Why have they brought the two of us here? What use could two cadets be?"

"Orders said it was for extra-curricular training."

"Whatever that means."

Axelrod indicated an adjutant marching towards the gate and Rickenbacker tapped the tobacco from his pipe to extinguish it.

The two young cadets were shown into a side room and told to wait. After twenty minutes, a fat young man entered, eating a flatbread stuffed with peppers and some form of meat. He sat down on a bench opposite the two cadets and looked them both up and down. When he'd finished his meal, he pulled a lump of gristle from between his teeth and flicked it to the floor. He dusted down his red tunic and licked his fingers. Axelrod noticed the pips of a captain on his collar.

"You here to see the ballrooms too?" the man suddenly asked.

"I don't... we..." Axelrod started.

"Keeping you in the dark, are they?" he offered a hand, lifting his large posterior from the bench, "I'm Captain Edgar Quine. You can call me Captain."

They shook hands and the two cadets introduced themselves as Axelrod wiped his palm on his overcoat.

"We were told we were here for training," Rickenbacker offered.

"Good for you. Let's hope you're up to it."

"Is it dangerous?"

"This is the Gramarye, old boy. There are more dangers and secrets here than anywhere else in the Empire. You've got the Ditch just on the other side of the mountains, and the only thing keeping them there are the monsters in the mountains."

"Monsters?" Axelrod scoffed.

"Then there's the Humps who'll eat anyone, local or Quillian. You've got your pyramids full of ancient Wonder, the cursed Cathedral of Tales from which nobody has ever returned, woods made of glass and the slideways haven't even reached this far yet. If the locals rise up, there won't be any reinforcements for months. If anything were to happen, the whole of the Gramarye colony could rely on you two, your training, and the ballrooms."

"What are the ballrooms?"

"That's not for me to say now, is it?"

"I don't know," Rickenbacker replied. "I have no idea what they are."

"I'm not sure anyone does. I mean, we know what they do, but nobody knows why or how."

"You're talking in riddles," Axelrod huffed.

"This place is a riddle," Quine replied, picking meat from his nails.

The adjutant returned and led the three men down corridors that still smelt of paint, deeper into the new building's bowels. Rickenbacker noticed that they always seemed to be going down, and wondered whether they were being taken to some underground bunker.

"Do you smell anything?" Rickenbacker asked.

"Wonder?" Axelrod replied. "Probably just the generators."

"I don't think it's Red Wonder," Rickenbacker said, and Axelrod frowned.

After some time of seeing no other Trade worker, they eventually caught sight of a large man with a blat gun on his lap behind a barred gate with three separate locks. As they approached he stood up and unlocked the middle lock. The adjutant pulled a key on the end of a chain from his tunic and unlocked the bottom lock. Captain Quine unlocked the top to allow the guard to pull open the gate. The two cadets were ushered through, and Rickenbacker looked down the corridor beyond as the three men locked the gate behind them. It resembled a darkened hospital, with walls and floor scrubbed clean and completely lacking in any ornamentation except for the red glow of the light bulbs. There were bolted doors either side of the passage, each with a small locked hatch at face height. Only one hatch was open, halfway down before the passage turned to the right. There was a silence more eerie than the constant sound of dripping water and the groans of prisoners, which Rickenbacker had expected.

"What is this place?" Axelrod whispered.

"This is just the beginning," Quine replied, with the excited smile of a small boy showing off a treehouse.

"Ghosts," said the guard.

Rickenbacker looked at the guard for the first time. His face looked anaemic in the red light, his eyes flashing so that he appeared albino. He put his key back into a pouch on his belt and sat back down on a small stool.

"What did he say?" Axelrod asked.

"Ignore old Joe. He's been down here too long," Quine said, looking at the guard with disdain.

"He said ghosts," Rickenbacker said. "What do you mean by that?"

"This is where ghosts come to die," Joe replied.

"Oh do shut up," scolded Quine. "You're scaring the children. Shall we move on?"

The adjutant nodded once, clicked his heels together and set off down the corridor, his footsteps clicking against the floor. The two cadets glanced at each other before following him, missing the glare Quine threw at old Joe.

Rickenbacker was aware of his own breathing as they advanced, his eyes locked on the one hatch that was open. He started to slow as they approached the door.

They reached the open hatch and Rickenbacker glanced inside. The cell was completely bare except for a cot and a lone light bulb. Seated on the bed was a man, his hands flat on his naked lap, facing a blank wall. Dried rivulets of blood, black in the light of the cell, crisscrossed his face and neck, and continued down his shoulders and back. On top of the man's bald head was a delicate mesh of copper or bronze strands like spun sugar, throbbing with Blue Wonder. In the split second it took to pass, Rickenbacker realised that the wiring was threaded into the man's scalp, piercing the skin. And some strands were buried into the man's eye sockets so he leaked tears of blood, and others were latticed across and into his ears, cutting into the skin, gristle and lobes.

"No dawdling," Quine called behind him. "Everything will become clear when we reach the ballroom."

"Did you see?" Rickenbacker hissed into Axelrod's ear.

"What?"

They turned the corner and were faced by an identical corridor. Rickenbacker shivered as he thought about more men like the one he had seen, a blood stained man behind each door, crowns of thorns burying into his head. The adjutant stopped at a door like all the others and knocked once. The hatch opened from the inside, and then bolts were heard being slid back. The adjutant nodded once at the two cadets and continued down the corridor, leaving the door open. Filling the doorway stood an Immolator in full battle gear, pistol and sword hanging from his belt, full-face helmet in place.

"It would appear the Viceroy is having some fun," Quine sneered, before giving a mock salute to the warrior in front of him.

Rickenbacker and Axelrod exchanged puzzled glances as the Immolator stepped back to allow entrance. The three men joined the armoured killer in the small cell, and Quine closed the door behind them before sliding the bolts into place. Rickenbacker was aware of each breath he took as his chest brushed against the armoured arm of his cellmate.

Axelrod stared into the lens of the Immolator's goggle, unable to discern anything. He raised his hand and Rickenbacker was shocked to see the man tap a finger against the fogged glass. A loud clunk bounced around the room before a rattling started, like something shaking the bars of its cage, and it grew louder. Axelrod withdrew his finger.

"Excuse me," Quine said, pushing his way past the other three to reach the wall farthest from the door. He knelt down, inserted two fingers into a crack in the bottom of the wall that could have been a mouse hole, and twisted. Quine stood up and pushed the wall so that it swivelled backwards to reveal another corridor that led to an elevator at the end, which had created the rattling noise.

"After you," he offered, and the two cadets entered the lift.

Leaving the Immolator in the cell, Quine pushed the secret door back into place and joined the cadets in the lift.

"Here's where the fun begins," he told the two men as the lift juddered once and set off on its journey beneath the Trade Headquarters.

The elevator grille allowed a view of the shaft, and as it trundled slowly downwards, Rickenbacker noticed the walls were dark, smooth and shiny, like polished leather. As he stared through the grille, he could see his own face looking back at him.

"Did the Trade build this?" he asked.

"The Trade found it," Quine replied, leaning back against the wall of the lift with a smug look on his face.

"This was built by the Elf," Axelrod uttered, stopping himself from reaching through the grill to touch the wall. "This was a part of Pearly."

"Is that what the ballrooms are? Some piece of ancient Elf Wonder?" Rickenbacker asked.

"You're the enchantment and chicanery operative," Quine smirked. "You tell me. All I know is that the power here will keep the Empire going for one thousand more years."

Axelrod ground his teeth, his heart a mixture of excitement and rage. What had the Trade found here? He knew that many underground networks had been created to support Pearly, including the underground carriageways and various correspondence channels. But why would this help them in their war effort?

The elevator ground to a halt and Quine pulled back the grille to reveal a passageway sheathed in the same dark material as the shaft. A blue shimmer filled the air, like a torch in fog, so that although there were no lights and the walls were pitch black, they could see quite clearly. Rickenbacker reached out a hand and brushed a finger against the wall.

"It's warm," he said as Axelrod did the same.

"It feels like skin," he said, as Quine closed the lift behind them.

"Follow the passageway down," he ordered, straightening his tunic and trousers.

They continued down the passage, their footfalls leaving no sound.

Viceroy Ambrose Willis had been given five files to review, and had whittled them down to two. One, Hilary Rickenbacker, was an incredibly talented hyperphysicist, capable of finding new ways to utilise Red Wonder, inventing new ways to tap its potential seemingly weekly. The other, Kevin Axelrod, was also extremely talented, only needed telling once how to create something hyperphysical before being able to replicate it immediately. He exhibited more traditional thinking when it came to the Wonder, but was very well versed in the Green Wonder, coming as he did from the regions nearest the Attar Mountains.

Obviously neither of them knew much about the deep Blue, and this ballroom might be the first time they had ever experienced it.

But the two cadets were very different, as reported in their psychological files.

Rickenbacker was from a mundane suburb of the capital. His father had been a greengrocer, running a small shop on the corner of a street remarkable in its lack of anything special, anything that set it apart from every other street corner in every other suburb of the capital.

The grocer's son, however, soon became a local celebrity. He excelled at his local primary school, leaving five years early to attend a decent grammar school. Whilst there, the deputy headmaster had recognised the talent of the boy immediately and had tutored him personally, so that young Hilary was able to achieve a scholarship to Fairport University, the youngest person to achieve such an accolade.

Hilary surpassed all expectations, excelling in the meritocracy of academia whilst always aware that he was lucky to have moved beyond his humble beginnings. He never looked down on his origins, always looked back, swearing to himself that he would find a way to allow everybody the same chances he had, whatever their background. Many of those around him at Fairport harboured political aspirations, and the quickest way into public life was through either government service or contacts within the Trade, allowing opportunity to rise through the bureaucracy of local colonies.

A greengrocer from the suburbs had no such connections in the Trade, and was torn between a career in academia or service for Grand Quillia. He was approached to be an operative within Enchantment and Chicanery Operations and it seemed to offer a happy compromise between the two; the ability to study the Wonder while keeping open the opportunity to move into government, to improve the world for everybody, for people like his friends and family in the unremarkable suburbs of the capital.

However, during his training, Rickenbacker had proved less than proficient in one particular area: combat training. Viceroy Willis had not been surprised. Both the lower middle class and the well-educated always seemed to display an ineptitude with physical violence, whereas the working class and aristocracy were made up of a gratifyingly sizeable percentage of psychopaths.

Which had led Willis to Axelrod's file. A working class boy from a remote hamlet near the mountains, young Kevin had little respect for the living, and a lot of respect for the power of pain. Much more than Quine, a bully who used violence casually, Axelrod's record was made up of the clinical application of violence, always well-timed and well-placed. One of his tutors at the academy had suggested his easy use of Green Wonder and its ability to reanimate the dead may have contributed to Axelrod's approach to 'the good fight'. He had once been overheard stating, "Be careful who you kill. You never know where you'll be seeing them again."

On his journey through Grand Quillian politics and Trade service, Viceroy Willis had always made sure he would never bump into any of his vanquished adversaries again. He buried them deep and he buried them far away, where nobody would find them.

Some people considered the Viceroy a bully, and Willis allowed these people to remain in power as they underestimated him. He was more than a simple bully. He had no doubts at all that he was better than everybody else. He knew he was always right. And if he wasn't stronger, then he'd bribe somebody who was, or blackmail them, or find somebody even stronger than the person stronger than him, and bribe or blackmail that person to destroy the person stronger than him. It was not Machiavellian. He kept things simple and he used common sense. Common sense and money and connections and threats and sex and violence.

It had always worked, and he could not foresee ever losing what he was entitled to. He had seen off the Melodys just as his father had seen off the Gleaves.

All he needed was the right tools to stay in power. And one of the young men in front of his had the potential to fulfil that need.

He already had the pontificating bully in place. Now he needed someone clever, powerful and hungry that he could keep in their place. The grocer's pacifist son or the parochial peasant psycho to take on the power of the ballroom.

As the two men approached, Willis made his decision. Some say you can't judge a book by its cover, but Ambrose had always wondered how on earth one would choose what to read without doing so. He was also the Viceroy of all of the Gramarye, ruling an entire colony for the Empire. All his decisions were correct, every choice he made the best choice, every road he took the optimum route.

One man looked like a badger, the other a vulture.

It was an easy choice.

The ballrooms had been found as soon as the Trade had entered the Gramarye, but it had taken fifty years to recognise their purpose.

The ability to identify and communicate with every Elf in the Gramarye would have been a very useful commodity, had the Empire considered the Elf could have been anything but a sad throwback to a forgotten world. But then some of the more Imperial-minded hyperphysicists had discovered that with a few invasive medical procedures, a few additions utilising Blue Wonder, a couple of useful little twists to young Elf brains, the Empire could have a soldier that never questioned orders, could report back instantaneously, and could receive instruction anywhere, with no fear.

The Immolators.

It was that sort of hyperphysicist that the Viceroy was seeking, the sort that repurposed the ballrooms and enslaved the remaining Elf. Somebody who really knew how to use the Wonder, and who knew exactly who he was working for.

CHAPTER 14

The Road to Chinsey
The Gramarye Region
Grand Quillia

June 1856

The Undead cannot march. Although they were moving in columns and rows, and despite the fact that when they had been living Trade regulars they had regularly pounded the parade square, these particular deceased soldiers could not march. One or two former regimental Sergeant Majors were obviously trying, but the Ditch troopers pointed at them with skeletal fingers and mocked them, their grins revealing teeth that were a mixture of apple and spinach green in colour.

The yellow tunics of the Trade platoon were caked black with their own blood and guts so that their uniforms resembled some gruesome mottled camouflage. Any attempt at concealment would never work, however, due to the astonishing stench of rot and decay.

Major Franks continued to shadow the Undead platoon, his back knotting as he stooped behind the hedgerows, a handkerchief held tight to his nose and mouth. He had cursed himself for not taking one of the ponies when they had set off, but that was all undoubtedly part of the traitor Axelrod's dastardly plan. He needed to get to Chinsey before this macabre army, and despite the lurching lope of the former soldiers, he knew he would not be able to outrun them without being seen.

So Franks bided his time. Once they reached the outskirts of Chinsey he would wait until they had engaged the Trade defence and then he would lead an attack from the rear. He would charge into the stragglers, hacking and shooting, perhaps attack even Axelrod himself, steal the traitor's pony and seize the day. He would be the saviour of Chinsey, would accept Colonel Quine's former role, and would be hailed a living legend.

He looked at Quine, who Axelrod had not entirely reanimated. A large chunk of the Colonel's head was missing, and he lolloped alongside Axelrod's pony like a toddler wired on sweets, his tongue dangling from his mouth and his hands limp in front of his chest like a clown bunny. And if that wasn't bad enough, Axelrod had stripped the man of his clothes, so his pale rotundity flopped about revealing hairy moles alongside bloodstains.

Franks shivered with disgust and fear. He sincerely hoped that if he were discovered, murdered and reanimated that he would not be stripped of his dignity. The last thing he wanted was for Mrs Franks to see him dead in another woman's knickers.

"I know you," Brennan said as the Viceroy entered the sitting room to inspect Lady Melody's party.

"Of course you do," Willis replied, "I'm the fucking Viceroy."

Willis looked the scruffy old man up and down, deciding that the individual looked used up, finished, exhausted. His comrades fared no better, although the women could be made to be appear more alluring. His guards had already searched one of the women, a boyish individual whose multitude of weapons were strewn across a table. Her hands were cuffed behind her and her clothes were dishevelled, allowing Willis a good eyeful. His guards knew what he liked. They were just handcuffing the old man, who had an ancient spinner pistol, as well as what appeared to be a large kitchen knife and some sort of battle hammer. Only the one-handed man in the Trade trenchcoat and the strumpet remained, and the barrels of several rifles were trained on them. The slut's good looks reminded the Viceroy of someone from his past.

"Where is Elena?" the boyish one asked, which Ambrose chose to ignore.

"I mean we've met each other before," the old man said.

"I am a man of the people," Ambrose smiled. "Perhaps I closed down your favourite tavern."

"I remember you as a young man. I was just a boy," said Brennan, his lip curling. "You used to visit the Gleave lodge."

"Ah, the good old days," said Willis wistfully. "My star in the ascendant, the Gleaves passing the proverbial baton as they finally faded into obscurity." He paused and regarded Laurel beneath an arched brow.

"Leave her alone," Brennan growled.

"So she is," Willis grinned at his own ingenuity. "Your manservant betrays you, milady Gleave."

The Viceroy shuffled forward, his stick tapping on the floor. He raised it slowly and pointed it in Laurel's face.

"I am an orphan," Laurel explained. "I never met my parents."

"Most would say you are lucky in that respect. You do look astonishingly like your mother, a beautiful woman. Let's hope you're not quite as spirited, eh?"

"Annabel Gleave was the only one worth a breath in that damned family," said Brennan, straining against his cuffs.

"What a satisfying day. A widow and an orphan, both enemies of the Empire, come to beg my assistance."

"I'm not begging for anything from you," Laurel replied.

"Oh, you will be, my dear, just like Lady Melody."

"Leave her alone, you foul corpse," cried Bunce.

She put her head down and charged at the Viceroy, her hands still shackled, but the guards either side of her kicked her legs from under her, and she skidded face first into the floor at the Viceroy's feet.

"My, you people are such fun," the Viceroy said with relish as he brought down his stick and pushed it hard into Bunce's cheek, "and so lacking in manners."

Hilt was aware of the conversation but wasn't really following it word by word. He had studied the eight guards since their surprise arrival. Three of them mistrusted him, seven of them were more interested in the women and two of them were more worried about the Viceroy than they were about their prisoners. One of them had cricked his neck recently and one had cramp in his calf. The two closest to the single door were not practised with their weapons and had enjoyed ogling Bunce's breasts. Of the two nearest the double door into the hall, one was torn between checking out Laurel and showing them he knew how to use his weapon, while the one closest to the door, and the eldest of the guards knew Hilt was hiding something.

When the Viceroy had entered, Hilt had recognised him as one of the many self-centred bureaucrats he had disposed of following the Meander Valley massacre, an arrogant pest unaware of anyone else's abilities. All that Hilt had to do was bide his time. His Twirler was still in his low slung cavalry holster beneath the officer's trench coat, but there was no way he could get it without being shot in the head. His sword's tip was still sheathed in his boot, his elbow and arm locked beneath the coat, and so while nobody could recognise the danger he posed, he posed no real danger. He had to rely on the search. As soon as his coat was opened, he would pull his Twirler. He believed he could dispose of three of the guards as he ducked for cover and pulled his blade, which he would use to somehow free the others. Bunce would grab her weaponry as Brennan grabbed anyone close by. He would down two others with his pistol from cover and anyone the others hadn't disposed of he would eliminate with his sword or anything else to hand. Now it was just a question of who to hit first.

Admittedly, gnawing into his brain was a certain niggling worry about the Lady Melody. His primary motivation at all times was self-preservation. After all, how could he avenge if he were dead? But he looked forward to making the Viceroy's final moments uncomfortable. He enjoyed the idea of coming to the lady's rescue.

As guards stepped towards him to start the search, Hilt hid his eyes beneath heavy lids so that none of them would suspect any planning, knowledge or ability on his side. The youngest guard, keen to impress both Laurel and the Viceroy, lay down his rifle and started to roughly unbutton Hilt's trench coat. The low slung holster fell into view and Hilt started to shake his shoulder to allow his blade to slide out of the boot quickly when Willis raised his stick and jammed it into Hilt's solar plexus, knocking all the wind from his lungs. As Hilt gasped for breath and doubled over, he heard the Viceroy speak.

"Always watch out for the quiet ones."

The old man leant over and drew Hilt's Twirler from its holster.

"I've heard many things about the last of the Torchlights," he continued, nodding at the youngest guard who grabbed Hilt's wrist and wrenched the blade from his boot.

"I had no idea it was true," revelled Willis, as he spied the steel attached to Hilt's hand. "Pin the abomination to the floor."

The guard cracked Hilt across the jaw with the butt of his rifle and the last of the Torchlights went down, his face hitting the floor next to Bunce's with a dull thud. Willis took one step forward and placed the heel of his boot on the flat of Hilt's blade. He span the cavalry officer's Twirler, raised the pistol to sniff the Red Wonder in the chamber and then lowered the barrel to aim it towards the floor.

Finally, Hilt felt his lungs start to fill with air and then the Viceroy pulled the trigger. There was a loud crack of gunfire.

"That was for all my friends who died at the end of that blade."

Hilt looked down and saw the hole in the sitting room rug, felt the jolt up his arm as though he had been struck by lightning and lifted his sword. His flesh was still melded with the hilt of the sword, but it was no longer a weapon. The blade stayed on the floor.

With the smoking Twirler in his hand, the Viceroy grinned and motioned for the guard to eliminate the man at his feet.

Then the windows exploded inwards, six of the guards were cut down in an initial salvo that was immediately covered up by a localised popping of ears that preceded a white out attack.

As the milky nothingness swamped the room, Hilt grabbed the Viceroy's belt and dragged him to the floor.

Rickenbacker tilted his head to one side, his nostrils flaring.

"Did you feel..?" he started to ask but Spicer's Twirler was already drawn.

The Professor didn't know if it was the improved reflexes or the *déjà-vu* that had rung the Elf's internal alarm.

"White outs," Spicer said, his eyes scanning the area around them. "At the barracks, the Trade headquarters and the Viceroy's palace."

"We must get to the others," Rickenbacker said, indicating the direction of the palace.

"No, the headquarters."

"But..."

"Whoever is on the offensive have taken out everywhere with accessibility to the murder. There's no way to get a message out of Chinsey except by foot or the Bester. Right now the remainder of the Trade battalion that didn't follow us to the Glasslands is being wiped out. The only ones left to defend Chinsey are…"

"…the Immolators, and the ballroom is based at the Trade headquarters."

"The ballroom?"

"We need to get to the headquarters and hold it until Colonel Quine's platoon returns."

"Something tells me that Quine and his platoon will be no help," said Spicer with foreboding. "What about the storyteller box?"

"I'm sure Mister Pinkerton has it in hand."

Although his ears had not popped and there was no sign of any Wonder, everything seemed to be moving in slow motion for Pinkerton. He knew this feeling, had felt it before in some of his boxing bouts. He'd also felt it falling from a pony or dropping a valuable and delicate piece of crockery. The trick was to turn this feeling to his advantage.

As he stared down the barrel of his undead former partner's gun, he found he was having some trouble grasping the advantage, especially as he watched the rotting finger slowly squeeze the trigger. Without aiming, Pinkerton fired the blat from the hip. Mandell's pony screamed with terror as shots pockmarked her chest and flank. It reared up as Mandell fired the spinner, the round going wide, and both pony and rider collapsed to the floor.

"Mister Elephantine!" Pinkerton heard Teddy call, and he saw Aldo Kendrick scoop up the box. The little man's shoes skidded on the cobbles and he was off into the fog.

Pinkerton swung his blat to fire at Kendrick but Teddy leapt up into the boxer's line of sight and scrambled after the man who had deprived him of the box. Pinkerton brought the blat back to bear on the undead knight, but the wounded pony thrashed in front of him. Pinkerton cursed in a most ungentlemanly manner and started into the fog, the wound he had received from Mandell's gun at the snowdrop spire already smarting.

Mandell hit the ground hard, feeling his elbow smash against the cobbles. He listened as the pony rolled across his foot, the bones making a crackling noise like screwed up paper. He pulled himself up as the pony screamed again and galloped away. Although Mandell could feel no pain, his foot was damaged enough so that he would be unable to rely on it. He roared in frustration and fired three shots in the general direction of the others before hobbling as quickly as possible after them.

As Kendrick raced blindly through the fog, he cursed his leather soles. He had won them from a man of diminutive stature who had passed through the lodge. The individual had financed a group's entire trip to the Glasslands and at the last moment had insisted that he joined them. He told Kendrick that he relied on his money and his luck to get him out of trouble. Kendrick had then played the man at cards and won his watch, collar, shoes and hairpiece. The man had taken this to mean this was the last of his bad luck and that his good luck would start when he entered the Woods en route to the Cathedral of Tales. Kendrick pitied the man, as he had no need for luck due to his capacity for cheating.

However, as his victim's shoes slipped over the cobbles, Kendrick cursed his fortune, and wished he had won shoes with more grip.

He did not feel any better that the man of diminutive stature had never returned, but then nobody ever had until this Rickenbacker fellow had arrived with the Gargoyle Key. The same key that he now held in his hand.

"Stop!" he heard the boy call from behind, and Kendrick prayed for more than luck, money or a capacity for cheating. He needed to do what many people had suggested he do before, especially women. He had to get lost. He scooted towards the flagstoned pavement of the cobbled street, reached out his hand to feel the rough brickwork of the tenements, and waited for a gap. A corner came within seconds and, hoping it was an alley, Kendrick swung into it.

He stretched out both arms through the fog and his fingertips brushed brickwork on either side, so that he knew he had found what he needed. Even without the smog, a random back alley in the tenements of Chinsey would provide anyone with an easy escape route, even a giant.

As he clutched the Gargoyle Key tighter and attempted to resist congratulating himself as he slowed to a jog, Aldo clattered into a steel dustbin. The empty lid rang like a bell as its lid crashed across the floor like a cymbal.

Kendrick cursed loudly as a pain rocketed up his shin and he stumbled into a back gate. He heard the ear-piercing yowl of an angry cat, and a dog started barking aggressively some way ahead, hopefully locked in a yard. Kendrick didn't want to look back but as he pulled himself up he couldn't help himself. As the gate swung open flopping him back to the ground, he saw the silhouette of the boy looking around at the end of the alley. He got back on his feet, the box still in his hand, and started to run again. Kendrick took two steps, and a sodden string vest from a washing line wrapped itself around his face. He screamed in terror, imagining the netting had burst from the box in his hands to punish him, and fought desperately to free himself.

The stench of carbolic soap and the addition of a damp sock sloshing against his wrist made him realise he was fighting nothing more sinister than washing hung out to dry, so he doubled over and continued down the alley, his eyes peeled for clothing, domestic pets or any other danger.

"Ouch!" he heard the boy call as he clamoured into what sounded like a dustbin, and Aldo Kendrick realised he might just have a chance. Then the dog leapt out of the fog, its jaws bejewelled with drool, and knocked Aldo to the floor, its paws on his chest. Kendrick dropped the box and rammed his thumbs into the hound's jowls, keeping the snapping fangs inches from the soft skin of his face.

He could hear the boy blundering after him and decided all was lost. Damn the box. He was free of the rotten rotting knight and he should cut his losses and run.

The boy raced out of the fog and his foot struck Aldo's head. He yelped in fear and fell face first at the dog, which growled with anger, forgot Aldo and rounded on Teddy.

Aldo rolled to one side, his hands flapping blindly in the fog like two fish slapping towards a net. He found the soft worn corners, pulled it to his chest and scrambled back to his feet.

"Get off me!" the boy cried over his shoulder, and Kendrick continued down the alley on his slippery shoes, reasoning that this was surely more dangerous than any tunnels beneath the Cathedral of Tales.

Pinkerton stumbled through the fog in the vague direction of Teddy and the ugly little man. A face loomed out of the fog and the pugilist was confronted by the puckered and lined face of a local washerwoman.

"Watch where you're bleedin' goin'," she chided him.

"Terribly sorry," Pinkerton said, "but have you seen a man and a boy?"

"They went a-racing down the back at an awful pace," replied the shrill woman, moving her wash basket to one hip to point at the shadowy opening of an alleyway to her right.

"Thank you so very…" he started to answer, and then the back of the woman's head exploded. A hole the size of a cockroach appeared on her forehead and there was the sound of a gunshot.

Pinkerton got his head down, fired the blat gun once in the direction from whence he'd come, and dived into the alley. He took two steps and one shin struck the dustbin lying on its side. He fell forward, dropping the blat as he used both hands to break his fall. One hand landed on the dustbin lid, and spurted forward so that his face smashed into the ground, cracking his cheek. He felt blood pouring down his face and his earlier wound open up. He heard a dog tearing at something ahead, and as he dragged himself over the dustbin he looked around the ground for his blat. A shadow reached the end of the alley, and Pinkerton realised the dustbin lid was still in his hand. He saw Mandell raise his pistol, and he held up the lid with both hands like a gladiator's shield. The bullet hit the lid, sending a shock up his arms, and he threw it in the direction of Mandell then continued running. He took four steps, heard the undead knight kick the dustbin to one side and then the boxer felt something fibre slice into his throat. He gagged as he was catapulted backwards to the floor, gasping for breath as two bullets buzzed past his face. As he pushed himself up, his hand squelched into something heavy and wet. He caught his breath, realised he had hold of a large vest and, as Mandell emerged through the fog, he flicked it towards his gun hand. The wet heavy netting of the string vest enveloped the hand and as Mandell tried to pull the trigger, Pinkerton yanked the vest hard. The spinner pistol and two of Mandell's rotting fingers came loose from the knight's hand. The knight reached for his sword, but the gentleman pugilist chose flight over fight, and, leaving his former partner's pistol on the floor, the finger still on the trigger, he used the washing line to propel himself further down the alley, hearing the swish of the blade behind him.

He managed to regain his footing, and started to run again when he heard the dog. His first thought was of Alexander the Western Isles wolfhound from the lodge, but this thing was a mangy mutt. He made out Teddy a few feet ahead of him and then the dog launched itself at Pinkerton. There was no way this dog would knock Pinkerton off his feet, he thought, but then he felt the icy crescent of the dog's teeth sink into his calf.

"You bastard!" he cried, rolling onto the ground.

The dog started rolling its head to tear muscle from bone, and Pinkerton clenched his fists to start pounding on the beast's head until it finally released his limb.

As Mandell hobbled into view, sword in hand, Pinkerton expected the dog to turn on his former partner, but the mutt had no interest in rotten flesh. As Mandell raised his sword, Pinkerton's fist wrapped around the animal's tail and he dragged it back into the fight. Sir Evan's blade swooped down and hacked into the dog's torso. The beast howled in pain and went into a biting frenzy, snapping at anything within reach. Pinkerton threw the dog at the knight, knocking him off his feet. He heaved himself upright, feeling a burning sensation in his calf, and hopped towards the end of the alley, telling himself it wasn't too late, that he would find Teddy or Kendrick and be back in the chase.

He came out of the alley and all Pinkerton could see was smog and brickwork.

They were gone.

As the milkiness of the White-Out subsided, Laurel shook her head to clear it.

"What was that?" she asked.

"A white out," Bunce groaned from the floor. "I have been through quite a few recently."

Bunce shrugged against the cuffs and opened her eyes.

"Oh my God," she whispered.

Inches from her face lay one of the Viceroy's guards, dead. But it was the cause of death that bothered her. The boy who had eagerly ogled her breasts now looked to have turned one hundred years old since the white out. His skin hung from his bones, his gritted teeth were discoloured and his eyes milky. She turned her head away and rolled onto her hip so she faced the opposite direction and was greeted by a sight no less macabre. Viceroy Ambrose Willis lay on his back, impaled to the floor through his throat by Hilt's blade, his blood glistening on the expensive rug.

She sat up and looked around. All the Viceroy's guards were dead, prematurely aged during the white out. Brennan and Laurel, still cuffed, looked down at her, both pale and shaken, and the eight guards were now replaced by three new guards and an officer, all in bottle green uniforms.

"Who are you?" Bunce asked, looking them up and down, not recognising the uniforms. The weapons were also mysterious, cruciform in shape with a phial of green liquid attached to one side. Inside the phials, suspended in the liquid, Bunce thought she could make out stars, and realised she was looking at Green Wonder. One thing she did recognise was the physiognomy of the three guards, as ears like Spicer adorned their heads. And although they weren't her type, they were extremely attractive.

"Elf," she whispered.

"Where is the Gargoyle Key?" asked the human.

"We don't have it," Laurel replied. "It's with the Professor." She felt like she had to impress the three Elf.

"Which one of you is the Gleave?"

"How do you know?" Brennan asked.

"We ask the questions."

"We'd be more inclined to answer if we knew to whom we were speaking."

"You are the Gleave, are you not?" said the Elf, pointing at Laurel with the cruciform gun. "You of all people should know who we are. You and your kin attempted to wipe us out."

"When are people going to listen?" Laurel asked with exasperation. "I am an orphan. My mother took me away from the Gleaves so that I would be free of their legacy."

"It is in your blood."

"Leave her alone, Fredo," said the human. "We're not here to bully young women. Where's Widdershins? Is he with the Professor too?"

"Widdershins?"

"The slasher? The last of the Torchlights?"

"You mean Hilt?"

And then they realised that the warrior had somehow escaped the room.

Sharp corners dug into Hilt's chest and arm. His ankle was twisting inwards and his nails bending backwards as grit ground into his bare flesh. At the same time, the lack of his blade had enabled his escape. He would never have been able to take this route with the sword still attached to his hand, and he took a certain pride in the fact that he had left the blade in the jugular of a Trade bastard.

Hilt flexed his shoulders and pulled himself up another six inches. He rammed the broken nub into a piece of blackened mortar and shuffled up another foot in the choking confined space. He could hardly tilt his head back but knew his escape route would take a final corner before continuing upwards.

As he carried on shimmying vertically, he went through what had just happened, as far as he could tell. The windows had blown in. As they were leaded lights, that would have required explosives. Then the white out had hit. He had decided that whoever had attacked would enter through the windows, and that any Trade reinforcements would come through the doors, so he picked the only alternative.

The chute angled as he knew it would, which made things slightly easier and he slid on his belly, feeling his ribs bruise with each movement, using his feet and ankles to keep moving upwards.

If he survived this, Hilt thought to himself, in future he would always tip chimney sweeps handsomely.

After what felt like hours but was closer to ten minutes, he reached the chimney stack. Using the blade nub, he prised loose the top of the chimney and sent it scooting down the tiles to the ground below, hoping that no sentries from either side would notice it. Then his arm was free, his shoulder and finally both hands were feeling the night air. Hilt heaved himself onto the roof of the Viceroy's palace, gasping down deep breaths.

He looked down across Chinsey and was not surprised to see flashes of red and green gunfire at the barracks. In the Trade headquarters, a sliver of smoke split the sky like a refugee from the fog that consumed most of the downtown and industrial area.

Hilt scoped out the rest of the palace, couldn't see any guards and saw a conservatory. He pulled the top of another chimney stack free and rolled it down the incline of the roof towards the glass below. It hit the lead guttering, bounced upwards and plummeted through the top of the conservatory. The sound of glass smashing seemed to continue for some minutes and Hilt carefully lowered himself further down the roof so that he could look over the guttering without being spotted.

Someone kicked in the door to the conservatory so that a thin blade of light illuminated the plants within. Hilt's eyes cast over the gutter and he saw a random piece of brick, which he picked up and cast into the hole in the glass. He heard the bark of an unknown weapon, and saw a flash of green that travelled from the open door into the conservatory, and then there was silence. He waited a beat and glanced over the guttering again to see that some of the plants had wilted and died, black and brown leaves dripping from limp plants that had moments before been full of life. Then he saw movement as an armed individual approached the plants he had killed. Hilt swung his feet over the edge of the roof and let himself drop. He had been silent and had avoided kicking anything from the roof that may announce his impending arrival, but nonetheless the guard seemed to sense his coming. As Hilt was mid-air, his target swung his weapon up but did not fire. He knew that even if he hit the man tumbling towards him, the corpse would still strike him, so he jumped aside.

Hilt hit the floor and rolled as two bolts of green burst from his enemy's weapon. He crouched for cover behind a giant terracotta plant pot. There was another green blast and the conifer in the pot turned brown and bowed towards Hilt, its branches wilting. Hilt's hand flicked towards his empty holster as his eyes looked at the useless stub of his blade.

"Come out with your hands up," said the man with the weapon and Hilt realised that this was the first time in decades that he could honestly prove himself unarmed.

A shadow crept across the floor of the conservatory as a man blocked the entrance.

"John," called a voice, "John Widdershins. You and the Brigadier were not the only survivors of the Meander Valley."

As his mind flashed to his mother and young Kip Evans, Hilt glanced around the conservatory for a weapon. There was a shovel six feet away.

"Who are you?" he called back, before throwing himself at the shovel, snatching it up and rolling into cover behind another pot.

"I'm the hyperphysicist," the man replied, "My name is Talisker."

"Prove it," said Hilt, immediately moving to fresh cover.

"Kip shot you in the shoulder before you were forced to cut him down," said Talisker, remaining in the door.

Hilt gritted his teeth.

"Then I threw the grenade and you tried to blow it out of the sky."

Hilt cursed quietly and moved closer to the door, sticking to the shadows.

"Like you, I have been taking revenge on the Trade ever since."

Hilt reached another pot and peered around it. The gunman was on one knee next to the man calling himself Talisker.

"You should join us, lead our troops, force the Trade out of the Gramarye, take back Maisy. Avenge the Meander Canyon."

Hilt thought the man might look like Talisker, and probably sounded like him, but he seemed a little taller than Hilt remembered.

"I carry the Meander Valley every day."

Talisker took a step onto the tiled floor of the conservatory.

"Listen," he suggested.

He shuffled with each step into the middle of the conservatory, never lifting his feet more than an inch from the ground. Each step sounded like rock on rock, like marbles being knocked together, and instead of footprints, great grooves and scrapes were scored into the tiles.

The gunman stood up and moved behind Talisker, the cruciform weapon pointing ahead into the shadows. Hilt had almost reached the door Talisker had entered through but his plan was not escape.

"Can you hear, Hilt?" Talisker asked. "I bring the floor of the Meander Valley with me wherever I go."

Hilt stepped into the light of the doorway, the shovel in his hand.

"Perhaps you should have stayed there," he told Talisker.

The gunman span and Hilt struck him once in the face with the shovel, knocking him off his feet. As Talisker struggled to turn around on his stone feet, hilt picked up the cruciform weapon from the unconscious gunmen and trained it on the dabbler.

"How did you sneak up on Elf?" Talisker asked, raising his hands.

"I have a knack for it," Hilt replied. "Now tell me what the Hell is going on."

"The tide is turning, Widdershins. It is time for the Grand Quillian Empire to crumble."

"And a new Empire to take its place? Walk with me," Hilt said, looking down at Talisker's feet, "if you're able."

"Where are we going?"

"I need to rescue a traitor. I take it the Elf from Pearly have returned and judging by the Green Wonder weapon, they are allied with the people of the Ditch."

"How did you know?"

"People think I don't listen but it's more that I'm not generally interested."

They reached a corridor and Hilt paused, checking each way.

"When you were planning to storm the Viceroy's palace, did you happen to note where the bastard's study is located?"

Talisker took his bearings and nodded in the direction they then took.

"This isn't just about the Elf, Widdershins. Do I call you Widdershins or Hilt or what? The slasher?"

"Call me whatever you want," Hilt replied, checking they weren't being followed. "Just do it quietly. It's bad enough you're incapable of creeping."

"This is about more than the Elf," Talisker continued at a whisper, so that his words were hardly audible over his stone footsteps. "Something is stirring. Something is stirring in the Attar Mountains and the people of the Ditch cannot fight it alone. The Green Wonder is drying up."

"You mean the Threat. The forces that fought the Elf of Pearly before they were betrayed by their own kind."

"Have you been studying Gramarye history?"

"The Ditch need the Wonder of the Gramarye to repulse the Threat and the Elf can help them utilise it. And I suppose Pearly would be their reward."

"Exactly."

"But it wasn't the Trade who took Pearly from them. Why not attempt an alliance to fight the Threat?"

"The great John Widdershins suggests an armistice?"

"I've fought just one mechnological beast of the Threat beneath the Glasslands. It'll take more than a few Elf, undead and a bit of dabble to take down an army of them."

"You have been busy."

"As have you. How did you escape the Meander Canyon?"

CHAPTER 15

The Meander Canyon
Near Talling/Maisy
The Gramarye

October 1840

After seeing Kip Evans' throat get blown out and realising that he too had been struck by his own paralysing floor, Talisker had fainted dead away. The fact that his feet were melded to the floor meant that his knees bent, and he fell backwards at a right angle, his head striking the ground with a crack.

He came round slowly, not knowing how long he had been out, having dreamt of church visits from his youth. Religious chanting and incantations seemed to fill the air, and there was a chill that always seemed to permeate churches, regardless of whether it was a wedding or a funeral.

His feet were freezing cold, as though immersed in cold water, and his thighs were cramping as though he had recently completed a marathon.

He cracked open an eye and the first thing he was his friend Kip, the skin around the hole in his throat flapping in the breeze coming down the canyon. The blackberry stain of the paralysing floor encroached on Kip's shoulders, bottom, thighs and feet. Some of the stain spread across his face like a dark purple spider's web.

"Kip," he called, knowing he would receive no answer.

Talisker had been a last minute addition to the Torchlights, and so had never received a uniform. As he saw a handful of Reclaimers pick their way through the bodies, looting their friends, some of whom were still living, and putting a final bullet or blade into any surviving Torchlight, he was relieved to not be dressed in the scarlet tunic of the now extinct regiment.

He was wearing a silk collarless shirt, breeches and riding boots. He raised his hands to his face to check they were free and saw parts of the cuffs melded to his wrists, like wine spilt on a rug. He tugged at the material and his skin moved with it as if they had been crafted from the same loom.

He closed his eyes, willing himself not to go into shock, and reached towards the top of his breeches, to check what other pieces of his body were now attached to his clothes. His fingers reached the waistband, tugged gently to see inside and realised the breeches were stuck solid to his hips, stomach and back. He bit his lip and sat up. Surveying his whole body, he found he was unable to wiggle his toes inside his boots. He attempted to undo the laces but they were meshed into the rest of the boots, the knot now one unpickable ball.

He felt his heart start to race and he started cursing hard under his breath. He was about to scream, he wanted to bellow like a newborn with nothing but lungs to use as tools, but he saw the looters were yet to reach the S-bend where the Torchlights had made their last stand. He could see the band of men cackling at their good fortune, blood dripping from the knives they had used to prise the loot from corpses.

His fingers reached for the sniper rifle, fumbled against the barrel but the rest of the weapon was stuck fast to the floor. He looked around desperately, his hands scampering around the floor like crabs on a beach as he looked for something that could help him. His eyes fell on his bag that had held the home-made grenade which had brought down the opening to the canyon. It held his wallet, now useless, and the tools of his trade, tools he had used that very morning to craft the paralysing floor that was working so well. He could see grains of Wonder that had escaped from the grenade at the bottom of the bag nestled into the lining.

He looked down the canyon to check the looters still hadn't noticed him and reached again for the sniper rifle. His fingertips touched the twirling device that charged the weapon, and he snapped it free of the main body. Although it was all merged together, he was able to scrape away some of the Red Wonder charge with his nail. He snapped one of his tools free of the bag and picked out some of the grains from the seam, the material coming with it.

He tried to measure by eye but knew it was all down to luck. Too little and he'd make enough noise to attract the looters and still be stuck fast, too much and he'd blow his own legs off.

But he needed to have something to work towards otherwise he would give up there and then. He would lie down and let death take him.

He spat into the palm of his hand to make a paste with the grains and smeared them around the soles of his boots where they met the ground. Then he struck the paste with the Red Wonder charge device from the sniper rifle. There was a momentary spark and then nothing. He tried again, to no avail.

Bless my sole, he hissed through his teeth, and then struck the paste once more.

His ears popped and Talisker threw his head and arms as far from his feet as possible, like he was trying to make a snow angel. There was a muffled thud of explosive then a flash of red, and he felt as though he had beaten on the soles of his feet with an oar.

Then he passed out again.

Talisker awoke face down, his mouth full of earth. His eyes shot open. The groaning incantation continued from the dead in the canyon. And approaching him were two looters, with three more standing at the mouth of the canyon, a look of fear on their faces.

Talisker attempted to move his feet. The left one, although it still felt encased in ice, moved upwards. The left one did too, so that Talisker was now arse-up with his legs akimbo. He looked at the two looters who had been approaching. One clung to the other, both had drawn their weapons. Talisker raised himself up on his elbows and turned towards the looter.

"Come," his voice croaked, he cleared his throat and tried again. "Come here, you two."

They both stopped dead and he raised himself to his knees.

"I said come here," he repeated.

"Who are you?" asked one of the nearest looters.

"I am the hyperphysicist who cast this paralysing floor. Come here now or I shall use something on the pair of you that will turn you into the swine you are."

"Swine?"

"I'll turn you into pigs, you scum."

The two men turned from Talisker to look at each other. He expected them to burst out laughing but one turned and ran headlong towards the others. On seeing this, the other three broke for the entrance of the canyon, leaving the one looter closest.

"Come here or I shall transform your spoils to fire," he called as theatrically as he could muster, and the last man looked to run.

But then doubt crossed the looter's mind.

"You varlet," he growled and his hand started to move towards his Twirler. Talisker squinted at him darkly, moved both hands to his right ankle and lifted it. He half-expected it to stay rooted to the blackberry floor, but it came up and he was on one knee.

"That does it," he called, and, hiding his own surprise, he stood.

Talisker tottered as he stood, spread his arms wide to keep his balance and saw the looter's eyes grow wide.

"You will be a victim of your own loot," Talisker called. "Abracadabra!"

The man dropped his bag and turned and raced back towards the entrance, throwing aside knives and guns as he hustled out of sight, glancing back over his shoulder with terror in his eyes.

As soon as he was out of the canyon, Talisker collapsed back to the earth with a thud and took a breath. He shook his head in disbelief, muttering the Capital's old music hall illusionist's cry once more.

"Abracadabra…"

It took Talisker four days to walk the length of the Meander Canyon, a distance that should have taken some twenty minutes. The rocks that had become a part of his body were worn down with each step until the bottoms were smooth as pebbles. He saw upright corpses, lolling together, their chests merged together to form an archway of flesh. As he reached the S-bend where the Torchlights had made their last stand, he could hear dying groans alongside petrified howls of terror. The living were joined to the dead, man to horse, soldier to sword, tunic to rock to flesh to bone like some hellish bleeding shrubbery, trying to tear itself apart but locked together forever.

Talisker was forced to crawl on his hands and knees to cross the horrific dam of death as hands grasped at him, horses' teeth gnashed at him and the eyes of the doomed followed him as his stone feet crushed fingers and noses under their weight.

He tried not to look at the victims of looters, their heads cleaved off to dig necklaces from throats, fingers snapped away for rings, pockets torn open and coins gouged out from the flesh and material mix, leaving gaping wounds.

Finally he reached the avalanche that had crushed the convoy of civilians from Maisy. The screaming was more muted here, muffled as it was by tons of rubble. He clawed his way across stone and dust, now glued together beneath the blackberry stain, his fingertips dripping with blood, his tongue thick in his mouth through lack of water, his knees and elbows showing bone and gristle through clothing while his thighs and calves burned, having dragged the dead-weight of his stone feet.

On the fourth day, Talisker saw the glistening sea of the Moon Docks at the end of canyon. The smell of soup or stew, probably pork, reached his nose and he realised he was probably the first survivor to reach the Moon Docks.

A troopship belching red smoke was heading out to sea, while two skiffs bobbed next to a short pier. A tramp pad-dleboat was just visible where it had been sunk, the surface of the sea lapping against the burnt out bridge.

The Dancing Bear Inn, which had served as a social cen-tre for the fishing community and a meeting point for sea-farers and passengers seeking passage, was a charred husk. Black pits pockmarked the pebble beach where Reclaim-ers had camped, awaiting any final survivors of Maisy. All that remained was a small group of privateers, who Talisker guessed was a few stragglers who had seen enough death in the canyon to sate their appetites for adventure. They stooped around the cauldron from whence the smell of soup emanated, stirring it with a holey spoon.

"Help," Talisker croaked, his mouth bone dry.

Nobody heard him, so he shuffled out of the canyon, feeling the warmth of the sun for the first time in days. It warmed his soul just as the sea salt in the breeze scalded his wounds. As his feet hit the pebbles, the sharp crack bounced against the cliffs and carried to the group of men, who looked in Talisker's direction, two immediately pulling their weapons.

"Wait," Talisker vocalised, knowing they wouldn't hear, "I won't hurt you."

The men looked on his approach with amazement, a few laughed, while one approached him, his pistol in his hand.

"So what do we have here?" he drawled.

"Soup. Water. Soup," Talisker tried to request.

The man turned back smiling.

"Hear that? Our sticky friend wants some soup."

The group laughed as a whole.

"He's welcome to it," said one. "Help him over."

The man nearest holstered his gun and started to drag Talisker towards the cauldron.

"Christ, he's heavy," the man remarked.

"He should be," laughed the man who had issued the invite, obviously a leader of sorts. "He's attached to half the canyon."

"Stuck to stones may break his bones," called another.

The men all laughed and Talisker didn't care. He smiled with them, grinned at his saviours.

"Thank you, oh thank you," he mumbled, over and over again.

"Shall we give him a little water? Cleanse his palate before the soup?" asked the leader.

"Yes," Talisker whispered huskily. "Water please. Water."

He was handed a flask and drank from it greedily, letting the water run down his beard and chest.

"And in payment," smirked the man at his side, "I fancy the shirt off your back."

He snatched away the flask and put three fingers around the top of Talisker's shirt.

"No, wait," Talisker groaned, the fear rising in his throat.

"Take it off him then," cried the leader and the man tore away the shirt, ripping a square foot of skin an inch deep from Talisker's back.

Talisker was surprised he was able to scream, and couldn't believe the sound he had made as it curdled in the sky. The pain was a searing burn immediately covered by boiling fat, and where the skin and shirt were still connected to his body, it continued to tear moment by moment, inch by inch. Talisker's vision started to cloud and he was suddenly freezing.

"He's passing out," came a voice. "More water," and the man gripping him threw what water remained in the flask in Talisker's face. "You don't want to miss out on the main course."

He was dragged by his shoulders to the edge of the cauldron and the leader gripped his hair and made him stare into the bubbling liquid inside. The soup had the colour of the paralysing floor's blackberry stain.

"Breast or leg?" asked one, before he dipped the holey spoon into the fatty soup.

He lifted out the spoon to reveal a right hand, snapped off from the arm below the wrist so that the white bone jutted out.

"Let me remove the bones," laughed the leader. "We don't want you choking to death." With a rag around his own hand, the leader took the hand and removed a ring from its finger. The ring came away easily from the finger bone, but there was some meat still attached. Using one end of the rag, the leader poked a corner through the hole to rid the ring of the last piece of flesh, wiped it on his trousers and held the piece of jewellery in front of Talisker's face.

"Delicious," he chortled.

He slid the ring onto his own finger next to a couple of others.

"These came from the same *sauce*," he joked, and then, while Talisker was still held by the shoulders, the leader grabbed him by his chin, forced open his mouth and reached for the holey spoon.

"The condemned man's last supper," he said, holding Talisker's head steady as he brought the spoon to his lips.

Talisker could make out a knuckle, probably from an index finger, and a sliver of pierced nipple.

"Abracadabra," he whimpered hopelessly.

The first shot hit the leader straight between the eyes. The next two took out the men holding Talisker's shoulders. Each shot found its target and within seconds all the men were dead. Talisker collapsed face forward, feeling the heat of the fire singe his hair.

"Abracadabra," he repeated until he passed out.

He woke up vomiting, opened his eyes and saw a white sheet billowing above him, beyond which lay a clear blue sky. He looked to his left and saw a snipers rifle. His heart leapt a moment, convinced it was all a dream.

"Kip?" he said, but his throat was still dry.

"Let me help you," came a steady female voice, and a flask of liquid was lifted to his lips.

"No. Not hungry," mumbled Talisker, desperately turning his head away.

"It's just water," replied the voice, "You are safe now, although there is still a long way to go before you're fully recovered."

Talisker accepted the flask and drank tentatively.

"Where am I?"

"You are aboard the Faraway Friend. We set off from the Moon Docks two hours past. Would you like to see?"

Talisker nodded and he was propped up so he could see over the edge of the skiff. Across the blue sea he could make out white surf crashing on the pale grey pebbles, the cliffs beyond and the crack in the middle of them that lead to the Meander Canyon. He realised he was leaning with his back against the edge of the boat but felt no pain.

"My back? The paralysing floor," he said, looking into the stranger's face.

All he could see were clear green eyes. The rest of the head was wrapped in scarves.

"I did what I could do with the medical kit I had on me," she said. "That and a little hyperphysics."

"You're a dabbler?" Talisker asked, taking the flask with his own hands to drink.

"In my own way," said the woman, removing the scarves. "Obviously I've never won a scholarship to Fairport like your good self, but let's say I have it in my blood."

The headscarf was off now and the woman looked as beautiful as her eyes. She had deep black hair that shone blue in the sunlight, her lips were full and she had an alluring dimple in her chin. She was the most striking individual Talisker had ever seen.

"How did you know I…"

"We Elf have our way," she replied, pulling her hair back to reveal a pair of pointed ears.

"Elf? But you… where did you…"

"Relax, young Mister Talisker. There will be time for questions on the journey ahead. There may even be some answers I can provide."

"Journey?"

"Across the Gramarye and over the Attar Mountains into the Ditch."

"The Ditch?"

"And don't try to run for it," she said, pulling a cheroot and match from an inside pocket, "or swim."

And then she struck the match on the stones still melded to Talisker's feet.

"A Fairport hyperphysics scholar will be very useful to the people of the Ditch. We have limited information on what you have learnt of the deep Blue Wonder since the dark age after the fall of Pearly," she puffed on her cheroot, "and I'm sure you would like to introduce Grand Quillia to a dark age of their own after what they put you and the rest of Maisy through."

Talisker's head started to spin. His past held only sorrow, his present was a puzzle and his future unfathomable.

"Sleep, Mister Talisker," she told him.

"Who are you?" he asked as his eyelids grew heavier.

"You can call me Isabella," she replied, "Isabella Petrosian."

And then Talisker slept, his dreams populated by an Elf named Petrosian.

Talisker continued with his story and Hilt checked over the cruciform rifle as they moved through the Viceroy's palace.

"So you and your beautiful Elf sniper saviour fell desperately in love and lived happily ever after," said Hilt, shaking his head at the hyperphysicist shuffling along next to him.

"Not quite. Isabella assured me she would be able to free me of my stone encumbrances but refused to do so until we had returned to the Ditch."

"How did that go for you?"

"Shall I continue?"

"Can you walk any faster?"

"We were at sea for some days"

"Stoneboots!" called an Elf as he turned the corner, and Hilt shot him in the chest.

The burst of Green threw the Elf back against the wall while an unctuous lotion spread around the surface of the man's skin, altering its victim so that he aged a century before he hit the floor, his eyes, like the rest of him, dead. The lotion immediately dissolved.

"Garabed!" Talisker gasped, reaching towards the expired Elf.

"What is this thing?" Hilt asked, looking over the cruciform weapon. "I like it."

"He was my friend," Talisker said, cradling Garabed. "He was on our side."

"Then honour his memory and get me to the Viceroy's study."

"I am," Talisker wailed as he pulled himself to his feet. "You're a psycho."

"Amongst other things. But we were discussing your life."

"Rest in peace, Garabed. Your death will not be in vain."

"We'll have to see about that," Hilt gestured at Talisker to move. "Let's go, Stoneboots."

After they had landed the skiff, Isabelle had taken Talisker by cart to a safe house. The next few weeks were torture as Isabella trimmed away any material that wasn't attached to skin, and then used a scalpel that she had sharpened after each cut to separate his breeches, shirt and undergarments from his body. Following a successful slicing away, she would apply an extraordinary salve that resembled green whipped cream, which, once dissolved, left behind a new layer of skin. It was only after the fifth skin graft that Talisker noticed part of a tattoo. The top line was an A and a D, while beneath it said VER, all inside one closing parenthesis.

"What are you doing to me?" Talisker asked, as he prodded the tattoo. "Where did you get my new skin?"

"The people of the Ditch have relied on Green Wonder for most of their existence," Isabella explained, unfazed. "The Green can keep people alive for as long as they wish, although without the correct processes they can begin to rot."

Talisker looked at her in terror.

"However," she continued, "some people die too far from help to be saved, or meet an end that keeps them dead. Occasionally people decide they don't want the longevity treatment."

"I understand. So this skin is extracted from the naturally dead?"

"The salve takes and then the salve returns."

"This is more than anything the Trade is capable of, beyond any lessons at Fairport."

"The people of the Ditch have had some help in their learning."

"From the Elf."

"Indeed."

They reached the Attar Mountains in spring. Talisker expressed doubt on their prospects.

"Any crossing of the mountains comes with risk, even for one who has made the journey before," Isabella shrugged.

"The paths and tunnels change daily, so maps are of no consequence."

"How can they change?"

"Something is alive inside the Attar, something that came before and will rise again."

"Are they the same as those that destroyed Pearly?"

"They precipitated the destruction of my ancestor's home. They were driven back but we know they will return within fifty years. We suspect they change the routes over the mountains to snare travellers that they can use to examine regarding how our cultures have changed, looking for our weaknesses, biding their time."

"So they use those they capture in much the same way you are using me."

"Who knows?" Isabela smiled sadly. "Nobody they have taken has ever returned."

The beginning of the journey was enjoyable despite the changes in temperature. As they climbed, they had to remove layer after layer of clothing as the sun beat down. They would enter the shadow of a valley or a mountain path on the dark side of an incline and would immediately feel the cold eat into them. Without the sunlight, their buckles and weapons would chill to the touch.

Talisker's patchwork skin already felt like his own, and although his leg muscles had improved so that the stones on his feet were no longer quite so cumbersome, there was still no way he would be able to escape Isabella.

He had learnt that the Elf always seemed to be one step ahead, always had a good idea what one might be thinking and were extremely empathetic. Whenever Talisker had considered escape, Isabella always seemed to know the right thing to say that would make the Ditch seem all the more alluring, the Trade all the more dastardly.

After three days' climbing, the air became so thin Talisker could only take ten steps before pausing to catch his breath, despite the leaves Isabella had given him to chew. Now, even walking in the sun was cold, while the shadows had become treacherously icy. Each time they reached what appeared to be a peak, they would round a path just to see it climb further upwards.

At one point, Talisker marvelled as clouds struck the tops of mountains below and curled in on themselves, while the sky above remained a startling blue.

Eventually they reached a path atop a peak that passed between a V-shaped break in the rocks.

"The Mobilus Path," Isabella said through her scarf, "The highest point of the path through the Attar Mountains."

"Why is it called Mobilus?"

"Because it is found in a different place with every journey."

Talisker looked beyond the pass and saw the civilisation of the Ditch laid out before him in the centre of the mountain range, which from this viewpoint resembled one giant hollow volcano. The grass did seem greener, literally, due to the preponderance of Green Wonder beneath, and the moister atmosphere caused by the mountains keeping the clouds inside the crater.

The main city sat directly in the centre of the crater against a large vermillion lake. There were just two other villages and a few farms, but it did not appear to Talisker that the Ditch was full to the brim with bloodthirsty killers.

He turned his head and looked back at the Gramarye. Already Chinsey had started to choke itself with fumes, which dissipated before they reached the Glasslands. Besides the chimneys, the tallest structures were the Cathedral of Tales and far beyond, shimmering in the distance, the pyramids of Maisy. The Green around Chinsey was already starting to disappear in the name of progress. The slideways spread beyond the curve of the earth into the rest of the Empire. One slideway was being built towards the Mood Docks, but the Hodgkinson Line had decided to blast a straight route through as opposed to clearing the Meander Valley. Talisker's mind boggled as he traced the route he had taken with Isabella, all with his stone feet.

"Come on," Isabella called to him. "It's all downhill from here." She laughed at her own words.

Talisker smiled, turned back take one final look through the Mobilus Pass at his former home, but the V-shaped cut through the mountain had already gone and he was looking at a sheer rock face.

After three days of descending into the crater, Talisker had to admit that climbing down was more arduous on his already over-burdened legs, especially his calves and thighs.

Isabella never stopped moving, scouting ahead and looping back behind her fellow traveller, always on the move. But on the fourth day, when they had spent two days passing through the clouds, walking in shadow and drenched in mist, Isabella turned to Talisker and retrieved a Spinner and dagger from her backpack.

"Today you will need these," she told him, "I do not know whether either of us will live to feel the sunshine again."

"That's heartening." Talisker said, slipping the knife into his belt and checking over the Spinner pistol. "Do you have any Wonder? I'm a better dabbler than a fighter."

"Look for yourself," Isabella suggested, throwing him her bag.

Talisker opened it and found a collection of pots containing different varieties of Wonder, both Red and Green.

"This is quite the collection," he remarked.

"It's just my travel bag," she said. "I suggest we find somewhere we can defend and wait for the attack."

"By whom?"

"I don't know."

Another two hours passed, offering no respite from the damp chill of the clouds. Now the path was the width of a doorway, with a sheer drop down to the left into the crater, and a smooth expanse straight up on the right. Talisker kept his right hand against the cliff face, terrified that one step with his stone foot too close to the edge would collapse the entire path.

"This is the place," Isabella said with an intimidating finality. "Lay out your defences as you will."

With that, she sat down cross-legged, her back against the rock, the sniper rifle cradled in her arms.

"Isabella," said Talisker, "you seem well-versed with the Wonder. Perhaps you could help me?"

"No," she replied, her eyes closed. "I have an idea of what happens here. My help is not required. I am inconsequential. It is you who will meet the Threat."

Talisker felt the chill strike his bones. If his feet were not imprisoned in stone, he suspected he would have simply started running headlong down the path at that moment, anything to get away from the Elf's fatalism and his own predicament. There was also a part of the hyperphysicist not keen to dabble again. His paralysing floor had caused so much terror that he had witnessed close up, he was loth to use his skills again. And that grenade that had brought down the cliff had also been a lot more powerful than he had expected. Isabella had explained that the seam of Red Wonder beneath the Meander Canyon had amplified his weaponised Wonder, but it had been the first time he had used his dabbling skills in anger, so he still wasn't sure of what he was or wasn't capable.

He had prepared two explosives that he could detonate remotely with a length of string, and a paralysing floor grenade. He had also rigged three of the Wonder containers to work as a wind funnel, something he had never done before but had seen demonstrated once by Hodgkinson slideway hyperphysicists who used Red Wonder to blow tunnels into hillsides and wind funnels to clear out the debris. They called the device a Blow Back. The example Talisker had Jerry-rigged would not have much reach, or power, or longevity, but with the limited resources and lack of help from Isabella, he felt he had done the best he could.

He lowered himself down to take a seat next to Isabella against the rock face and waited. He had no idea what to expect. A small part of him thought it may be some form of test by Isabella to prove he was worth bringing to the Ditch, but he didn't know what else but sit and wait. One piece of string was wrapped around the index finger of his right hand, the other on his left, both leading to the explosives. The grenade was in his right hand while the wind funnel device, which resembled bolas, sat in his lap. Isabella had not stirred, her face wrapped in the headscarf, and despite the damp and cold, Talisker felt himself drifting off into sleep.

He awoke to the sound of a whispering laugh, a wheezing that bounced off the mountains around him.

"It's here," said Isabella, standing up slowly.

Talisker pushed himself upright and gripped the strings with both hands, while resting his thumb on the trigger of the grenade.

The mist still hung around them, and Talisker could see no stars above. The coughing grew louder and Isabella readied her rifle. Talisker watched the path to his left, staring at the point it disappeared around the mountainside, but still nothing came. He looked past Isabella in the other direction, hoping to see the swinging of lanterns illuminating the lasts wisps of mist but nothing presented itself.

The dry belching continued to grow louder.

"What is that sound?" he asked Isabella, and for the first time he saw fear etched into her beautiful face.

A small rock popped against Talisker's shoulder, then another hit his scalp. He looked above, seeing the mist dispersing against the rock face. Gravel rained into his eyes.

As he wiped them, he noticed that there were different colours of mist. The natural silver grey that he had grown used to from his time in the mountains and a black sootiness that seemed to ebb into the sky at regular intervals.

Then Talisker realised the dark smoke was pumping into sight in time with the puffing sound that had woken them.

"Above us," he whispered to Isabella, reaching out a hand so she turned to follow his gaze, the dust peppering her eyelashes.

Skittering down the rock face came a black metal spider crowned by a chimney. It was the size of a small carriage, and instead of eight legs its limbs resembled a grass skirt. Some limbs revealed themselves as multi-jointed legs tipped by barbed hooks, while others were folded beneath the beast. Talisker likened the unused legs to a multi-purpose penknife, with various tools tucked away inside until they are needed.

Atop the legs was what appeared to be a spider's head, which seemed to rotate above the limbs picking which to utilise, while at the rear, where a natural spider would have a furry abdomen was a dark smooth orb, jutted the small but busy chimney. A gyroscope cradle enabled the chimney always to point skywards.

Besides the puffing, Talisker became aware of the hooked limbs as they slammed into the rock, always keeping three embedded so that the spider appeared to be in no danger – a perfect animal for the mountains.

Talisker knew there was nothing natural about the beast above. He could see bolts and gears, metal and some malleable sponge material at the joints, and the nearer the mechnological beast came, the more deafening the puffing noise became.

Isabella brought up the rifle and fired twice, the rounds bouncing off the abdomen with the howl of ricochet. Talisker struggled to unloop the strings from his fingers as the beast continued towards them.

When the strings of the explosives fell free, he triggered the fuse of the paralysing floor grenade and felt the blood drain from his face.

"Here," he said, pushing the live grenade into her hand. "You throw it."

She looked down at the grenade and then the panic in Talisker's face. She didn't need to feel his thoughts to know exactly what he was thinking. She nodded once and threw the grenade.

It struck the rock face directly below the spider and their ears popped. The blackberry stain spread across the wall like spilled paint as Talisker and the Elf shielded their eyes.

The three legs extending into the wall were covered by the paralysing floor. The spider tugged at one leg, then the other two and realised they were stuck fast.

"It's caught," Talisker gasped with relief.

Then there was a deafening whistle from the creature like a howling banshee and they covered their ears. The spider's trapped legs made a metallic snap and slide noise, like a bolt being removed from a locked door. One leg removed itself from the hook attached to the wall at the nearest joint. The limb spouted another hook and the leg telescoped out from the joint to create a replacement leg. The hook sunk into the wall through the paralysing floor's blackberry stain and it repeated the process with another trapped leg.

"Run," Talisker cried. "We need it on top of the explosives."

Isabella nodded and raced down the path, Talisker spooled out more string from the explosive furthest away and followed her, careful as he shuffled backwards not to stumble over the edge.

The spider reached the path and straightened itself so that it was horizontal, the chimney puffing clouds of darkness into the mist above.

Two legs were selected by the selector mechanism at the front and locked into place, pointing in the direction of Isabella and Talisker. Isabella fired again so one bullet struck the selector mechanism and the other skidded off the dark abdomen. Talisker hobbled past her on the path, still spooling the string to trigger the explosive, his back to the beast. He stepped over the other explosive and kept moving.

Then he heard a terrifying whoosh, like the crashing of the ocean or a great hurricane striking a town. Talisker felt a burning at his back. He could hear flames in his hair and on his clothing, and ten he heard Isabella's screams of pain.

Instinctively he pulled the string, his ears popped and there was a dull boom as the explosives behind the fire went off. The force from the explosion knocked Isabella and Talisker off their feet and extinguished most of the flames that were licking around their bodies.

The spider rotated its abdomen and limb selector, creating a ticking sound, and took a few steps towards the dust cloud created by the Red Wonder explosion with its fire spurters still extended.

Talisker rolled Isabella over and baulked at the blisters and sears across her face.

"Isabella," he called, his hands on her shoulders. "Isabella, speak to me."

One of her eyes, its lid melded together in one corner, opened as far as it could.

"I am alive," she moaned.

"Can you keep moving down the mountain?"

"I can try," he muttered and helped her to her feet.

"What about you?" she asked.

"I'm not running anywhere," he told her, nodding towards his stone feet. "Now go."

With one arm against the rock face and smoke still seeping from her clothing, Isabella continued down the path. Talisker followed her a few steps until he felt he was far enough away from the second explosive, and waited for the spider to show itself.

He picked up the remaining string from the floor and unhitched the wind funnel bolas from his belt. Then he waited, alone.

He heard a ticking as the spider's body rotated again and it came out of the dust cloud with its spurters still extended. Talisker heard the whoosh as they fired up and he swung the bolas. Within moments they were up to speed, his ears popped and as the fire streamed from the spider's limbs, it looped back over the spider's own body. He heard dust and rock pinging against metal and saw the flames flash across the spider. The beast took one step back and then extended two more legs to stand its ground against the force of the wind funnel.

Finally the two fire squirters were retracted and Talisker let the bolas wind down, unsure of how much energy was left in them.

The spider's dark metallic body was smeared with dirt and scorched by the fire. Small dents and pockmarks were scattered across the abdomen. It regarded Talisker motionlessly but for the continuing smoke belching from its chimney. Talisker faced it, moving the string behind his thigh for fear of warning the creature. It seemed to sink slightly, its limbs closing up a little so that for a split second Talisker thought it was about to collapse.

Then it gave another screech and launched itself from its prone position, pouncing towards Talisker. He yanked at the string, falling backwards, his ears popped for a third time in as many minutes, and the second explosives blew.

The spider's trajectory was blown off course and it slammed into the rock face above the path, dropped and rolled before plummeting over the precipice.

Talisker picked himself up and moved to look over the edge where the path had been completely obliterated. As the dust settled and his ears cleared, he immediately heard the steady wheezing puff of the spider.

Instinctively he pushed himself away from the edge as he saw the spider clinging to the rock face below by one leg. He noticed that it seemed to be missing a few limbs, and the abdomen was cracked, but within seconds he heard the sound of a blowpipe once, then again, and two grappling hooks shot past him to embed themselves above him. He crawled back to the edge and looked down as the spider winched itself upwards, back towards him. The hooks were in too high for him to dig them out and Isabella's rifle had been destroyed in the explosion. He pulled the pistol she had given him and fired it wildly over the edge, watching the rounds bounce from the shell. He withdrew the knife and hacked at the vine attached to the grappling hooks but they were not made of rope and refused to fray.

He picked up the bolas and checked them over, knowing they were almost spent. He looked down again, his eyes streaming as the black smoke from the chimney was expelled into his face. Between each cloud of smoke, Talisker spied flames within the belly of the beast.

His eyes scanned the floor and he saw a large round stone not unlike those connected to his feet, slightly larger than the diameter of the spider's chimney. He climbed to his feet at the edge of the path, his stone feet poking over, the rock in one hand and the bolas in the other and looked down at the spider levering itself towards him. He squinted in concentration, lobbed the rock into the air in front of him and spun the bolas. As it reached its height and plummeted back down inches from Talisker's face, he used the last of the wind funnel to speed the rock up. It struck the top of the chimney as fast as a bullet and sank deep into the chimney, only stopping when it was wedged fast.

The two winches stopped turning and the steam whistle started to wail. Then the abdomen exploded with a force that blew Talisker against the rock face and slid to the path.

Burning metal plopped around him and then a hand, as small as a child's but as weathered as an adult's, landed in his lap. Talisker stared at it in shock before getting to his feet. The ropes to the grappling hooks were limp and all that was left below the path was a giant black smear.

He heard coughing and saw the blood drenched face and charred clothes of Isabella as she stumbled back towards him.

"You're alive," he called, resisting the instinct to hold her.

"As are you, Mister Talisker. I have found the end of the path. We are hours from the Ditch. My people will meet us there," she raised a singed eyebrow. "They will be impressed you destroyed a beast of the mountains."

"I even have a trophy," Talisker told her grimly, holding out the small hand.

"You can carry that yourself," she said, wrinkling her noise and then hissing with the pain.

They took each other by the arm to aid their journey and hobbled down the path, the ropes from the grappling hooks flapping in the wind.

"This is the door," Talisker told Hilt.

The warrior indicated for the dabbler to stand aside and he opened the door to the study. He stepped inside, the cruciform rifle at chest height with his finger on the firing mechanism. He saw Elena's hair sparkle in the light, her back to him as she sat slumped in the chair.

"Elena," he called, reaching towards her shoulder. As his fingers touched her, he could feel her warmth and he put the rifle on the desk before turning to face her.

"Elena," he repeated, both hands on her shoulders as he looked into her face.

Forgetting Talisker, he leant forward and kissed her gently on the lips. Her eyes flickered open and he saw anger and fear.

"It's me," he assured her. "Hilt."

The fear faded but the anger remained. There was a trickle of blood from her ear lobe across her shoulder that ran into her cleavage.

"I've come to rescue you," he said with a mixture of pride and embarrassment.

She rolled her eyes, mocking him.

"She's paralysed," Talisker told him, lifting her hand and letting it drop. "Poisoned."

"She can't move?" asked Hilt, still facing her.

"It'll fade with time."

"Yeah," Elena growled through her closed mouth. "Don't get any ideas."

"I would never…" Hilt blustered.

"I can speed the healing process up," Talisker offered, "if you get me back to the sitting room and stop killing Elf for just one minute."

"Very well."

"Is she your girlfriend?"

"She's a fan," he answered. "What about you and your Elf sniper woman?"

"Isabella and I never became lovers, but I did find a wife in the Ditch. I have five children."

"Five is good going."

Elena cleared her throat.

"Oh sorry. Perhaps we should go?"

"With your blessing, Milady," said Hilt, and he scooped her up into his arms.

"Where's your blade?" she mumbled.

"In the Viceroy's throat?"

"Good."

CHAPTER 16

Chinsey
The Gramarye Region
Grand Quillia

June 1856

Flashes of Red and Green could be seen on all three floors of the Trade headquarters, while smoke belched from the window nearest the entrance.

At the gate, Rickenbacker and Spicer could see dead Trade soldiers in the guard hut. Three replacements in bottle green uniforms ensured nobody asked any questions.

"So this is how you got in when you snatched the Gargoyle Key?" Spicer triple-checked as they stood at the perimeter fence.

"Yes, but I had more Wonder, more power then. And I didn't actually enter myself," Rickenbacker replied as he measured out Wonder from different vials from his bag.

"Do you want to wait here until I can fetch you?" Spicer offered, already knowing the answer.

"We can't risk either of us being hurt," Rickenbacker said, sweat dripping from his face as he concentrated. "It's best for both of us if we stay together."

"Then let me go first. I'll be able to clear the way before you get there."

"Very well," The Professor replied, nodding towards the pile of Wonder he had measured out. "The bounce is ready. Step onto it, bounce once and then push down hard, angling yourself towards roof."

"And this worked before?"

"It worked perfectly for Pinkerton and Mandell. Then they rappelled down the walls..."

"I know what happened next," Spicer reminded the Professor.

"Good luck, Lieutenant."

"See you on the roof."

They shook hands, Spicer checked his Twirler, shook out his limbs like an athlete and stepped onto the pile of dabble. He pushed against the bounce and was catapulted twenty feet into the air. He looked at the roof of the headquarters and saw the smoking remains of the cage that housed the crows for the murder. As he reached the apex of his first jump, he saw a green tunic on guard on the roof reach for his cruciform rifle and then he was falling back towards the Professor. He hit the dabble again and pushed hard in the direction of the roof, pulling his Twirler as he was flung through the air. He spun it once, a burst of green energy flashed past him and he fired at the guard until the Twirler stopped spinning. Then he was tumbling towards the flat roof, readying himself for the impact. He hit the structure and rolled past the corpse of the guard, then slammed into a chimney stack and spun his Twirler.

Now that he was on the roof and over the perimeter fence, he could hear cried of terror and the discharge of weapons. He stood up and waved at the Professor. He could understand the older man's hesitancy. It was a fall from high, and his bones hadn't entirely appreciated it. He was also a veteran soldier, as opposed to an aging college Professor.

From his vantage point, Spicer watched as Rickenbacker slammed one foot onto the remaining pile of Wonder and was spat into the air. However, the Professor had misjudged the angle, or perhaps was all too aware that their supply of Wonder was fast running out. Instead of going straight up and then angling up and over to the roof, the Professor was propelled straight towards the headquarters with his first jump. Spicer raced to the edge of the roof just in time to see Professor Hilary Rickenbacker fly through the air and smash through the third floor window below. Spicer shook his head in dismay and raced towards the door leading downstairs.

The fog downtown showed no sign of clearing. It generally didn't until the weekend came around, when some of the factories would close. Pinkerton limped, beaten, bruised and gasping for breath, his eyes scanning the fog ahead, his ears wide open for any movement.

"Pinkerton," he heard behind him. "Pinkerton. You're going to die here, Pinkerton."

The voice was a parody of his friend's, raspy and lisping due to the swollen tongue.

"If not me, then one of the others. You will die today, Pinkerton."

The gentleman pugilist stopped and turned to face the direction from which he'd come. He could see the shadow of the knight stumbling towards him.

"You should let me kill you, Pinkerton," Sir Evan reasoned. "Let your old friend kill you, Pinkerton. You never know. If you're lucky, Doctor Axelrod might find your corpse and bring you back to do his bidding, Pinkerton."

Pinkerton exhaled sadly. His gunshot wound was throbbing, the dog bite burned and his cheek was cold with blood, the bone probably broken.

"We could work together again, Pinkerton. Mandell and Pinkerton. Back in action."

Due to the dense smog, Pinkerton had no idea where he was, which saddened him as he would have liked to have known the name of this final battle's location. He cracked his knuckles and stretched his muscles, clicking his shoulders. He tightened his boots to better support his ankles and jogged on the spot to get his blood pumping.

As Sir Evan emerged from the fog, his trusty blade in a hand two fingers short of the full complement, Pinkerton raised his fists.

"I'm sorry it has come to this, Evan," he said, turning his leading shoulder towards the dead man.

"I've been rather looking forward to it," the dead knight replied, swishing his blade through the air as he approached.

Finally the two men faced each other, two feet apart, the boxer and the knight.

"Let's be having you then," said Pinkerton, beckoning his best friend forward with two fingers. Mandell raised his blade and took a swipe, which Pinkerton side-stepped.

"We were friends, were we not?" Mandell said, the point of his sword levelled at Pinkerton's chest.

"Indeed we were."

"Then I'm going to fuck you in the arse as you lay dying," Mandell told the pugilist, stabbing forward.

Pinkerton stepped back, let the sword pierce the air an inch from his chest and swung with his left. There was a loud crack as his fist connected with the dead man's chin. The jawbone burst from Mandell's face and flew into the fog, where both men heard it clatter to the ground.

"That should shut you up, old boy," said Pinkerton, hopping away as the knight span in the opposite direction.

With no working heart to pump the blood, there was no bleeding and Mandell glared at Pinkerton, his nose and top row of teeth all that was left beneath the milky eyes.

The two men squared up again. Adrenaline had hit Pinkerton's system now, and he could feel none of his wounds.

Mandell slowly moved his blade through a figure of eight and then lunged at Pinkerton's hip. As the boxer stepped back, Mandell swiped through a backhand, cutting into Pinkerton's side beneath his arm, the blade only stopping when it hit his rib cage. Pinkerton roared with anger as Mandell wrenched out the blade, a smile written in his eyes. Mandell spun three hundred and sixty degrees to cut into Pinkerton's other side, but the boxer grabbed his old partner's wrist and slammed his fist into Mandell's once beautiful face, ramming the nose into his skull. The dead man stumbled backwards, teeth dropping from his palate, nothing left of his nose but a triangular hole.

Pinkerton put one hand to the gash at his side, feeling the warm blood pulsing through his clothing, and Mandell was on him again, chopping downward with his sword. Pinkerton raised his good arm and grabbed Mandell's hand. Then the boxer felt the muscle that had been bitten by the mutt spasm, and his foot slid sideways. As he stumbled backwards, Mandell punched him with his other hand and Pinkerton spun, crashing to the floor on his side, bones cracking. He felt himself start to pass out, could hear the referee start to count.

He rolled onto his back and looked into the undead eyes of his former partner, seeing victory as he raised his boot to crush the old boxer's face. Pinkerton screamed with every last piece of energy left in his battered frame, snatched the boot poised above his head with both hands and twisted hard.

He heard tendons ping and bones crack as he grappled the foot around so that the toes were where the ankle should be. Then Pinkerton pushed hard and Mandell tumbled backwards, the sword clattering to the floor.

Pinkerton crawled to the blade and used it to lever himself upright. He stood swaying, looking down at his former friend as the creature he had become attempted to stand, despite one crushed foot and the other almost twisted clean off. Pinkerton stood over his friend, and, as he raised the sword to cleave the head from the shoulders, he swore he could see thanks in the man's eyes.

"Up the Reds," Pinkerton said calmly and then he put his friend out of his misery before collapsing next to him, the sword still tight in his hand.

Teddy wandered the tenement blocks with tears and snot rolling down his face, completely sure that he was without doubt the unluckiest wretch to ever walk the Earth. If not that, then he was definitely the most unfortunate chosen one. The hound had bitten him on the hand - well, more scraped him with his teeth, but it still really smarted. He also had a rather nasty bruise where he had stumbled into the dustbin in the alley, and he was starving hungry, having not eaten a thing, not even toast, since they had left the Bester.

But worst of all he had lost Mister Elephantine. The Professor may have given him opportunities, taken him out of the gutter, but Mister Elephantine had revealed him as the chosen one. The Chosen One. And that snotty little short man had stolen him.

As he stumbled forward, kicking at stones, his hands deep in his pockets, the fog seemed to clear. A familiar smell came to his nose and he recognised the sound of chanting. He frowned into the fog at the building ahead and recognised the foul structure that seemed to ooze against it. The Fairy rookery. He sniffed back more tears at the proof of his own uselessness. He had managed to go round in one big circle and end up where he had left the others.

"Professor?" he called, unsure whether he wanted his employer to find him or not. "Sir?"

He continued on towards the rookery, sniffing and wiping his eyes.

"I smell the Blue," said one lazy eyed fairy, fart-flying his way towards the boy.

"The Blue," another chanted, "the Blue," as he approached.

Teddy wiped his hands on his trousers, trying to tub away any traces of the Storyteller Box but Fairy still showed interest.

"Forget it," he moaned, "I lost it. I lost the Blue Wonder. I lost the box and I lost Mister Elephantine."

"Oh dear, deary me. Everything is lost, misplaced, missed, gone, doggone," Fairy said as they flittered around him. "The rest of the one that we have a part of has departed."

And then it struck Teddy. He knew Fairy were weird and stupid and everything, but they could still smell the Blue Wonder on him. And the short man couldn't have gone far. So he would enroll Fairy to find Mister Elephantine.

And when they did, he would keep the box closed and escape with Mister Elephantine, leave this horrible place, go back to Fairport and make the Elf ghost man in the box tell his mother he was the Chosen One. Mister Elephantine would be able to find her and he'd tell her how important her son was and she would make toast with lashings of butter and everything would be alright.

"Fairy," Teddy said, mustering all his courage to talk to the diminutive gaggle, "I need your help."

Laurel could feel the eyes of the Elf guards on her, and knew it wasn't through physical attraction. She could feel the hatred simmering within them and felt her own bitterness towards the family that had been so foul to her mother. She had been given away: it was better to have honest loving parents than the privileged cold murderousness of the Gleaves.

"You don't feel the way I expected a Gleave to feel," said the closest Elf.

"Thank you," Laurel replied. "I hope I have nothing in common with them."

"So do I," the Elf replied. "You seem to have a good heart."

"She does," Brennan said. "My family were in thrall to the damned Gleaves for generations and she was the only one worth a penny."

"You have suffered loss," the Elf said as he regarded Brennan. "You have lost someone recently."

"My son," Brennan replied. "He died defending the key that allowed us entry to the remains of Pearly."

"They really exist?" asked the other Elf, his eyes lighting up. "You've been there?"

"We were inside the Library of Senses," Laurel explained. "We freed the prisoners."

"The traitors?" the guard snarled.

"We didn't know at the time," she added quickly.

"The precious Blue Wonder that has enabled the traitors to stay alive had enough energy to run a city for a week. Where is the Storyteller Box now?"

Laurel and Brennan looked at each other and shrugged, seeing the faces of the Elf harden.

The door opened and Hilt entered with Elena in his arms, Talisker following.

"All I'm saying is that isn't it strange that your Doctor Axelrod invented these Cruciform rifles," Hilt was saying, "and that they work on humans and Elf but not his undead army or the manmade beasts of the Threat?"

"Kevin Axelrod is a hero of the Ditch, our greatest double agent."

"Ever thought he may be a triple agent?"

"Never," Talisker scoffed. "He has planned the whole thing."

"But what is the whole thing?"

"I've never seen Hilt so engaged," Laurel mumbled to Brennan.

"This is what he does," Brennan replied. "Look for the worst scenario."

"He's a psychopath.

"He's a warrior," Brennan shrugged. "One of the best."

Elena was placed on the sofa and Talisker pulled some herbs from his bag.

"The Viceroy used a bog standard paralysing potion," he explained. "No Wonder is required."

"You said you could help me with my hand," said Hilt, looking down at his snapped blade.

One of the Elf guards stepped forward.

"Must we really help this animal?" he asked. "He has already killed Garabed and wounded Hraztan."

"If John Widdershins is working with us we cannot lose," Talisker smiled. "Look inside yourselves. Look inside him and you will know what I say it true."

"That's the thing, Talisker," one of the Elf said. "He's a blank. We can't feel his feelings and everything about his future is missing."

"You mean he's going to die?" asked Laurel.

"I mean nobody knows."

Talisker turned to regard Hilt, who was recovering his blade from the Viceroy's throat.

"Do you know what they're talking about?" Talisker asked him.

"It would appear that ever since the Meander Canyon, dabbling has no effect on me, unless it's very strong."

"No effect?" Talisker asked, completing the herb concoction for Elena and passing it to Bunce.

"I think I overdosed at Meander or something," Hilt shrugged, "The Storyteller Box was able to look into my mind but most manufactured Wonder doesn't touch me."

"The Storyteller Box is extremely strong Blue Wonder," Talisker pondered.

"Why didn't you tell us?" Brennan asked.

"Why would he want anyone to know?" Bunce asked as she lifted Elena's head so she could take the medicine.

"So," Hilt continued, ignoring the conversation, "what was Axelrod's plan?"

"We kill the crows so that nobody can use the Murder to call for reinforcements, take control of the ballrooms to shut down the Immolators and then Axelrod arrives with his undead army of occupation."

"Why use the Elf for the first wave?"

"They can sneak up on anyone and are more likely to be able to shut down the ballrooms."

"And you?"

"I'm well versed in Red Wonder hyperphysics."

"So the Elf get Pearly back while the Ditch continue the rape of the Gramarye's Wonder and turn it into a battlefield as they take on the Trade. Once again the people of the Gramarye are in the firing line."

"You don't understand," reasoned Talisker. "The Storyteller Box is right and the Elf can feel it too. The Threat is returning and the Ditch cannot take it on alone. There are secrets buried within Pearly that the Elf can decipher and use against the Threat."

"Secrets?"

"The power of the Blue Wonder and the knowledge to use it."

"Did the Elf forget?" Hilt scoffed.

"Many refugees were lost when the Elf crossed the Attar Mountains. Books and other storage devices were destroyed..."

"Storage devices?"

"The Elf of Pearly had methods of storing hundreds of books on one page."

"What does that even mean?"

Talisker shrugged.

"The secrets of Pearly. The hyperphysics of Pearly surpass anything you can imagine."

"We've seen some of it," said Laurel. "Moving pictures, living walls..."

"And the Threat is that powerful?" Hilt asked.

"You've seen the beasts they can create. Imagine an army of them. Imagine metal monsters against the innocents of The Gramarye."

Laurel and Brennan shook their heads as Hilt surveyed the room, his eyes falling on Elena.

"Very well," said Hilt, "who can re-attach my blade?"

"If you are immune to the Wonder..."

"I am. The sword is not," Hilt said, anger flashing in his eyes. "The blade is attached to me. It is not part of me."

"Then I can merge the blade back in place using a localised version of the paralysing floor," said Talisker.

"Are you sure you want to use a paralysing floor on a Torchlight?"

Hilt regarded the dabbler darkly. Talisker would not meet his eyes.

"Do you trust me?" he asked.

"The only man I ever trusted was killed by an Elf," Hilt replied. "Now do it so I can help you shut down the Immolators."

"Hilt," Elena said, raising a hand while Bunce knelt beside her.

Hilt crossed the room to her side.

"Are you feeling better?" he asked her.

"I can feel sensation returning. What about Spicer? What about Mister Elephantine and the Professor?"

"I'm sure they have everything in hand."

Spicer kicked open the door into the building, his Twirler spinning, and two rounds smashed into the wall next to his face. He fired once, hitting a Trade guard in between the eyes and leapt down the stairs four at a time. He reached the dead guard, grabbed his Twirler and spun in before cracking open the entrance to the third floor.

He saw a barricade in front of him manned by two Trade guards firing in the opposite direction. A dead old man in uniform lay expired on the floor. One guard turned, expecting to see his colleague.

"Wait," he suggested and Spicer shot him with one Twirler and then his friend with the other.

Two bursts of green flew down the corridor from beyond the barricade. Spicer returned fire with both guns and leapt for the closest open door. Once through it, he glanced around and recognised Franks' room, where Tork had revealed the Gargoyle Key to the Wonder censor so long ago. He knew that over the corridor and two doors down he would find Quine's old office, which he guessed would reveal Rickenbacker, judging by the window he smashed though.

He looked back through the doorway and two Green bolts screeched down the corridor, lighting up the walls.

"Professor!" Spicer called, before firing around the corner with both pistols.

He looked at the closed door to Quine's office, and fired down the corridor with one Twirler while he fired the other once, blowing out the lock. Green bolts hit the wall around him and seemed to make no mark, but Spicer did not mistake them as harmless. He got down on one knee, prone, and then threw himself across the corridor, firing from the hip all the way. He clattered into the office, rolled once and took cover behind a chair. He could see the shattered panoramic window and Quine's large desk.

"Professor Rickenbacker!" he tried again and heard a groan.

Keeping one Twirler on the door, the Lieutenant walked towards the desk and as he approached, he saw the old man face down. He ran to the man's side and rolled him onto his back.

"Are you alright?" he asked.

"Not entirely," said the Professor as Spicer sat him up, "What's going on?"

"It's looking like the Elf have complete control of the building."

"Above and below ground?"

The door was kicked in and green bolts flew over their heads and through the window out into the sky above Chinsey. Spicer threw his shoulder against the desk and tipped it over, spun the pistols and fired them both over the top in the direction of the doorway.

"Throw down your weapons and surrender," said a woman's voice from beyond the door.

"Are you from the Ditch?" Spicer called.

"We are Elf from the Ditch and we don't need to kill you."

"I am an Elf," Spicer replied. "An Elf of the Gramarye."

There was a brief conversation on the other side of the door.

"There are no Elf in the Gramarye," the woman replied. "Now stop these games and surrender now."

"I am a Yossarian," Spicer called back, feeling both lost and empowered as he used his family name.

There was a pause.

"Show yourself."

Spicer looked at the Professor and inhaled. He put one Twirler on the floor, the other in his holster and stood up, his hands at a distance from his gunbelt.

A face wrapped in scarves peered around the edge of the door and Spicer saw the eyes grow wide with surprise.

"Now you," Spicer called, "I am not here to fight you."

There was more dialogue out of sight and then the woman stepped into the doorway. A curved sword hung from her waist, a sniper rifle was strapped to her back and she wore a bottle green uniform.

"Let me see your face," Spicer instructed the woman, feeling a rush of excitement at seeing his first living Elf. She unwrapped the scarves from her head, revealing jet black hair that shone blue in the light then clear green eyes. Spicer felt himself gasp as she finally showed herself, her white teeth biting at her full bottom lip nervously. Poking from her full hair he could just make out the points of her ears.

"You are Elf," she said in hushed tones.

"As are you," Spicer said, feeling rooted to the spot.

"You look like a Yossarian," she said, looking him over, "or at least how I imagined one to look."

They stood at opposite ends of the Trade Colonel's office but Spicer thought he could feel warmth coming from her body. He couldn't tear his eyes away. They both blushed.

"Isabella," said a trooper from behind the door, "We are needed downstairs."

The trooper paused and repeated himself.

"I am needed downstairs," Isabella told Spicer pointlessly.

The Professor stood up but the two Elf ignored him, entranced.

"I can help you find the ballroom and release the Immolators," Rickenbacker announced. "My name is Hilary Rickenbacker."

"Why would we want to release the Immolators?" the trooper asked, frowning at the Professor.

"They are Elf," he replied.

"Nonsense," the trooper guffawed. "Isabella, who cares if he is Elf. We have to go."

"It's true, Isabella," Spicer said, his eyes still on hers. "The Immolators are Elf. We have to free them from the yoke of the ballrooms."

"But our agent said we should destroy them," Isabella said, finally breaking out of Spicer's spell, looking over at the broken window beyond.

"Axelrod has been lying to you," Rickenbacker said.

"Axelrod is a hero. He found a safe route through the mountains. He would never betray us to the Trade," the trooper said, raising his rifle instinctively.

"It is not the Trade he is working for," Rickenbacker continued. "He has no interest in the Elf or the Ditch."

"Who then?" Spicer asked, puzzled.

"The Threat," Isabella said, shaking her head. "He pits Elf against the Trade, takes control of the Immolators and then his undead army can destroy Chinsey."

"Leaving both the Ditch and the Gramarye wide open for an attack by the Threat," Spicer added.

Isabella walked towards Spicer, past him and looked out across Chinsey. They all turned to join her looking across the frontier town, at the chimneys on the outskirts, the Spirit of Bester loading up as Ashburton Station, smoke rising from the barracks as the sun started to dip.

"Axelrod and his legion should be here within the hour," Isabella told them. "We will not be able to stop him with our weapons and the Trade barracks is already in flames."

"Then we need the Immolators," said Rickenbacker.

"And we need to find the Storyteller Box," said Spicer. "It holds the key. It always has."

Isabella was staring directly below into the grounds of the headquarters.

"Is that man a friend of yours?" she asked as Hilt's pony leapt the front gate. Hilt held the reins in his teeth, a Twirler in one hand and his blade flashing in the last of the sunlight.

"You need to let him through," Spicer nodded, "or we could lose even more of our men."

Isabella nodded in the direction of the trooper who left the room at speed.

"Has it ever struck you that people like Hilt never seem to be on the winning side?" Rickenbacker asked no-one in particular.

Spicer looked at the woman next to him, and in the last rays of sunlight he noticed a cobweb of scarring across her face. They made him feel like he was home.

Kendrick put the box on the bar and searched his pockets. He put a pile of business cards on the sycamore wood in front of him next to the box, then a few shillings that had been secreted in his watch pocket. He waved two fingers at the barman, and when he came over he pointed to the change between them.

"What can I get for that?"

The barman reached beneath the bar and pulled out a rag, soaked in gin and any other dregs of alcohol left in glasses at the end of the night.

"Is that it?" Aldo asked.

The barman picked up the gin-soaked rag, wiped down the bar and gave it back to Aldo. He picked up the change and retreated to the other end of the bar.

Aldo glared at the man polishing glasses and inserted a corner of the rag into his mouth, which he proceeded to suck like an alcoholic baby with a comforter.

"Who are you?" someone asked, and Aldo instinctively reached for a card, before realising that the pub was empty.

"Who said that?"

The barman glanced over his shoulder and rolled his eyes.

"What is it with you people?" the voice continued. "Just think the words and I will listen."

Aldo concentrated and thought hard to form words in reply.

"To whom am I speaking please?"

"I am Mister Elephantine. I reside in the box. Who are you?"

"I am Aldo Kendrick, gentleman, entrepreneur and friend. I rescued you from the others."

"You are indeed a friend, Aldo Kendrick. You may even be the chosen one."

"Well I probably am, actually. I've always suspected as much."

"Indeed."

"Tell me. Is there any money in being the chosen one?"

"Indubitably, Aldo Kendrick. Now all you need to do is get me to someone with power and they will thank you a million times over."

"Power?" Aldo racked his brains. "Would a Viceroy do? I'm sure there's one around here somewhere."

"Let us visit this Viceroy then, Aldo Kendrick."

"Can I just finish my drink first, Mister Elephantine?"

"I suppose so, Aldo Kendrick."

"Thanks."

Aldo returned to sucking his gin-soaked rag with a smile on his face, occasionally casting a smug condescension in the direction of the barman.

"Which was for the Viceroy's palace?" he asked the man's back.

He looked down at the business cards in front of him and considered the new title he needed to add. He was surprised he hadn't done added it before.

An Elf trooper handed Isabella a note, which she opened with some trepidation.

"Including the troopers here, we have thirty one left, four of whom are wounded," she told the others.

"Twenty seven against three hundred undead," said Rickenbacker.

"And we still need to get to the Immolators."

"We need to dump those cruciform rifles and salvage what we can from the barracks. How many do you need to take the ballroom?" Hilt asked Isabella.

"Twenty?" she smirked.

"You can have six," he answered. "I'll take Talisker and Bunce to take the undead."

"What about Mr Elephantine? The Storyteller Box?" Spicer asked.

"Pinkerton must have it in his hands now," Hilt replied. "How hard can it be taking it from the boy?"

Pinkerton didn't know how long he'd been unconscious but the fog had been replaced by the darkness of night. He opened his eyes to see Mandell's jawless skull glaring at him, while the rest of his body was crawling away.

Pinkerton pulled himself up on a lamppost as it flickered to life. He reached up, took the orb of glowing Red Wonder and threw it at the knight's body. As the orb burst into flames and engulfed the knight's body, the boxer searched his clothes for a cheroot and Sir Evan closed his eyes for the last time.

Pinkerton puffed on the cheroot and saw two young scraps staring at him from beneath their caps.

"Either of you two boys know where the Viceroy's palace is?" he asked.

One shrugged, wide-eyed, while the other used one hand to point uptown and the other hand to ask for money. Pinkerton flicked a coin into the upturned palm, gave a gentle salute and limped in the direction indicated.

"You boys should head home," he said over his shoulder. "Tonight is going to be busy."

Hilt had left them just five minutes and Isabella led the Professor and Spicer down the stairs to the barred double gate. They paused at the bottom of the stairs and Isabella turned to them.

"Here is our impasse," she said. "Watch."

She took a scarf from around her neck and waved it around the corner. They heard two shots from a Twirler and the scarf bucked. When Isabella brought it back to her chest, she poked her fingers through two bullet holes.

"I think it's just two men," Isabella told them. "A jailer and a soldier."

Rickenbacker had stocked up his bag with any Wonder he could find from the desks above, including Franks' and Quine's, with raw material and some confiscated grenades.

"Rickenbacker could blow them out," Spicer suggested.

"But the door will remain locked," Rickenbacker reasoned.

"Then blow the doors too."

"But that could bring down the roof."

"Wait," said Spicer, his eyes narrowing. "I have an idea who this might be. I may have met him when we delivered the Gargoyle Key."

"You were delivering it to the Trade?" Isabella asked.

"A lot has happened in the last few days," Spicer reassured her before turning his attention to the people beyond the gate. "Pendle? Is that you?"

There was silence.

"Pendle? It's me. Lieutenant Spicer."

"Who?"

"We met when Rickenbacker stole the Gargoyle Key," Spicer continued, "I was the leader of the Reclaimer squad that brought it in."

"So what?"

"So I'm on your side."

"If you were on my side, sir," Pendle called back, "you would be on this side of the door."

"Pendle," Spicer countered, "if I wasn't on your side, I wouldn't be talking to you."

It went quiet again. Spicer turned to Rickenbacker and whispered as the Professor went down his bag of tricks.

"What have you got?"

"I have no idea," Rickenbacker replied, "unless I put something together from scratch."

"How long will that take?"

"I don't know."

Spicer rolled his eyes.

"Show yourself," Pendle called, "and then we'll talk."

"Very well," Spicer called back. "What do I do?" he asked the others.

"Go," Isabella suggested.

"I didn't look like this when he met me."

"We all get older."

"We met a few days ago."

"What's different?" Isabella asked.

"I had a scarred face," he replied, "And I wasn't an Elf. Not in body anyway."

Rickenbacker glanced around and saw a Trade soldier's corpse. He picked up the man's hat and passed it to Spicer.

"I wear a hat? That's it?"

They all looked at each other.

"I'll cover you," Isabella suggested, taking her rifle from her back.

"Well?" called Pendle from beyond the gate.

"I'm coming out," Spicer called out.

"Unarmed."

"No. Wait."

He reached into his pack and pulled out his old wig.

"Is your pet going to attack him?" Isabella asked.

"Just shoot him if he looks like he's going to shoot me," Spicer told her before he put his old wig on his stubbly scalp.

Then he stepped around the corner.

There was a bright light from the other side of the gates that made him squint, the shadows of the bars from the gates were painted on the floor. Spicer pulled the Twirler from his holster and the sword from its scabbard and handed them both to Isabella. He took one step forward, then another.

"Pendle?" he called.

The silhouette of a short skinny man appeared in front of the light, holding a blat gun that was pointing directly at Spicer.

"What's happening, Lieutenant?" Pendle asked, his face in shadow.

"Doctor Axelrod has betrayed us all. He is marching on Chinsey now with an army of undead. Our only hope is to use the Immolators against them," said Spicer as succinctly as possible.

"I never liked the Doctor," Pendle replied. "That doesn't mean he's a traitor, mind."

"Trust your instincts, Sergeant."

"It's not the undead that have attacked us here though, is it now, Lieutenant?"

"No, but..."

"It's the Elf, isn't it, sir?" he cocked the blat gun. "And from what I can see, sir, you're one of them."

Spicer was suddenly aware that he was too far from the corner to duck back to cover. He prayed Isabella had him covered.

"The Elf have come to defend us against Axelrod and his followers," Spicer said, feeling his mouth dry and his forehead moisten.

"According to you, Sir," said Pendle, raising the blat gun.

There was a scream behind him and the shadow behind the gate turned.

"I knew it," Pendle cried and he fired the blat twice. Then they were on him.

Spicer couldn't see clearly but he could still hear Pendle. He no longer had the blat but he was kicking and screaming as hands grasped and tore at him.

"Get away from me, you buggers," the Sergeant cried and then there was silence. Seconds later the bright light on the other side of the gate went out and they were plunged into subterranean darkness.

"Spicer?" Isabella called out, but Spicer couldn't help himself. He walked towards the locked gate and the darkness beyond.

He reached the bars and waited for his eyes to grow accustomed to the darkness. There was a gap between the gates, occupied by a solitary stool, and then another gate.

All was shadow.

Then Spicer could make out forms on the other side of the gates. Hands grasped towards him, and he could feel the breeze from their desperate flailing. Isabella and Rickenbacker were behind him.

"Oh my God," Isabella whispered.

Spicer's knuckles whitened as he clung grimly to the bars. As he saw the lost souls ahead, he forgave his parents for burning his heritance from his appearance. In the little light there was, he could make out the latticework of brass pulsing with Wonder, weaving in and out of skulls, piercing eyes and burrowing into ears. Their faces were blank, but their desperate yearning to harm anybody on the other side of the gates was clear.

"Immolators," Rickenbacker said. "Not yet fully turned, but already under the control of the ballroom."

"They are Elf," Isabella said, her face draining of blood.

"The mind control can only work on the Elf," Rickenbacker said, staring with sorrow at the mass ahead of them. Isabella handed Spicer his sword and Twirler.

"Do we kill them?" she asked.

"The ballroom is beyond the cells," Rickenbacker said.

"Axelrod wouldn't think twice," Spicer reasoned.

"Whoever is controlling them probably works for Axelrod. When he arrives they will stand down to admit him."

"We can't kill them," said Isabella. "We need them."

"And they are Elf. They are people, despite their appearance."

It was hard to recognise the damaged killers as anything that could have ever been reasonable. Spicer was sickened to see women and children caught up in the morass.

"Professor," Spicer shrugged, "it's up to you and your bag of tricks."

"Yes," Rickenbacker replied, "it would definitely seem so."

As the undead reached the outskirts of Chinsey, they started to pick up speed, almost jogging in their eagerness to show their creator, to show Doctor Axelrod, how well they could carry out his bidding. They were also keen to feel the warmth of the living as they died on the end of their blades and under the salvos of their firearms. They had orders. They were to take the Trade headquarters first, the building some of them had left a few days previously very much alive, with wives, families and work pressures. Now they were returning to kill whoever held it, Elf or human.

Immolators were the only beings to be spared. With no soldiers to defend them, the townsfolk would kneel before anyone who would stop the slaughter, be it Axelrod or anyone else.

Little did anyone but the good Doctor know that there would be no survivors, no mercy would be given, and that the Threat would destroy them all once they had taken what they wanted. And they wanted their Wonder and their flesh.

As the sound and the smell of the undead army permeated the Gramarye evening, night watchmen and workers on the late shift came out to see the new arrivals. They were all cut down. As screams echoed around the factory walls and gunshots rang out, the people of Chinsey cowered behind their front doors, barricaded their windows with the furniture they had been eating their dinner from moments before and thanked their lucky stars that the Trade were there to defend them. If there was just one good thing about being occupied, it was that you knew the occupying force would work to retain their property. And it had been explained that the Immolators had been conceived with the express intent of fighting off the undead threat from the Ditch.

As the night went on, more Immolators took to the street. But instead of moving to intercept the undead army, they headed for the burning Trade headquarters, their weapons drawn.

CHAPTER 17

Chinsey
The Gramarye Region
Grand Quillia

June 1856

It took Isabella twenty minutes to scrounge together earmuffs and goggles for the three of them. As she scoured the Trade building, she saw the first of the Immolators approaching the perimeter fence and despatched two Elf troopers to take it down. When she reached the ground floor before heading into back into the below ground cells, she saw four more skirmishing with more troopers.

By the time she joined the others, the Professor was rigging the white out and had already prepared the Blow Back. Luckily he had found two grenades that he could use to blow both set of gates.

"The Immolators are moving in," she told them all. "We need to get this done."

"Almost there," the Professor replied.

"Impressive," Isabella noted, "you can put it together so fast."

"It works too," Spicer told her. "I've been at the receiving end of one of the Professor's treats in this very building before."

"There are a lot of variables," Rickenbacker warned them. "The Blow Back could be too strong and crush those poor souls against the wall, or too weak and they'll get caught in the explosion."

"But the white out will work," Spicer said.

"I did not procure this Wonder myself," Rickenbacker said, shaking his head. "I have no idea how potent it will be. It could cripple them for life."

"Or they could regain their senses and cripple us before we reach the ballroom," said Isabella.

"Exactly."

The three of them looked at each other.

"Do you trust him?" Isabella asked Spicer.

"Do we have a choice?" Spicer replied. "Let's go, Professor."

He reached out his hand and the two men shook. The Professor eased on his goggles and positioned the earmuffs. Isabella leant forward and kissed Spicer gently on the cheek.

"Good luck, Yossarian," she said, before setting her own protective gear in place.

Spicer looked the Elf woman in the eyes, the feel of her lips still on his face, and then he noticed something in the reflection of her goggles. He pulled his Twirler and spun in one, firing low. Two Immolators charging down the corridor were struck in the legs and fell forward, fumbling their weapons. He saw the Professor turn and, recognising their predicament, step around the corner to start the Blow Back. As he did so, another Immolator came down the stairs, weapons drawn, and while Isabella brought the invader to the floor, Spicer pulled on his goggles and earmuffs and readied himself.

As Hilt rode in, he saw the man stumble and right himself against the wall before continuing on, one hand locked to his side and one foot dragging behind him. Hilt looked around to ensure whoever had done this to the man was not still around, and dismounted his pony, drawing his Twirler.

"Pinkerton?" he called as he saw the familiar mutton chops caked with blood.

Pinkerton paused and turned his head, in too much pain to move his whole body to face his colleague. Hilt holstered his pistol and threw his arm around the big man's shoulder blades.

"Who did this to you?" Hilt asked, guiding the pugilist towards his pony.

"Mandell," Pinkerton coughed.

"Did the bastard take the box?" Hilt asked.

"No."

Hilt turned Pinkerton so they could face each other.

"Where's the box now, Pinkerton?"

"I don't know," Pinkerton replied, unable to meet Hilt's eye. "Kendrick has it."

"Kendrick? What the hell is Kendrick doing with it?"

"Is this your pony?"

"Yes."

"May I sit on it please?"

Hilt looked over the battered individual in his hands, saw the blood and bruising and realised he would get no more answers as the boxer's head lolled and he passed out, propped up against the pony.

As Hilt hoisted his unconscious colleague onto the back of his steed, screams and gunshots reached his ears from downtown. He climbed onto his ride behind Pinkerton's prone body and kicked onwards towards the palace.

Lady Melody watched from the sofa while she sipped some sweet tea as Laurel, Brennan and the Elf completed barricading the sitting room window.

"I hear hooves," Talisker called.

"Hilt's riding in," Bunce replied from her vantage point at an upstairs window.

"Thank God," said Laurel as Brennan joined her to meet Hilt galloping up the drive.

The pony ground to a halt and Brennan immediately recognised Pinkerton face down across the saddle.

"What happened to him?" Laurel asked.

"Mandell," Hilt replied, "Axelrod's army have entered the town and the Professor is still fighting to get inside the ballroom."

"And Mr Elephantine?"

Hilt shook his head.

As they carried Pinkerton inside, Laurel looked at the warrior.

"What's going to happen, Hilt?"

"Ask an Elf," he suggested, closing the front door behind them.

From the shadowy doorway of Mulligan's Haberdashers shop opposite the palace, Aldo Kendrick shook his head in disbelief. If he was the chosen one, then why was he so unlucky?

He always seemed to be stuck on the losing side. If Hilt was in the Viceroy's palace, then it was a foregone conclusion that the Viceroy was already dead. The Trade headquarters was under attack by Immolators, which made no sense, and flames had engulfed the Barracks. That meant he had the choice of turning to the vindictive Colonel Quine, who had made him plead for his life, or a psychopath he had already betrayed. He decided on the Trade platoon, and set off towards the road that Mandell and he had taken from the Glasslands. He stepped out from the shadows and looked up at the Viceroy's palace one last time, before heading back downtown.

Bunce loved this new rifle she had acquired from the corpse at Wyman's base. It was a sincerely thrilling piece of weaponry. With the Wonder-assisted scope she could make out each hole on the straps on Hilt's saddle. She rolled the sight across the shops across the street from the palace, taking in a haberdasher's and a confectioner's, wondering if anyone had ever been window-shopping like this before. Then she caught some movement by the sweet shop. She lowered the rifle and squinted into the shadows with her naked eye. She spotted a diminutive figure scuttling from one doorway to another, obviously keen to be unnoticed. She put her eye back to the sight and zoomed in on the figure, releasing the gel full of Wonder across the lens to enable its full telescopic range.

First she recognised the scared little man as the card-carrying traitor from the lodge, the first to surrender to Colonel Quine.

"What are you doing here, shorty?" she mumbled, using the sight to look him up and down.

The Wonder in the gel seemed to react to something in the man's hand, making it glow a bright blue so she could almost make out the bones in the man's fingers.

Then she realised she was looking at the Storyteller Box.

"Elena!" she called down the stairs, "I've found the Storyteller Box! I can see Mr Elephantine!"

Rickenbacker glanced over his shoulder and although he could only just make out gunfire through his earmuffs, he could see the flashes of red as Isabella and Spicer discharged their weapons around the corner, attempting to keep the armoured Immolators at bay without killing them.

Not only would the death of an Immolator mean one less Elf and one less potential ally once they took control of the ballroom, it would also cause the warrior to burst into flame, starting a chain reaction that would block their only escape route.

He looked back towards the two gates ahead, at the morass of scarred monsters grasping through the bars towards him, their eyes submerged under the fine mesh that pulsed with Wonder. He held one grenade tight in one hand and started to spin the Blow Back device with the other, his ears popping.

First, the air in front of him started to fill with swirling dust, resembling spinning dervishes, and then the lights started to flicker. The wooden tiles on the floor started to ripple and clack together. The device meant that Rickenbacker didn't feel anything pushing back against him and he couldn't resist looking behind him, which, besides the gunfire around the corner, looked completely untouched. He faced the gates again, looking through the dust for signs of grasping arms or the glint of wire mesh, which would mean the half-made Immolators were still there, beating back the wind.

All he could see as the dust and dirt moved further down the corridor in the relentless wind was one last fist grasping the far gate. The Professor stepped forward while swinging the Blow Back device more strenuously. The knuckles on the hand grew white with the strain of clinging on to the bars and then suddenly they were gone, thrown backwards as the Elf was beaten back. Reducing the swing of the bolas, he pulled the fuse on the grenade with his teeth and rolled it along the floor. It bounced across the uneven tiles, hit the bottom of the first gate and flipped over it. Rickenbacker fought the urge to drop the Blow Back despite imagining the grenade hitting a group of Elf and exploding, and watched in terror as the grenade rolled on.

It finally came to rest against the hinges of the second gate.

Rickenbacker breathed a sigh of relief knowing the grenade wasn't going into the rabble beyond and then he felt his ears pop.

The grenade exploded in a flash of red, and a burst of flame lapped towards the Professor then swept back when it hit the last of the Blow Back. He felt a wave of heat as he dropped the bolas, the typhoon immediately dissipating. As the carnage of the corridor settled, Rickenbacker was relieved to see both metal gates on the floor, blown from their hinges.

"They're open!" he called to the others. "We're in!" He was unable to hear his own words through his earmuffs. He turned round to get back to the others and let them know, but something stopped him. Caked in dust and smoking from the explosive, the half-made Immolators were picking themselves off the floor, the Wonder still throbbing in the mesh.

"Oh dear," said the Professor as his hands flittered into his bag for the white out bomb.

He looked up as his hands closed on the round container full with a mixture of Wonder and saw the lead half-mades start to sprint towards him, a grim determination scored across their damaged faces now that the gates that had kept them from their prey were no longer an obstruction. In their blind eagerness to reach him, they stumbled over the twisted metal that had once been the gates, as Rickenbacker's fingers found the trigger.

Then one of the mind-controlled killers was over the gateway and racing towards him.

"Oh dear, oh dear, oh dear," the Professor repeated as the thing knocked him to the floor and wrapped his hands around the old man's throat, the white out rolling from his hands.

When the shop window shattered next to him, the first thing Kendrick considered was what he could nab from the window display. Then he saw the rifle barrel poking from one of the palace's second floor windows, and leapt through the broken glass to take cover in the shop.

He peered over the windowsill and saw the rifle still trained on him as Laurel and Brennan ran down the drive towards the road, the old man holding a blat gun. Hilt, with a face like thunder, stormed out of the front door and down the steps, grabbed his pony's reins and swung into the saddle.

Kendrick supposed they hadn't shot him because they probably thought he knew where the boy was, whatever-his-name-was…Terry, was it? He considered this and decided that if they caught him he would tell them where the boy was, and lead them somewhere that would enable his escape.

But then he pondered his luck and thought of the last time he had used that ploy, which had resulted in him sharing a ride with a rotting, rutting killer. Kendrick shrank back behind the window and looked around the shop, his eyes alighting on his favourite sight, a back door. He started to crawl further inside and another couple of rounds slammed into the counter in front of him. He lowered himself to his belly and slithered onwards through the gap in the counter. Bullets shattered jars on shelves above and Kendrick sheltered his head as glass and a variety of sweets rained down on him. He reached the back door, and his little hand grasped the door handle and twisted as more bullets slammed into wood. As he ducked through it, he considered dropping the box and grabbing handfuls of boiled sweets, humbugs, wrapped toffees and fudge. They would probably bring him more joy than this Chosen One rubbish. They would not, however, be quite so valuable to Colonel Quine and the Trade platoon he calculated were just roads away, judging by the sound of gunfire, swordplay and screaming.

He had never thought he would ever be happy to see someone of the Colonel's ilk, but then the Colonel had probably never expected someone like Aldo Kendrick to actually complete what he had originally been asked to do. As he bumbled through the small storeroom and reached the exit to the street, Kendrick pictured the Colonel's impressed face now, perhaps even offering Kendrick a medal for services, a tour of his favourite bawdy houses and restaurants and eventually they would become best friends.

The door to the street slammed open and the smell of blood, Red Wonder and fires assaulted Kendrick's senses. The first person Kendrick saw was Colonel Quine, which would have pleased him no end if the Colonel had not been naked with raw meat in his mouth, an erection in one hand and a sword in the other. If that was not disturbing enough, the man was quite clearly undead.

To the half-made Immolators, the corridor had been consumed by an all-encompassing milkiness that had also stripped them of all sensation. To Rickenbacker, Spicer and Isabella, shielded by their goggles and earmuffs, their surroundings had become dazzlingly white, with flashes of lightning dancing around the edge of objects.

The hands that had been throttling the Professor had fallen away after Spicer had found the White-Out on the floor and triggered it, so the half-made was seated on the floor waving his hands in front of his face blankly.

Spicer reached down to help the Professor to his feet while Isabella couldn't resist reaching forward to the half-made's pointed ears. The two men saw tears behind the goggles, and Spicer put a hand to her shoulder, both to reassure her and to get her moving.

They jogged down the corridor. Nothing had changed since Rickenbacker had been there decades before except now all the doors were open. A thick trail of blood led from the entrance down to a dismembered body that had Pendle's face on its caved-in head. Damaged prisoners, half-mades in different states but all whited out stumbled around in somnambulist trances, the Wonder still pulsing through the mesh threaded through their eyes, ears and skulls.

Eventually Rickenbacker recognised the door he had entered all those years before with Axelrod at his side and the three of them went in, guiding a half-made back into the hall. The Professor reached down, inserted his hand into the handle, and pulled back the wall to reveal the passage to the lift beyond.

As his finger reached to summon the lift, Spicer noticed the lightning edge start to fade from his sight. Then the bright whiteness started to dim. He pointed at the secret door and Isabella reached to close it as the white out dispersed as quickly as it had come. Spicer tore off his earmuffs and listened for the sound of the lift.

"It's not coming," he warned the Professor, attempting to look through the door at the lift shaft below.

Isabella shook her head bitterly as she started to push the secret door closed.

"How could anyone do this to anyone?" she said, looking at the others with anger in her eyes.

"Can you do anything to bring the lift up?" Spicer asked, ignoring Isabella's bitterness.

"I don't know," Rickenbacker admitted, opening a maintenance hatch next to the lift door.

Then a hand reached round the closing secret door and grabbed Isabella's wrist.

"Spicer!" she called, attempting to crack the fingers from her wrist as half-mades threw themselves against the open door.

Spicer pulled his Twirler, spun it once and aimed at the gap by the open door.

"No!" Isabella screamed, raising her hand to protect her kindred.

Spicer cursed and ran towards the door, throwing his full weight against it, and heard a crack as bones in the hand gripping Isabella's snapped. The hand withdrew and they slammed the door shut.

"Professor?" Spicer asked. "Any luck?"

"If this were a bomb and I was defusing it, I would feel more confident," Rickenbacker shared with them.

There was a heavy thud from the other side of the door as more half-mades threw themselves against it.

"It might have to be them or us," Spicer warned Isabella, his pistol still in his hand.

"But they are us," she countered.

There was a metallic moan and the lift weights shuddered into life. Rickenbacker turned to look at them, but showed no optimism.

"Was that you?" Spicer asked him.

The Professor shook his head.

As he kicked the flanks of the pony, Hilt found himself wondering if he had ever seen Bunce actually hit anything. He knew they had agreed to keep Kendrick alive, but why not wing the little bastard? After the time he had spent with the annoying conman at the lodge, he would have enjoyed seeing him have to endure a little pain.

Laurel and Brennan had just reached the front of the sweet shop and, with a signal to Bunce, Hilt decided to check the back door, taking a road down the side of the terrace.

As he turned the corner, the first thing he saw was Kendrick racing directly towards him, the Storyteller Box in his hands. Pursuing him was Colonel Quine, naked and missing most of his head. Being naked may have stripped him of his dignity, but being undead had added a danger to the Colonel he had never possessed in life.

Hilt drew his gun and levelled it at Quine.

"Don't shoot me!" Kendrick pleaded as he saw Hilt spin the chamber.

Two bullets slammed into the wall next to Hilt, throwing brick dust into the pony's eyes. The animal, already exhausted and never bred for fighting, reared up in shock as Hilt tried to get it under control.

Laurel and Brennan burst out of the shop's back door and looked both ways for Kendrick. Gunfire forced them back inside the shop and, with the naked dead man chasing him, Aldo Kendrick resigned himself to the fact that he was probably the unluckiest man alive,

Then he stumbled and fell to the floor, cracking his head on the cobbles and dropping the Storyteller Box. He shook his head groggily, looked around for the box and then Quine was standing over him, the sword raised above his head.

Kendrick looked into the dead man's face and words failed him. Then, over Quine's shoulder, Kendrick saw Hilt in mid-air having thrown himself from the saddle, the pony bolting in the opposite direction. Hilt slammed into Quine, forcing what was left of the man's skull into the street, so that it shattered against cobbles.

"Get the box and stay behind me," Hilt ordered, pulling his Twirler.

Further down the street a squad of undead advanced, swords in their hands. Behind them, riflemen were firing at the sweet shop and Hilt. Kendrick looked in the junction Hilt had arrived from and three more undead rounded the opposite corner.

All of the undead looked like they were thoroughly enjoying themselves. Hilt fired at the riflemen, hitting one in the head, one in the chest and one in the stomach. None of them fell and none of them bothered to take cover, or even look down at their wounds. The fresh bullet holes only seemed to improve their demeanour.

"Run to the others," Hilt said to Kendrick, firing a salvo at the approaching swordsmen, which knocked them back a few steps but did nothing to stop them. More shots thudded around him, and Hilt dropped to one knee, rested the hand gripping his pistol on the other's wrist and aimed carefully at the riflemen, He fired at the one he had already hit in the head, blowing out an eye, fired at the second, hitting his rifle so that it exploded in his undead face, and then he was suddenly aware of a cracking sound, like a falling tree.

He turned and saw Kendrick's head in Quine's hands as the Colonel crushed the life out of the little man's head, his fingers buried knuckle deep in his eye sockets, his legs jerking spasmodically. Hilt automatically fired his Twirler point blank into Quine's demolished head so that he released Kendrick, who collapsed to the floor, blood bubbling from his eyes, ears and mouth. Hilt fired low at the closest swordsmen, blowing out their kneecaps, holstered his Twirler and bent to grab the Storyteller Box from Kendrick's dead fingers as the three undead from around the corner moved to hem him in against the wall. He heard the sound of Brennan's blat gun firing from further down the street, and readied himself to barge his three attackers aside and make a break for the back door when Quine's blood-soaked hand reached up from the floor and grabbed his ankle.

Then the first swordsman on Hilt's right lunged. Hilt knocked the blade aside and decapitated the undead in the middle. As the swordsman to the left swung at him, Hilt ducked, the sword rang as it struck the wall and Hilt rammed the Storyteller Box into the undead's face. The swordsman on the right swung with a backhand and Hilt raised his sword so it connected with the man's wrist, disconnecting his hand from his arm.

"You're dead," cackled the head from the floor as its body threw itself at Hilt.

Hilt buried his sword into the body's chest and used its momentum to swing it to the side, blocking a blow from the swordsman before collapsing on top of Quine, who continued to grip Hilt's ankle. His blade still deep in the undead's chest, Hilt threw the Storyteller Box high into the air, drew his Twirler and raised it as the final swordsman brought his sword down again. It hit the Twirler's chamber, Hilt pushed up so the Twirler spun, and then he fired two rounds into the undead's face. Its head snapped back and it fell backwards as Hilt holstered the Twirler and caught the Storyteller Box before it hit the floor. He withdrew his sword from the headless body, hacked off Quine's hand at the wrist and kicked the decapitated head across the road into the gutter. He extricated himself from the mess of writhing bodies as bullets struck the wall around him as the vanguard of Axelrod's army of undead streamed into the street from both ends.

"Hilt! Run!" Brennan called, and the old man started firing his blat over and over again. Hilt started moving towards the open door, leaping over the kneecapped undead, Quine's fist still wrapped around his ankle.

Teddy couldn't guess how many Fairy had joined him in his quest for Mister Elephantine. Their wings flapped fartily as they fluttered about in front of him, careering into walls and occasionally dipping so their feet dragged along the floor. Some dangled from his clothes and hair, too lazy to flap their own wings. At each junction they came to, a conflagration would break out as the Fairy fought amongst themselves on which direction to take, and as the fight continued, the Fairy behind would pick a road, apparently absent-mindedly, but by the fifth junction he knew they were being innately drawn to something.

Turning another corner into another salubrious back alley of the tenements, Teddy heard a steady pattering, like hail against a window. Fairy were throwing themselves against the closed door of a public house, picking themselves up and trying again. Teddy stopped, leant against the wall by the pub and caught his breath.

"The Blue stayed here, strayed here, sprayed here," the Fairy were gibbering, hardly aware Teddy was there.

"In the pub?" Teddy asked, knowing he would receive no clear answer.

Instinctively, Teddy flattened his hair and collar before entering. The Fairy swarmed in with him.

"Get out, you grotty little vermin," called the barman, stepping from behind the bar and snapping a dishcloth at the Fairy as they entered.

"Excuse me, Sir," said Teddy, putting on his deepest voice.

"Are these little bastards with you?"

"Yes," Teddy replied, but as he saw the barman's face changed he reconsidered. "No, no idea where they're from. Have you seen a little man with a box?"

"What's it worth?"

"I could get rid of these Fairy for you?"

"He was here. He was on his way to the Viceroy's palace."

Teddy was about to thank the barman when the door behind him burst open. He turned, expecting a violent drunk and instead an undead swordsmen, grinning maniacally barrelled into the pub. Teddy fell backwards over a stool and collapsed spread-eagled onto the floor. The undead raised his sword and then turned to the barman.

"Just a short for me," he cackled, and then there was the sound of a blat gun.

The undead was lifted off his feet and propelled through the pub window as smoke issued from the barrel of the barman's blat.

"Only one thing worse than Fairy in your pub," he said, racking his gun, "and that's undead."

Fairy tugged unhelpfully at Teddy as he climbed back to his feet. The undead soldier's hand appeared at the window as he pulled himself upright. Three more undead arrived at the window and the barman fired at them, taking off their heads.

"Which way was the palace again?" Teddy asked, "And is there another way out of here?"

When Rickenbacker first heard the coughing, wheezing and puffing, he thought it was the lift itself, looking over at the maintenance hatch for some sort of problem.

But as the lift got closer, he heard scuttling and he looked down to see the lift itself swaying against its cables. It was then he knew the sound was coming from within.

"Spicer? Isabella? I may need a little help here," he called over, still staring down.

"We're busy," Spicer called back, his back against the secret door, his feet sliding in the dust as the half-mades battered themselves senseless against the other side.

"There's something coming up and I think it's big."

"So blow it up."

"The grenade will destroy the lift."

Isabella looked over at Spicer, her shoulder tight against the wall, beads of sweat running down her face.

"If we can't get in the lift, it ends here," she told him.

He nodded once, and as the top of the lift came into view through the grill door, she stepped away from the door and approached the Professor, who was staring at the inside of the lift as it shuddered into view.

"What the hell is that?" he whispered, causing Isabella's hand to tighten on her Twirler.

As the lift reached their level, black smoke belched from within and Isabella immediately flashed back to her trek over the Attar Mountains with Talisker.

"It's the Threat!" she called, stepping back and firing into the dark smoke.

There was the shriek of ricochets, Isabella's rounds bounced back out of the list and pounded the walls around them.

Then came the loud screech of a whistle.

Rickenbacker pulled the grenade and the bolas for the Blow Back from his bag as they both backed away. The smoke started to dissipate and there was a rumbling from the lift. A ball wrapped in plates of metal shot from the lift, causing Isabella and Rickenbacker to leap aside. It hit the wall, rolled up and then rolled directly at Spicer at speed. He leapt over it awkwardly, landing on his shoulder and the secret door cracked open. Spicer rolled onto his back and pushed at the door with his feet as the ball hit the wall beyond him and flew back towards him.

"Spicer!" Isabella called, firing her Twirler at the ball.

It thundered over Spicer's hips and chest and he screamed in pain, clenching himself in the foetal position. The door opened again as the ball trundled towards Isabella and Rickenbacker.

"Get in the lift," Rickenbacker ordered as he spun the bolas, "now!"

He barged her aside with his shoulder so she stumbled into the lift, her ears popping. The Blowback kicked in immediately, throwing Spicer against the wall and the half-mades on the other side of the door away from the door, but the ball, although slowed, did not stop, the wind slipping over its smooth sides. The Professor walked backwards into a corner, his slender frame tightening itself in an attempt to be stick thin.

The ball thudded against the two walls either side, pinning the Professor but unable to crush him.

"Professor!" Isabella called from the lift.

"Go!" he ordered her through gritted teeth.

She slammed the lift doors closed and pulled the lever to descend as the ball slammed against the corner again, sending cracks up the walls and causing masonry to tumble from the ceiling. With the Professor's arms trapped against his sides, the Blow Back stopped and Spicer dropped to the floor, still clutching his ribs.

The lift juddered once and started to shudder down into the gloom. As the floor rose to Isabella's eye-level, she saw the secret door crash open and half-mades burst into the room, carrying makeshift clubs from beds and other wreckage in their fists, desperate to do some damage.

Everything was going to plan. Axelrod had hoped his apprentice in the ballroom would not lose his nerve so that he would be able to utilise the Immolators for himself, but never mind. He had sent undead scouts ahead and they had reported that the Elf had control of the strategic targets. He had watched his own troops spread into Chinsey unhindered and was now en route to the headquarters to take control of the ballroom.

Then the Threat would arrive to finish the job, while he finally found and harnessed the Blue Wonder of the Gargoyle Key, so that they could launch an attack on the rest of the Wonder-using world.

And then his day got better. The undead he had created from Quine's platoon were racing back from the battleground around the Viceroy's palace to report they had found the evasive Key, but he had learnt from bitter experience that the recently reanimated were so keen to impress their creator that there was a tendency to embellish the truth. It was only when troops he had brought with him from the Ditch started to reiterate the same facts that he believed it, and he instructed his captains to mobilise his troops in that area.

Apparently the box was with a man attached to his sword, which convinced him of the truth. He looked forward to Hilt's death, as he would prove a very useful addition to his own undead platoon. The man was already dead in so many ways, and it was really just a matter of restarting his heart so that he could be given some productive instruction. Psychopaths were a welcome addition to a battle given the correct direction.

Hilt pushed the Storyteller Box into Laurel's hands as he pushed stacked shelves against the sweet shop's back door.

"Get to the palace," Hilt told her, already out of breath. "Don't stop until you get there."

She nodded as they picked their way through the battered sweet shop, their feet skidding on glass and gobstoppers.

"Good luck," Brennan said, kissing her gently on the cheek.

Already the back door was being broken down, and they could hear the sound of Bunce's rifle as she picked off the first of the undead advance in the street at the front of the shop.

"Let's go," Hilt said, swinging his legs over the broken window. "Aim for the legs. Preferably their kneecaps," he told Brennan.

Laurel breathed out nervously and followed Hilt out. Before his feet had touched the ground, Hilt had taken down two undead as they raced towards them.

"Run," he roared at her, firing in both directions and Laurel picked up her skirts to sprint across the road. She focused on the front door of the palace and refused to look left or right as the undead approached. She heard the blat and the Twirler behind her, and whenever an undead warrior came up in front of her, it was blown to the floor by a shot from Bunce in the upper window. Melody was joined by an Elf at the front of the palace and joined the fray, firing into the attacking hordes without pause. But Laurel couldn't hear the gunfire over the sound of her own blood pumping in her veins and her ragged breath as her terror grew.

Hilt ran behind Laurel, shooting and hacking as more undead arrived from either end of the street and from the sweet shop behind him. It was good to be back in battle but he had a bad feeling, stemming from the fact that although they had recovered the Storyteller Box, he didn't know what they were going to do with it. Without Rickenbacker, only Talisker would be able to help them, and until a few short hours ago he was allied with Axelrod. He wiped such thoughts from his head as more undead pressed down upon him, and then he became aware that something was missing.

He hadn't heard Brennan's blat gun for a few seconds. He took out the nearest undead and turned around to look for the old man.

Brennan was swinging wildly with the hammer he had used to destroy the beast beneath the Library of Senses, as more undead surrounded him, giggling while poking at him with their sabres. He looked back at Laurel, tearing ahead towards the palace, and heard an order shouted through the ranks of the undead that chilled him to the bone.

"Rifles only!"

The swordsmen didn't stop, but all the undead armed with rifles raised their weapons and fired. They didn't need to avoid hitting their comrades, and Hilt ducked instinctively as bullets tore through the ranks of the undead into his friends. He saw Laurel spin as she was struck in the shoulder and roll to the floor. Looking back, he saw Brennan struck three times, twice in the back, once in the leg, and the old man sunk to one knee. Undead dropped to the floor laughing, holes in their chests and heads, and then they started to rise again.

Hilt buried his sword into the back of the nearest undead, and used him as a shield as the warrior thrashed about attempting to escape so that he could look for where the order had come from. Then he saw him, Doctor Axelrod, arrogant enough to still be straddling a pony so that he was higher than anybody else. He glanced up Bunce's window to tell her to take him out, but she was under fire. The Elf at the entrance to the palace was dead, and Melody was making her way towards Laurel, both guns blazing. Hilt took out two more approaching undead with his pistol and sunk to the ground using the dead man on his blade as cover, dimly aware that he too may have sustained some injury he was unwilling to admit to. He lay beneath the thrashing undead and waited for Axelrod to come closer.

Talisker peered through the cracks of the barricade they had built at the window and shook his head with sorrow.

"I have to get out there," he said, shuffling towards the door.

"What's going on?" Pinkerton asked, swathed in bandages on a sofa soaked in his blood.

"The old man and the girl are both hit," Talisker said, "and I can't see Hilt. There is no way to stop the undead."

"There is," Pinkerton called. "I've already killed one today myself."

Elena was firing from the hip, not bothering to aim, knowing that there were so many attackers, she was bound to hit something. When the others had been hit, she had felt the bullets buzzing around her, and was shocked when they had missed, but her own fortune immediately paled when she saw Laurel go down.

"Bunce," she had screamed over the battle. "Protect Laurel!" She started down the drive to cover the twenty yards to the young girl.

She saw Laurel raise her head and struggle to get to her feet as two undead bore down on her, but Bunce took them down before they got close to the girl. Then she heard Talisker's voice behind her, calling to them all desperately.

"Shoot the lights!"

The lift descended agonisingly slowly, and Isabella found herself pacing the cramped space, breathing fast. She didn't know how deep she was going, where she would arrive or what would be there to greet her. She was painfully aware that there was no reason to believe that either Spicer or Rickenbacker was still alive above, and she couldn't even guess what was happening above ground. She had felt so many of her kinsmen die already, and the few left alive were terrified and exhausted. As he wasn't an Elf, she couldn't feel Talisker at all, but she knew he had already survived so much. Perhaps this would be the end of his long run of luck.

She became aware that she could only hear the grinding and swaying of her vehicle now, the ancient lift showing its age, having been installed by the Trade when they had first built their headquarters. The gentle swing and noise almost made her feel secure, the creaking like a heartbeat, the movement like a rocking crib. She put her face against the grill and tried to look back up at whence she came, hoping to see the flash of Spicer's Twirler or have her ears popped by one of the Professor's devices, but nothing was forthcoming.

She concentrated on what was coming and tried to feel it, but knew it hung in the balance, just as it had when she had come through the Attar Mountains with Talisker. There was a decision she would have to make. One way would lead to her death, the other to more danger. She could not see beyond her own oblivion, but if she did survive she knew she would find true love for herself, but heartbreak for her people. She wished she were only human, and not aware of anything in her path.

Light cracked through the grill at her feet and she drew her Twirler, spun it, and unsheathed her sword as the lift reached its destination.

A dull blue glow ebbed from beyond the grill, but she could see nothing more. She flattened herself against the side of the lift and kicked the grill open. Her breathing was hard but it was all she could hear, besides a strange humming inside her head, as if she had her fingers in her ears, and the mosquito buzz of her Twirler. She stepped out of the lift, flicked the lever to send it back up, and threw the grill closed. There was a heavy clunk as it shut, and then came the clanking as the lift moved out of view, leaving her to her fate.

She put her back against the wall and edged down the curved corridor. The wall was almost warm to the touch, like skin, and although it gave off a blue shade, it did not have any reflective qualities.

As she descended further, she saw the ballroom for the first time, and she inhaled in awe despite herself, her eyes flickering around the walls. It resembled a rib cage, columns curving inwards to a central support that looked like it was constructed of vertebrae. If she were not so far beneath the earth, if she hadn't taken a very man-made lift to get here, then she would have sworn she had entered the remains of some giant creature, the skeleton of a long dead dragon, the corridor from the lift its tale, the main chamber its chest. As she reached the ballroom itself, she saw a globe of Blue Wonder where the heart would be.

At the globe stood a young man, not out of his teens, his face etched with terror. He was drenched in sweat as he concentrated at the globe that he gripped with both hands. Isabella could already feel the strength of the globe. She could feel the whispers, the hushed tones of thousands of thoughts and feelings and fears and inanities, and she knew what the ballroom was immediately, innately.

The ballroom was some great communication exchange, used by the people of Pearly to speak to each other across great distances, a beautiful thing that allowed families to look after each other, loved ones to check on each other, new friendships to be forged without the need for travel. It was like the Trade's Murder network, but instead of requiring the intermediary of crows, the ballrooms allowed people to communicate directly with each other within the boundaries of the Gramarye.

But the Trade had mutated it, twisted it into something inhuman by ramming it into the brains and senses of the Elf they had caught. They had used this incredible device to find and enslave the last of the Elf in the Gramarye, and this boy, this pathetic apprentice, was controlling the Immolators with a view to his own promotion, an eye on finding the approval of his superiors, people like Axelrod, the great traitor. This young man didn't care about the ethics of his power, he just wanted acknowledgement.

She didn't care if the boy had information about Axelrod or the Trade or anything. She just wanted him to stop existing. Isabella shot the boy in the head, holstered her weapons and placed her quivering hands on the blue globe in the centre of the ballroom, the first Elf to do so in hundreds of years.

Spicer, every bone in his body throbbing with pain, was wedged behind the secret door. As the half-mades had flooded into the area, it had taken a while before they had noticed him, and as soon as they had, he had hacked with his sword, swinging it to keep them at bay but avoiding stabbing at the unarmed devils. On the other side of the door that pinned him to the wall, he knew there was a different battle, a fight with something worse than the half-mades, but he had no time to think about anything but keeping the half-mades at bay with the edge of his sword.

However, he could hear the metal ball grinding filth into the floor as it slammed itself against the corner in an attempt to crush the Professor.

And then the half-mades stopped. They dropped to their knees and lifted their faces as though considering something, their eyes deep in thought, their weapons dropped to the ground.

Spicer put his feet against the door and pushed it forward hard enough to knock anyone on their knees out of the way. He stepped around the door, his Twirler drawn, and saw the metal ball roll away from the skinny man locked into the corner. The metal sheathing retracted and the ball flattened to resemble a woodlouse. The shell of the metallic ball ridged back into itself and steam burst from its underneath. It let out a great whistle, its multitude of legs swamped in the steam it had built up as it had expelled energy attempting to crush the Professor.

As Spicer appeared from behind the door, his chest the same height as the Elf kneeling before him, he caught his breath and spoke to the Rickenbacker, the words rasping out.

"Grenade," he hissed.

Rickenbacker, unfolding himself from the corner glanced up, tearing his eyes from the genuflecting Elf, looked at Spicer.

The last of the steam dispersed from beneath the metallic woodlouse and the whistle turned to a hiss. Spicer spun his Twirler and started firing over the heads of the half-mades, his bullets bouncing from the armour of the unwrapped ball. And then he saw it start to close up.

"Grenade!" he called again, ignoring the lift as it ground closer from below.

Spicer watched as the intelligence flooded back into the Professor's countenance, and he saw the old man's hands reach into his bag of tricks for the final grenade. Spicer continued firing at the metal beast and then he saw the middle plating rise as the woodlouse started to close up. The rear of the animal scooped up dirt as it protected itself in retracting itself, but the Professor knew what to do. He flicked the trigger of the Red Wonder grenade and chucked it gently towards the stomach of the monster. Spicer continued to fire his Twirler, and as the animal closed up tight as a fist to avoid the bullets, the grenade was scooped into the belly of the beast.

Spicer jumped back behind the open door as Rickenbacker bunched himself up into a ball of flesh. Both of them glanced around at the Elf around them, knowing that Isabella had freed them, but also aware that their own lives depended on the death of this metal insect.

The beast from beneath the Attar Mountains closed up. There was a puff of steam as the ball locked back into place as its dark smoke dissipated and then the Professor heard the grenade explode, muffled to sound like a sneeze. The ball's metal plating bulged outwards like a pulsing heart, black clouds streaming from the gaps between the dark metal plates, and it rolled gently to one side, lacking all aggression.

The Elf remained on their knees as Spicer and Rickenbacker dared open the eyes to regard each other.

The metal ball, once so terrifying, let out a rasping sound and slumped, as though it had melted, becoming a dark broken oval.

Spicer stepped from behind the open secret door and regarded the Professor.

"I think we killed it," the Professor said.

Spicer did not have the nerve to tempt fate with a reply.

Teddy huddled behind a locked down market stall, feeling concealed but knowing the swarms of Fairy around him were as incongruous as the undead soldiers advancing on the palace. He watched as Brennan crumpled to the floor and Laurel was struck down with a bullet. He saw Lady Melody start down the steps and Hilt disappear in the throng. If Kendrick was in the palace with Mister Elephantine, then all was lost.

Above it all, surveying the chaos of his own creation, sat Doctor Axelrod, a self-satisfied grin on his face. Teddy watched as the smile disappeared from his lips and he frowned into the battle. He followed the Doctor's gaze and saw Elena helping Laurel to her feet, and in Laurel's hand, the Storyteller Box. Teddy gasped and broke cover, desperate to reach it, as Axelrod spurred his pony forward.

Elena was bringing down the undead left and right, blowing away knees and ankles and a more-than-required amount of genitalia, firing at rifles to cause them to explode in their owners' hands, but the undead came on, roaring and cackling. The crippled on the floor reached towards the two women, clawing at their ankles as they dragged each other back to the doors of the palace.

Teddy saw Elena stumble once as more undead approached, ignoring the others to concentrate on the two women and the box. Indeed, nobody had even noticed the approach of Teddy, the cloud of Fairy twirling above his head like a typhoon.

Then the lamp atop one of the lampposts in the palace drive exploded in a burst of Red Wonder, showering the undead below with glass and burning sparks of energy. As soon as the smallest flame touched the dried parchment skin of the undead, they ignited with a whoosh, the red wildfire spreading across their entire bodies. The rapid oxidisation was caused by the raw Red Wonder mixing with the concoction of Green Wonder Axelrod used to reanimate his servants, and he knew it.

"No!" he called shrilly, as five undead lit up.

The flames started to spread across the soldiers as more streetlights exploded under fire from the palace.

"Take out the sniper!" Axelrod called, pointing towards the upper windows.

Riflemen opened up at Bunce's position, forcing her to take cover as Melody took out all the lights nearest her on the drive, turning the palace grounds into a flaring holocaust of undead.

As Axelrod advanced slowly through his platoon, he passed the area of Brennan's final stand, the undead that had brought him down already advancing towards the palace. The old man, pale with blood loss and shaking with shock, his torso soaked in his own blood, reached out his hand and grasped the blat gun. He pulled it closer to him, as though it was a child he was protecting from the marching feet around him, raised the barrel as the Doctor grew nearer, and fired once.

As the blat gun blasted, the undead around the old man turned and finished him of in a hail of bullets, but the last thing Brennan saw was Axelrod, the man who had brought so much death and destruction into his life, the bastard who had caused the death of his beautiful son, lift into the air out of the saddle by the blat gun fire, skin flailed from his body as the shot slammed into him at close range.

As their leader went down, the undead platoon did not react like most soldiers. They cheered, free of the man who commanded them, and continued their attack on the palace, the last order they had received from their master, bringing a fresh blood-thirsty fervour to their attack, despite the large percentage of them in flames.

"Run!" Talisker called from the palace doors as Bunce renewed her fire at the streetlights.

Talisker pulled a device from his bag, primed it as Laurel and Melody hobbled closer, and lobbed it over their heads.

The soldiers advanced past Hilt buried beneath his living corpse and the warrior pushed the undead from his blade, picked up a burning rag from the undead next to him and dropped it onto the dead man he had used for cover. The body flared, but his comrades did not turn as they ran headlong at the palace.

Hilt's ears popped and he saw Talisker's device burst. Before it exploded, he knew instinctively what it was and climbed a lamppost as the blackberry stain spread behind the two women heading for the palace doors.

Undead soldiers fell as their feet and boots stuck to the ground, roaring with frustration, as Melody and Laurel reached the stairs. Talisker dragged his stone feet across the doorway and reached out to take Laurel from around Melody's shoulders and bullets whizzed around them.

From his vantage point halfway up the burning lamppost, Hilt's eyes fell upon Axelrod's body, its clothes shredded, and he saw movement. Hilt dropped to the floor and drew his Twirler, training it on the corpse in front of him.

Doctor Axelrod lifted his head and glared at Hilt. His eyes were obsidian, darker than coal and he drew himself to his feet. Hilt started firing, the bullets slamming into Axelrod's torso and face before howling away, each bullet hole revealing a dark metal skeleton beneath.

"What the hell are you?" Hilt said, staring in shock at the mechnological half-human in front of him.

"I am the first of many," Axelrod replied through dark sharp teeth.

Then the Doctor lifted his chin like a wolf about to howl and let out a screeching whistle that echoed around the palace grounds, the tenements of downtown and the factories beyond. The air around him shimmered in a haze of heat and steam seemed to seep from beneath what was left of his skin.

Hilt holstered his Twirler and brought up his blade.

"Then you will be the first to die," he told the Doctor, as the metal man took his first steps towards the Torchlight officer.

Spicer heard Isabella's voice inside his head. He liked the feeling.

"Yossarian," she called to him, "you need to get to the palace. Lead the Immolators."

"What's going on?" Rickenbacker asked when he saw Spicer's face concentrate.

"It's Isabella," he told the Professor, "she has control of the Immolators."

The half-mades rose from their knees and faced Spicer.

"Should I go down to the ballroom and relieve Isabella so that she can join you in battle?" Rickenbacker offered.

"No human will enter this place again," Isabella said in Spicer's head, and he could feel her rage.

"I'm not sure she would appreciate that," Spicer smiled at Rickenbacker.

"I have no more Wonder. I will be of limited use."

"Professor, you have survived this far. You should see it through to the end."

Rickenbacker looked at the terrifying half-mades around him and shuddered with horror.

"I suppose you are right," he said, and the two men led the half-mades through the secret door back up towards ground level.

They left the Trade headquarters, picking their way through the corpses of Elf and Immolators towards the column of smoke that rose from the palace across town. Spicer was aware of Isabella's instructions to the half-mades and

Immolators buzzing in his ears, telling them to follow him and take on the undead of Doctor Axelrod.

The crackle of gunfire carried down the streets, accompanied by the smell of the fires. And then something new filled the air, a noise so alien in the Gramarye that all of Chinsey seemed to settle afterwards to take it in. It was a whistle, but not from a human being. It was astonishingly loud, a whoop that lasted too long and sustained the same note.

"What the hell was that?" Spicer asked.

"I don't think it is just the undead we need to worry about," Rickenbacker replied.

"Oh good," Spicer replied, "Because things aren't bad enough."

"The palace is about to fall," Spicer felt Isabella communicate.

"I need to move," Spicer said, his eyes alighting on the stables. "Get the Immolators who can fight on ponyback."

Spicer raced ahead, clambered onto the nearest pony and dragged it round to gallop in the direction of the gunfire, the smoke and the terrifying whistle when another sound carried through the air.

A dark rumble carried down the streets like distant thunder. All heads glanced towards the Attar Mountains and saw one of the tallest peaks collapse in on itself. There was another momentary silence and then a rumbling drone started to emanate from the mountains.

"What's happening?" Rickenbacker asked.

"One thing at a time," Spicer replied, before racing off to the palace.

The undead spread across the palace ground, skirting their comrades caught in the paralysing floor and encircled the building. Bunce fired down at the vanguard hacking at the front door with her Twirler, exploding skulls and taking off limbs.

"We need to burn it," Talisker said. "We need to burn the palace."

"You may not have noticed, but we are inside the palace," said Laurel as Melody bandaged her wound.

"Bunce, what's happening?" Melody called.

"We're completed surrounded. The Fairy have even come to watch."

"The Fairy?" puzzled Talisker. "Can you see Hilt?"

"He's taking on Axelrod."

"The Doctor?"

"Look, I'm pretty busy up here..." Bunce reminded them, continuing to fire into the undead at the front door.

There was the sound of glass breaking from a window nearby.

"They're coming in through the conservatory," Laurel called.

"Get me my guns," said Pinkerton, sitting up slowly.

"You shouldn't move," Laurel told him.

"Neither should you," Pinkerton replied, pulling himself to his feet, "but if we're going to ignite this place, I'd rather be elsewhere."

Then there was a screech from the palace grounds, followed a minute later by thunderous rumbling from the Attar Mountains.

"What's happening?" Talisker called again.

"I have absolutely no idea," Bunce replied.

Hilt and Axelrod circled each other, sizing each other up.

"You think you're unique, don't you?" Axelrod taunted the warrior.

"I hope so, for your sake," Hilt replied.

Axelrod shook out his right wrist, as if he were an athlete limbering up, and a long blade slid from the skin of his wrist. As it passed through his hand, it drew blood. The Doctor didn't notice, and swung at Hilt, who stepped back and knocked it aside.

"What comes out of your feet?" Hilt asked, parrying a lunge. "Rollerskates?"

He extended his sword and Axelrod met it.

"I am not alone," Axelrod explained. "My kindred are coming."

They engaged their blades. Hilt was exhausted, knew he was bleeding and broken in places, but would not let his brain admit the pain. Axelrod's attack were incredibly strong, his full weight behind each blow, but he obviously did not use his blade as often as Hilt. Hilt knocked Axelrod's attacks aside.

"Bring them on," Hilt nodded. "I've already taken out some of your dead friends."

Axelrod swung again and Hilt sidestepped to bring his blade round behind him, slicing through Axelrod's back with a blow that should have shattered his spine. He felt metal strike metal and Axelrod grabbed Hilt's sword arm hard, the blade still in his flesh. He turned, forcing Hilt to stumble to knees and raised his other hand. Another blade burst from Axelrod's wrist and brought it down at Hilt's chest. Hilt pushed himself backwards so Axelrod's second blade hit the floor, and Hilt stamped his foot onto it. He drew his Twirler and rammed it sideways into Axelrod's mouth, smashing teeth and nose and cheeks, pulled it out so that it spun and fired it into the Doctor's throat. Axelrod heaved up his blade, sending Hilt's foot into the air so that he rolled away as the first blade cut the air where his head had been. Hilt rested on one knee, catching his breath, as Axelrod attempted to straighten up, stumbled and spread his legs to stay upright.

The two men regarded each other. Axelrod's face had lost its skin so that the black metal beneath was revealed. Steam pumped from each of his joints and Hilt could hear the ticking of clockwork. In the centre of Axelrod's torso, beneath a breastplate and above the stomach, Hilt saw the gentle rocking movement of a mechanism.

"You will lose, Hilt," Axelrod told him. "You will lose everything, just as you did at the Meander Canyon."

Hilt threw himself forward from his kneeling position like a sprinter leaving his blocks at speed. He knocked aside one blade and got in close as he felt Axelrod's second blade slide into his stomach.

"Goodbye, Hilt," Axelrod hissed, and Hilt fired the Twirler trapped between the two of them into Axelrod's midriff, the barrel angled up so the bullets would get under the breastplate.

The two men remained standing, keeping each other upright, slumped together.

"Goodbye, Doctor."

Teddy watched Hilt and Axelrod locked together slide slowly to the floor, their heads nodding forward onto each other's shoulders. He stood up and started towards the entrance to the palace grounds, the Fairy still buzzing around him. He heard the sound of hooves on cobbles, and was ready to turn back to cover when Spicer galloped into the street, flanked by mutated men and Immolators on ponies. Spicer brought his pony to a halt next to Teddy.

"What's going on?"

There was the sound of breaking glass and one of the ground floor palace windows blew out, allowing flames to billow outwards. Several undead lit up, screaming with anger.

"Get in there and defend that palace," Spicer called to his tiny cavalry, and they broke forward to engage the undead, who turned away from the palace to face an enemy altered from birth to fight them.

"What are all these Fairy doing here?" Spicer asked, looking at the swarms still fluttering clumsily around Teddy.

"They were helping me," Teddy said, feeling foolish. "Helping me find Mister Elephantine."

"Where is the box?" Spicer asked.

"Laurel took it in there," Teddy replied, pointing with a shaking finger at the palace.

"You're with me," Spicer said, grabbing the boy's extended hand and pulling him onto the pony behind him.

The Elf kicked the pony forward and followed the Immolators. As he reached Hilt and Axelrod he slowed, looked down at the two men locked together before pushing forward down the drive, feeling Teddy trembling against his back, the Fairy following them like a cloud of smoke.

The Immolators smashed into undead, hacking and shooting, pushing them into the flames of the palace. As Immolators fell, they too flashed afire, bring more undead down. The undead looked for escape but found none, and an inferno flashed around the palace.

Spicer pulled back on the reins as he felt his pony spook at the explosions of fire.

"Is Laurel in there?" he called over his shoulder. "Is the box in there?"

"Yes, unless they've escaped."

Spicer spurred on the pony and circled the palace, looking for a way out for the others, a part of him hoping he would find none. Then, in a top window flashing with red gunfire, he saw Pinkerton's broad back silhouetted against the flashes in the room. Spicer fired high, smashing the glass and immediately Bunce was at the window with her rifle. She raised it, saw Spicer, and looked around as if he would have a miraculous means of escape. Spicer closed his eyes and hoped Isabella would understand him as he willed more Immolators to come round to this side of the building as flames started to engulf the palace.

He saw Laurel stagger wounded towards the smashed window and she waved the box at him.

"Mister Elephantine!" exclaimed Teddy.

Spicer immediately felt a change in the Fairy around him. The raspberry beats of their tiny wings seemed to take on real purpose and their inane chatter quieted. He heard the whisper to each other, just discernible over the sound of their wings, the gunshots and the crackle of the fire.

"The deep Blue. The Blue."

And then a new noise caught on the wind and grew louder until it filled the air. It rumbled like a thousand hard wooden wagon wheels on a bridge, like the dark incantation of worship in an enormous cathedral, like a billion bees.

From the mountain missing its peak rose a small black cloud, which moved so fast that it was within the boundaries of Maisy within a minute. A whistling joined it, and the cloud started to drop enormous black hail as big as pineapples that exploded with enormous effect when they hit the ground. One of the chimney stacks on the edge of town toppled, but the sound of its multitude of bricks was drowned out by the buzzing.

As they came closer, Spicer was able to see the individual entities within the cloud. They were shiny black, the shape of dragonflies the size of shire horses. The melée at the palace stopped as everybody looked up, only turning back to the battle when the bombs started dropping closer.

Spicer drew his Twirler, but knew that the metal dragonflies from the Attar Mountains were both too armoured and too high. As he looked up, he realised the Fairy had left them and were making a beeline for the Storyteller Box. He saw Laurel take two steps back and then the Fairy were on her, buzzing around her like a hurricane. She screamed and dropped the box and there was a flash of Blue Wonder. It came out of the shattered box like a perfect disc, thinly pristine, shining bright like a diamond. The Fairy moved from the funnel they had built around Laurel and spun into the disc.

As the Fairy moved into the still-expanding disc, spinning faster until they too became a blue blur.

The dragonflies drew closer, a wall of fire behind them as they rained down bombs on Chinsey. Spicer's pony reared back and he climbed off, helped down Teddy and spanked the animal's rear to send it racing away.

"What are they?" Teddy asked.

"It's the Threat," Spicer replied.

"Will they kill us? Are we going to die?"

"No."

The first Fairy broke out of the disc and shot towards the dragonflies, a blue trail behind it. More Fairy followed, splitting up to aim at specific dragonflies within the dark cloud. As the Fairy struck each dragonfly, the beast imploded in on itself with a soft 'thup' noise as the Fairy came out of the other side and aimed at another. The thundering buzz started to lessen as more dragonflies disappeared. Some broke from the cloud and tried to escape, but the Fairy, barely visible but for their trail, pursued them and brought them down, making them disappear whenever they met them midair.

"What's happening?" Teddy asked Spicer.

"The deep Blue Wonder," Spicer mumbled, staring upwards.

Then the Elf shook his head in disbelief, drew his Twirler and headed towards the smashed window where his friends were fighting a final battle with the undead. The blue disc had gone, leaving tracers of a blue sparkling spiderweb that trailed the Fairy attack.

As he approached, he saw a ladder against the edge of the ruined conservatory and nodded at Teddy to take the other end. As they lifted it up beneath the window, they felt their ears pop. Laurel was the first out of the window, but she could only use one arm to get down each rung. Spicer climbed up to help her down.

"What's going on?" Spicer asked.

"Talisker is using something called a Blow Back," Laurel told him.

They reached the bottom of the ladder and Teddy helped Laurel sit down on the grass.

"Have we won?" he asked her.

EPILOGUE.

Chinsey,
Capital of The Gramarye region
Grand Quillia

June 1856

He had lost everything by refusing to be a part of what had happened in these subterranean chambers, but here he was, beneath the Trade headquarters, where the Elf had been cut open, probed, and violated.

Rickenbacker had to admit to himself that he was relieved to be back in a laboratory, however fleetingly. His adventure had started here, and the now he was ready for the next chapter, a part of his story that would give him more knowledge of the Wonder than anybody in Gramarye had known for decades. Before embarking on the journey across the Attar Mountains to the Ditch, he was determined to find out as much as possible about the Threat, and the more he found, the more impressed he became.

"I've never seen such astonishing mechnology," he said in hushed tones, regarding the cogs and levers within the chest of what was once known as Doctor Axelrod.

"Not just mechnology," Talisker said, as he removed the top of the metal skull. "There's flesh in here."

Blood, almost black, spread from the cavity like the blackberry stain of a paralysing floor. Rickenbacker joined Talisker as they marvelled at the human brain inside its metallic container.

"It would appear the Threat had much the same idea as the Trade," Rickenbacker noted, glancing at the Immolator guarding the door.

The two hyperphysicists regarded each other with respect.

"You know I am jealous of you going back to the Library of the Senses."

"And I of you," Talisker replied. "You will give my wife a message from me?"

"Of course. I hope you will join us all. That we will all be together. Eventually."

"If this monster doesn't bring us together," Talisker said, shaking his head, "Nothing will."

The whistles petered out as the sailors caught sight of the Reclaimer Lieutenant's ears, rising to the unmistakeable point of the Elf.

"Welcome aboard the Spirit of Bester, Lieutenant Spicer," said Captain Conrad said, snapping to attention and saluting.

"Lady Jerham and Miss Gleave," said First Officer Gower, stepping forward. "If you and your bodyguard would accompany me I will show you to your rooms. You will appreciate we are somewhat over-subscribed for the journey to the capital today."

"I'm sure we can find them for ourselves," Bunce remarked. "We have been on the Bester before, I assure you."

Bunce enjoyed putting the man in his place. She also found herself enjoying being called Elena's bodyguard.

The women looked down at Ashburton Station below them, thronging with desperate émigrés. Elena raised her eyes to the town beyond, scarred with black pockmarks of bomb sites, and pockmarked with the shrapnel of fallen mechnological dragonflies. At first, the people had started to loot the wreckage of the invaders, but once they had discovered the scraps of flesh inside, they had retreated, mumbling of curses and old evils.

For the first time she could remember, Elena could see a clear blue sky, with one industrial chimney sitting dormant, the other demolished.

Beyond she could see the jagged edge of the crater in the Attar Mountains where the Threat had started its destructive journey. Beyond that, black smoke was rising from what she imagined was the Ditch. With their undead armies and Elf commandos invading Chinsey, she wondered who had been left to defend them against the mechnological terror.

"I think I would prefer to stay on deck until we disembark, Mr Gower," Elena said, "so I can survey the damage."

"There would have been a hell of a lot more damage had you not stepped up to lead the resistance, Milady," Gower grinned.

"I think you should be thanking Lieutenant Spicer, sir," she snapped back.

"Of course," the Captain blustered, stepping forward as Gower flushed.

"Captain Conrad," Spicer interrupted, feeling Conrad's embarrassment and Gower's antipathy, "Without your quick thinking, Grand Quillia would still be in the dark about what happened here."

"We were lucky the invaders," he cleared his throat, not differentiating between the Ditch or the Threat, "we were lucky the invaders did not take into the account the Bester's Murder of Crows, Sir," he finished, his chest inflating with pride.

"There's a part of me that wished they hadn't sent that message," Laurel murmers to Elena, "I don't like being summoned. Especially to the capital."

"They have to be warned. We need Grand Quillia to join with the People of the Ditch to ensure the Threat do not try this again," Elena replied, as they leant against the railings and stared out.

"Do you really think they will help?" Laurel asked.

Spicer stepped behind both women and rested his hands on their shoulders.

"If I didn't feel this journey was worth something, do you think I would surrender a chance to meet my people on the other side of the Attar Mountains?"

"That's if anyone is left," said Elena, looking at the dark smoke beyond.

Without looking, Bunce gently took Elena's hand.

"I had hoped to open my eyes to something a little more like Laurel's face than your bewhiskered flesh bucket."

"Hello, Hilt."

Pinkerton reached out his hand from his infirmary bed and Hilt took it in his own.

"You're awake."

A woman's voice.

"You're here."

Hilt turned, hoping to see the Lady Elena, and was surprised to see the scarred Elf girl.

"Are we prisoners?" he asked.

Pinkerton smirked.

"You're being hailed the saviours of Chinsey," said Isabella. "Congratulations."

She stepped forward to shake Hilt's hand.

"Why is everybody so insistent on shaking my damned hand?"

Hilt looked down at his two hands, one in the battered fist of a boxer, the other held in the slender fingers of an Elf.

"Where's my…"

He threshed around until he saw it. His sword was sheathed in a scabbard hanging from his bed.

Teddy was not sad when the Fairy lost interest in him. After their transformation, their defeat of the Dragonflies and the subsequent exhaustion of the deep blue Wonder in the Gargoyle key, they had reverted to their former selves, their little wings farting them back to earth, and had found him again. Some had gathered up the remains of the Gargoyle key and returned it to him, gibbering their foolishness, and he had taken it. They continued their never-ending nonsense conversation while Mr Elephantine remained silent. Then they had retired to the filth of their rookeries.

Teddy ate his toast with relish, the butter running down his chin, as he looked out at battered Chinsey from its most premier guesthouse. The steward, a boy of Teddy's age, had regarded him with awe as he cleared Teddy's wardrobe of the previous occupant's clothing, a mixture of Trade dress uniforms and high class suits. It had reminded Teddy of the basement of the Lodge, full of adventurers' weapons and kit. He was surprised to have made the connection, and considered that being the chosen one, however briefly, may have rubbed off.

He cleared his mind of such thoughts, tasting bitterness at his susceptibility to Mister Elephantine's lies.

He finished his toast, pulled the curtains closed, and moved the deep eiderdown aside on his bed.

As he snuggled down into the enormous bed and turned down the Red Wonder valve on his lamp to dim the light, he was aware of a familiar voice, deep inside his head, words uttered but not heard.

"You know there is more than just one Gargoyle key, don't you, Teddy?"

The Wonder Glossary – for those short of time and/or memory.

AIR – Alien and Insurgent Research – Department of Imperial Operatives investigating foreign and non-human movements within the Empire and beyond. They wear black.

Ashburton Station – The only official and most important Slideways Station in The Gramarye.

Attar Mountains – an impenetrable range of high peaks that separate the Gramarye from The Ditch. They are rumoured to be inhabited by monsters, but so few people have returned, nobody can verify these old wives' tales. Doesn't stop the tales being hailed as truth though.

Axelrod, Penfold G. Dr. – An advanced hyperphysicist employed by the Trade whose speciality is Green Wonder. His background is not known, but it is suggested he is an orphan.

Beasley, Mycroft - Brigadier– Leader of the Torchlight Cavalry at the Battle of Maisy. Killed at the Siege of the Glasslands.

Blat Gun – Named after the noise it makes, a short range heavy discharge weapon popular with people with bad eyesight.

Blue Wonder – Hyperphysical power – Plentiful in The Gramarye but not so common across the rest of the Empire, Blue Wonder is known to bend people's minds and senses.

Its full capabilities are still being discovered in laboratories across Grand Quillia and in the studies of Fairport. It is suspected that the Gramarye was once powered by a culture with a profound understanding of Blue Wonder, now apparently lost to the ages. It is known colloquially as the "Deep Blue".

Blundstone Hall – Palatial home of Sir Ambrose Willis, Viceroy of Chinsey.

Brennan, Alfred junior – From a family of housekeepers that has run the Gleave Lodge in the Glasslands for generations. Lovely boy, caring, thoughtful, destined for great things. Killed at the Siege of the Glasslands.

Brennan, Alfred senior – From a family of housekeepers that has run the Gleave Lodge in the Glasslands for generations. A widower and former inebriant.

Bunce, Geraldine – Ex-Grand Quillian Military sniper, now a member of Spicer's Reclaimer group. Not a fan of lifts.

Chinsey – the Trade Capital in The Gramarye. Once the most important bustling market town in the region, the Trade has demolished the original conurbation and rebuilt it as just another outpost of the Empire. Serviced by the only Slideways in the Gramarye with Ashburton Station.

Conway, Jeremy - Ex-Grand Quillian Military hyper-physicist, now a member of Spicer's Reclaimer group. Killed at the Siege of the Glasslands.

Creslow, Teddy – Nephew of a Fairport landlady and currently employed as a manservant. Currently on the run from the Trade.

Ditch, the – The Gramarye's neighbour and previous nemesis until the invasion by Grand Quillia. They are rumoured to be very well versed in Green Wonder but anybody who has ventured there has either been forced back by the Attar Mountains or has never returned.

ECO – Enchantment and Chicanery Operative – Hyperphysicist employed by the Trade around the Empire to utilise the Wonder as required, sometimes within the realms of espionage and subterfuge.

Elephantine – A charming children's tale about a man who only had nice things to say. Also a creature created before the fall of Pearly, made up of the memories and aspirations of the ruling elite. And you know how they can be...

Fairport – Located in the green hills of Grand Quillia, a pretty town that's home to its most important seats of learning.

Franks, Rupert – A Major in the Trade Headquarters at Chinsey, where, much to his own frustration, he has the role of Regional Enchantment Auditor.

Glasslands, the – A forest of glass and crystal, created at the same time as the fall of Pearly. The location of a siege when Trade forces and a group of Reclaimers lead by Lieutenant Spicer attacked the Gleave Lodge.

Gleave – An old and powerful dynasty who once ruled The Gramarye after the fall of Pearly. Not known for their humility or open-mindedness.

Gleave, Laurel – Apparently the last member of the fabled Gleave Dynasty. Known for her humility and open-mindedness, as shown in her work as a nurse, dancer and landlady. Currently on the run from the Trade.

Gramarye, the – A small corner of the Empire ruled by the Trade, who are stripping it of every source of Wonder they can find. It was once the centre of a mysterious culture whose use of the Wonder was far in advance of what the Empire is capable of today.

Grand Quillia – Motherland of an Empire that stretches from sea to shining sea. Made up of people who love pantomime, male voice choirs and subjugating other countries to strip them of resources and quash them with guns followed by bureaucracy. Good gravy; stodgy puddings.

Green Wonder – Hyperphysical power – Rare and very valuable across the Empire but rumoured to be most common in The Ditch, Green Wonder has the power to cure the sick, raise the dead and change the very constitution of the body. It is known colloquially as "Verdant."

Hilt – Survivor of the Meander Canyon Massacre. Some stories suggest he is a hero, some a serial killer, but they all agree he has a sword attached to his hand. It is suggested he got the name Hilt due to this affliction, and not vice versa. Currently on the run from the Trade.

Hyperphysics – The study of the Wonder and how to mix its constituent parts to create the required result. The main factor in an incredible Grand Quillian industrial revolution built around the Wonder.

Immolators – Horrific troops clad from head to toe in thick leather used by the Trade in the Gramarye alone. Humanoid in appearance, they are apparently controlled from afar and burst into flame at death. As you do. They are the dark secret of the Empire.

Kendrick, Aldo – A long term guest at the Gleave Lodge. Fixer. Entrepreneur. Friend. What a guy.

Library of Senses, the – also known as the Cathedral of Tales, the only remaining building of Pearly in the middle of the Glasslands with a tower that curves like the flower of a snowdrop. Fabled to contain the riches of the Gramarye, many treasure seekers and looters have entered. None has returned.

Maisy – A now destroyed village that stood where Talling is reputed to have been located. The last stand of the rebels of The Gramarye against the might of the Trade.

Mandell, Sir Evan – Son of Prince Edmundsen of the Bullen Protectorate and brother of Lord Ethering of the Grand Quillia Parliament. Former Grand Quillian cavalry officer. Killed at the Siege of the Glasslands. Since raised from the dead and working with The Trade to find his former colleagues.

Meander Canyon, the – Known for the Last Stand of the Torchlights.

Melody, Lady Elena Drew Hynes Melody (widowed) – A lady of dubious virtue lucky enough to marry into one of the most powerful of Grand Quillian families. Before her marriage, it is rumoured she was involved in the underground network run by the Pick. Since widowhood, she has embarked on a series of "adventures".

Melody, Lord Runciman Drew Hynes (deceased) – Member of Grand Quillian aristocracy, a humanitarian who made his money in off shore gaols, gulags and slave mines. A true philanthropist.

Moon Docks – located in the crescent of a natural harbour, the fishing outpost for Maisy, now deserted.

Pearly – Once the capital of Gramarye, now only one building remains – The Cathedral of Tales, known in its day the as Library of Senses . Its fall from power is a thing of legend. Scholars say its name is from its fame as one of the Five Pearls of The Gramarye.

Pendle, Geoffrey – A Sergeant Major in the Trade, a veteran of many skirmishes, especially in the Western Isles, who has since been working a desk in the Trade Headquarters of Chinsey.

Pick, The – A shadowy underground figure in the Capital said to run most of the criminal gangs, if one believes the lower class penny dreadfuls and less reputable circulars.

Pinkerton, Corporal – aka Ten Fingers Pinkerton the Gentleman Pugilist, the victor at the battle of Langtry Common against Bill Edlington. Best friends with Sir Evan Mandell until his resurrection. Currently on the run from the Trade.

Quine, Edgar – Holds the rank of Colonel and is proud to be the bureaucratic Head of the Gramarye region for the Trade. Well connected in Grand Quillia. Lovely fella. You'd like him.

REA - Regional Enchantment Auditor – Individual employed by the Trade around the Empire to log and if necessary, confiscate relics of the Wonder that may be of interest.

Reclaimers – Mercenaries employed by the Trade to "reclaim" Trade property. Many so named are worse than bandits, pirates and cut-throats.

Red Wonder – Hyperphysical power. Very common throughout the Grand Quillian Empire and the fuel with which they expanded their regions. Harnessed for industry, Red Wonder lights the streets of its cities, transports the ice yachts of the slideways, constructs the buildings, digs the mines and fires the weapons of the Empire. It is known colloquially as the "Blood Red".

Rickenbacker, Hilary – Former ECO and Professor of the History of Wonder. Currently on the run from the Trade.

Simon Insley G Zero – Standard issue rifle for Trade personnel. Boring but functional.

Spicer, Valentine – Ex-Grand Quillian Military. Retired at the rank of Lieutenant. Now the leader of a successful group of Reclaimers. Recently went through a change after the opening of the Cathedral of Tales. Much better looking than he once was. Which is a relief for everyone.

Spinner – the first pistol to use Red Wonder, it needs to be spun before each shot to recoup enough energy to discharge.

Talisker, Felix – A hyperphysicist of the Torchlight Cavalry who fought at the Battle of Maisy.

Talling – Once the Wonder powerhouse of the Gramarye, with ancient pyramids unwilling to surrender their secrets to modern archaeologists. An area so strong with Wonder of various flavours, it is dangerous for hyperphysicists to practise their skills.

Tork, Aaron - Ex-Grand Quillian Military, now a member of Spicer's Reclaimer group. Killed at the Siege of the Glasslands.

Trade, the – a commercial entity that pursues business across all regions of the Empire on behalf of Grand Quillia. It is empowered to employ and command its own armies to police the furthest regions of the Empire, which is sometimes supplemented by freelancer irregulars, known as Reclaimers. Most shares in the Trade are owned by the aristocracy.

Twirler – The weapon of choice for any violent man. Using Red Wonder to discharge powerful energy from one of its six barrels, it need only be spun once for multiple shots.

Western Isles – A group of islands off the Coast of Grand Quillia that occasionally flare up and rebel against its closest neighbour. The perfect place for the Empire to test its troops and weaponry.

Willis, Sir Ambrose – Former darling of Grand Quillian society and one of the first men of power to see the possibilities of The Gramarye for the Empire and the Trade. Instrumental in bringing down the Gleave family. His reputation may be tarnished, but his power is not diminished.

Terri Pray

Published by Under the Moon, LLC
Pelican Rapids, MN

This book is a work of fiction. Any resemblance to actual events, locales or persons, living or dead, is completely coincidental.

Shadows of the Past
ISBN: 978-1-938339-25-7
Copyright © 2015 Terri Pray
Cover Art Copyright @ 2015 Samuel Pray and Terri Pray
Editor in Chief: Terri Pray
All rights reserved.

1

Shadows of the Past

Prologue

Lily was home. He didn't have to turn on the monitor and bring up the cameras to know. The GPS attached to her vehicle had already confirmed her location, and he would indulge in the footage later when it was safer.

He glanced at his phone. If Lily followed her normal routine, she'd have something to eat, perhaps a glass of wine, and then she would settle down with a book as she ran her bath. Bubbles and a tempting scent, candles and low light, a fresh glass of wine prepared along with thick, warm towels and a matching robe. Everything in its place before she stripped and stepped into the welcome embrace of the warm water. His imagination eagerly filled in the details: the way the water and bubbles would caress her skin, cup her breasts, and slide between her thighs. She'd reach for a large soft sponge and build up the foam before she eased it over her body.

He bit back a groan and shifted in the chair. He didn't need to imagine the scene. Before the end of the night, he'd see it for himself. He'd taken care to cover each room and every possible angle in her home with tiny, well-hidden cameras. Not a single visitor or phone call occurred without him knowing about it.

Not even her decision to hire outside security would change it.

Security, bodyguards, and precautions. He snorted and shifted in his chair. Some overconfident firm who could never understand his Lily or her need to create would walk into Lily's life and disrupt it. With her creativity came a desire for space and time alone to get her work done. Her studio, the place she'd wandered into, was off limits to most people, and he doubted a stranger would be allowed within her art room.

Perhaps he would have to change a few things, but the cameras were carefully hidden. Lily hadn't found them, and the police hadn't even bothered to check. Not that they knew what to watch